The Legend Begins

The Legend of Chip
The Legend Begins

STANLEY CAMPBELL

LEGEND WRITER PUBLICATIONS

LEGEND WRITER PUBLICATIONS

Printed in the United States of America

Library of Congress Control Number: 2017917749

ISBN: 0-9995971-1-6
ISBN-13: 978-0-9995971-1-8

Visit www.legendpublications.com

I dedicate this book to anyone who has ever struggled with anything in their life and wondered why. For those who have never struggled with anything in their life, please pass this book to someone else, as it isn't for you.

CONTENTS

---·---

ACKNOWLEDGMENTS

———•———

This book would not have been possible without the support and encouragement of my beautiful wife, Melenia. For understanding my long nights at the computer, I'd like to thank my children, Jacob and Caleb. I would also like to thank Adam Wayne for the outstanding work he did on designing and illustrating the book cover. Finally, I would like to thank God for giving me the opportunity and the inspiration to write this story.

The Legend Begins

———— ◆ ————

PROLOGUE

Christopher MacDougall was sitting near the fireplace, reading his father's favorite book, when a sudden booming ripped him from his thoughts. He turned to see his wife Mary sitting at the table looking alert, her eyes focused upon their cottage door. Christopher rose quickly, wondering who might come calling at this late hour. He opened the door to see his friend, Marcus Brown, looking quite alarmed.

"Marcus, what be the trouble?"

"Chip, ye must come with me at once! The reds hath Gow in the square, accused of treason!"

"Latch the door until I return."

Mary gasped as Christopher fetched his coat and hat. "Should ye take yer father's sword?"

Christopher glanced at the claymore which rested on the mantle above the fireplace. "Nay, me love. The reds shall slay any Scot bearing the blade."

Christopher kissed his wife goodbye before joining Marcus outside, snatching a torch from the porch as he went. They passed through the outer pastures to save time, arriving to find most of the men already assembled in the square. English soldiers had formed a circle, keeping the townsfolk from reaching the center.

Christopher's heart pounded as his eyes fell upon the face of his friend, Andrew Gow, standing atop the gallows, bound and gagged with a noose about his neck. The fear on Gow's face sent sparks of anger through him.

An English soldier addressed the growing crowd, reading from a scroll of parchment. "People of Balloch! On this, the eighteenth day of September, in the year of our Lord seventeen hundred and forty-two, this man has been found guilty of treason to the crown."

The gathered townsfolk roared their disapproval, shouting obscenities at the soldiers who brandished their riffles threateningly.

"Where be yer proof?" Marcus shouted over the commotion.

The soldier glared at Marcus. "He was found fashioning swords within his shop. A practice which has been banned by the King. The punishment for anyone caught conspiring—"

The roar of the crowd drowned out the red's final words. None gathered there needed hear any more. Any moment, the normally peaceful townsfolk of Balloch would become a raging mob.

"Audience with yer commander!" Christopher shouted, his words lost among the turmoil.

Two soldiers fired shots into the air, silencing the crowd.

"We shall have order!" The soldier shouted, climbing to the top of the gallows platform. "This man has been found guilty of treason and shall be hanged by the neck until dead."

Without warning, the soldier grabbed hold of the lever and pulled. The trap door beneath Gow's feet swung open and the night descended into chaos. The crowd pushed forward, attempting to reach the gallows, but the soldiers held their ground. The enraged mob began swinging torches and tossing rocks.

Using their riffles like batons, the soldiers retaliated, striking Christopher and several other townsfolk. Christopher fell to one knee, pain spreading through his midsection. Eyes watering, he looked up in time to block a blow to his head with his forearm.

In a fit of rage, one of the soldiers took hold of a torch and tossed it into the blacksmith shop. Fire engulfed the building, quickly spreading to nearby stores. Horror set in as Christopher realized what was happening. Marcus's cobbler shop, his bakery and all the other shops which lined the square would burn. The crowd erupted as more shots were fired into the air.

In a moment of confusion, a dozen men, including Marcus, broke past the line of reds. Christopher tried to follow, but was shoved back.

"Halt or we'll fire!"

He saw the soldiers raise their riffles, then heard the blasts.

"Marcus!" His heart failed to beat as he watched Marcus fall to the ground.

The thunder of hooves pounding the ground filled the air as he looked up to see several soldiers on horseback riding into the square.

"What's going on here!"

"Commander!" The soldier shouted from the platform, addressing the lead rider. "The local blacksmith was found guilty of treason. The townsfolk—"

"We are here to maintain order!" the commanding soldier boomed. "We're not here to punish or execute!"

Seizing the opportunity, he ran forward past the reds, sliding to the ground to avoid being shot, and cradled his friend in his arms.

"Chip … me friend," Marcus breathed, his voice ragged.

All other sounds about them became muffled. "Hold to me, Marcus!"

"Listen to me, Chip. Me time hath come."

Christopher could see a dark shadow forming on Marcus's coat. "Nay, Marcus! Ye hold to me!"

Marcus held his chest, coughing violently. "Tell little Marcus and Anna their uncle Marcus loves them."

"Ye shall tell them."

He stared down into the eyes of his best friend, as a thousand unspoken words passed between them. Then, as the glow from the growing fire filled his eyes, he felt his friend slip away. Shaking with rage, he held his friend close.

The commanding soldier addressed the square. "Disperse back to your homes. There shall be no more violence this night."

The square continued to burn, but the reinforcements of additional soldiers had extinguished the fury of the raging crowd. Several men eased forward and collected the bodies of their fallen townsfolk, while another retrieved Gow's body from the gallows. The rest of the crowd continued to shout obscenities at the soldiers, but had focused their attentions to gaining control of the fire which burned in the square. Christopher could see flames etching away at his bakery. What had stood for nearly a hundred years was disappearing in smoke and ash.

"Be this what ye call order?!" Christopher shouted, glaring up into the eyes of the soldier before him. "Burning the square? The slaying of innocent men?"

The soldier looked down at Christopher, who continued to hold his friend's lifeless body. "Sir, this is not what I call order. The actions of my soldiers tonight shall be addressed."

Christopher began to push himself to his feet when a pair of hands pressed down upon him. "Time to go home, son," his father-in-law's thick accent whispered from behind. "Marcus be gone and the bakery be lost. Let there not be another loss to mourn tonight."

Christopher focused his rage into strength as he scooped up his friend, rising to his feet. His father-in-law guided him as he carried the man he had called brother away.

"We shall fetch a cart for Marcus."

Christopher shook his head, unable speak.

"Christopher, ye need not carry—"

"Leave him be."

"Bobby, please let us help."

"Nay, Jamison," his father-in-law replied. "This be something me son needs to do."

The men nodded, bowing their heads as Christopher passed. He walked without knowing or feeling. His mind couldn't grasp the calamity the night had brought. Not even when Marcus's father cried out at the sight of his fallen son, did he feel the weight of all which had transpired. It wasn't until he beheld Mary's face, did the fire of vengeance finally fade from his chest.

Mary tore her eyes from Christopher's face to see the same sorrow filled expression reflected in her father's. "What hath happened?"

Christopher fell to one knee. "Marcus. Dead." was all he could muster.

The night's events began to crash against him like waves against the shores of Loch Tay. Every time he closed his eyes he could see Marcus's face staring up at him. Mary dropped down, wrapping her arms about him as silence filled the small cottage. Only the crackling of the fireplace could be heard. No words were said. No words were needed. Christopher was thankful the children were in bed, fast asleep.

When he finally regained his composure, he recounted the events of the night as Mary listened, too overwhelmed to speak.

Bobby McKinney lingered on, standing sentinel near the door. Christopher knew he wouldn't leave until he was sure his son-in-law wouldn't rush back out into the night seeking revenge.

Once his legs had returned, Christopher pushed himself back to his feet. He reached up and took hold of his father's claymore before turning to Mary's father. "One day this shall be young Marcus's. Until then, keep it from me. For the day I hold it again, an Englishman shall lose his life."

Mary's father accepted the sword from Christopher. "I shall keep it safe. Ye hath made the right decision, son."

Christopher nodded before collapsing into the chair nearest the fireplace. He covered his face with his hand, sorrow suddenly consuming him like the fire had his future. He felt his wife's arms surround him once more. He could hear his father's voice, telling him to prepare for tomorrow. At that moment though, tomorrow was beyond what he could fathom. All he knew was he would never forget the night Balloch burned.

ONE

———◆———

THE DOCKER

It was a quiet evening as Christopher headed home from the wharf, where he worked as a docker. Tossing his haversack over his shoulder, he stopped to peer out over the harbor waters at the burning red sunset. While admiring the shades of color that reflected off the now calm surface, he contemplated how his life had changed. Even after three years living in Edinburgh and working in Leith, his teeth still ground at the thought of what he'd lost.

"No mermaids a comin' today, Chip!" A young red-headed man said, slapping Christopher on the back.

"Ye never know," Chip chuckled at the notion, "one might swim me way right this moment with a chest full of treasure!"

Both men laughed, staring out over the waters. Chip was the name Christopher had gone by ever since he and his family moved to Edinburgh. The subtle reminder was like having his friend and brother with him, helping him in a way he could never explain.

Chip sighed, "Ah, just numbering the waves before heading

home, Jonah. There be days I feel as though I live here and visiting me wife and children when I be home."

"Aye, I know the feelin'. Join me in givin' the bottle a black eye before headin' on?"

Chip shook his head. "Nay. Every sixpence be needed for food."

"Then keep yer bender and hath a pint on me." A bearded bear of a man slapped Chip on the shoulder.

"Nothing doing, sir. I be owing ye enough as it be."

"Ye be a good lad who works hard and takes care of his family," the man said. "Nothin' wrong in acceptin' a little generosity."

"I'd take it. Ol' Malone never shows any generosity on the wharf, so best be takin' it as a bit of measure."

Malone growled, "I never give ye any generosity, Jonah McCullah, cause ye never be earnin' it! What Chip here doth in a single day takes ye a fortnight."

"Not be so hard on him, sir. Jonah be a carpenter. They be known to be perfectionists."

"That's right," Jonah said proudly. "We be known for our skill, not our speed."

Malone huffed loudly, "Show me some skill and I be showin' ye some copper. Now," he lifted his eyes and looked farther down the way, "I be in search of perfection in the form of the new wench at O'Gills."

Chip sighed, "Alas, maybe tomorrow. By now I be certain

me whither shall hath the stew on the fire."

"Very well, Chip, me lad. But tomorrow, ye shall not be gettin' away."

The men bid Chip farewell and he headed for home. While home wasn't a cottage amongst the open fields along the shores of Loch Tay, like the one where he'd once lived, it was a pleasant enough clay bungalow on the outskirts of Edinburgh with enough room for Chip, his wife Mary, and their two children, Anna and Marcus. The house served its purpose. It kept them warm during the winter and sheltered during the summer. They were far more fortunate than Jonah, who lived in overcrowded housing near the wharf.

After a thirty-minute hike across Edinburgh, Chip reached his modest abode, and breathed in the aroma of the stew his loving wife had prepared for them.

"Mary, I be home, me love!" Chip announced, tossing his haversack into the corner.

"Papa!" Anna and Marcus shouted, running forward to greet their father.

Chip sank low, taking both of them into his arms before standing and swaying them back and forth. As fast as they were growing, he would not be able to do that much longer. Anna, with her strawberry-blond hair pulled back into pigtails and brilliant blue eyes, would soon be six. While Marcus, a stout lad with coal black hair and dark blue eyes, would be eight in only two weeks' time.

"He still needs to wrestle some wood in for the fire before

ye two tire him out," Mary said, wiping her hands on her apron.

Mary was beautiful with soft brown hair that laid delicately at her shoulders and warm chestnut eyes that glowed in the firelight. Her slight stature and tender disposition led most to believe her easy-going, but Chip knew firsthand how fiercely strong-willed the woman who stood before him, the woman he'd fallen hopelessly in love with, could be.

"Good to hear me chores still be waiting." Chip lowered his children to the floor, both of them groaning in disappointment.

"John McClure stopped by today." Mary set the stew on the table and waited for him to erupt.

Chip growled, "What did the blaggard want?"

"Language, Christopher, language."

"Then doth not be mentioning his name in front of the children," Chip retorted, hanging his coat up to take a seat at the table.

"I shall remember that." Mary narrowed her gaze at her husband, while setting out the bowls and spoons. "He stopped in to inform us that a new occupancy tax levy was passed by parliament."

"That be the third new tax this month!" Chip pounded his fist upon the table. "How doth they expect us to eat? Be we dogs they shall kick whenever it pleases them?"

"We shan't speak of this anymore tonight," Mary said sharply. "Children, supper be ready."

Chip blessed the meal before Mary ladled the stew into their bowls. The burden of a new tax continued to weigh on his mind.

Any new tax, no matter the amount, was too much. There were no more hours to be had at the wharf, and today's round of stew marked the third portion of potato, merely flavored with leftover beef broth.

Mary finally broke the strained silence. "Where be William today, Marcus? He did not come by to play after his chores."

"Gone." Marcus stared down at the table.

"His family left for America aboard the *Perth*," Chip said, not looking up from his stew.

"Smuggled?" Mary covered her mouth with her hand.

"They had not a sixpence to their name, and William's father could not find any honest labor."

"Aye, Chip, but shall they survive the voyage?"

"Which be better, Mary? To meet the reaper in the streets of Edinburgh or in the belly of the *Perth*?" Chip stared at his wife, waiting for her response.

"Be we going to die, Papa?" Anna's face filled with fear.

"'Course not," Mary snapped, before softening her tone. "Yer father hath work, and we hath food to eat."

"Suppose something happens, Mama? Like before?"

Chip stood up, unable to take much more. He strode to the fireplace, pounding his fist against the mantle before covering his eyes with the palm of his hand. He felt the soft form of his wife's hand close upon his shoulder.

"Christopher, come back to the table," she said softly. "Ye supper be getting cold."

"Mary, I shan't." Chip refused to look at her. "We spend every copper we hath as it be. How shall we afford another tax?"

"Starvation shall not help. Ye need yer strength."

"I need to know me family be safe. They shall not take all we hath. Not again."

Not wanting to see the look in her eyes, Chip crossed the room in a single stride, pulled on his coat then placed his cap upon his head.

"Christopher James MacDougall! What in the name of all that be holy be ye contemplating?"

"I must speak with Malone."

"Speak to him in the morn." Mary crossed her arms while glaring at him.

"This shall not wait till morn."

Without another word, Chip headed out into the wintry night. His focus set on finding some way to assure his family's well-being. He would work twenty hours a day if it meant that his wife and children had food and a place to call home.

The trip back through town seemed longer this time, the weight of the world pressing down upon him. When Chip reached O'Gill's pub he hesitated, gazing through the large stain-glass window at the shadows dancing beneath the shimmering lights. The tavern drew crowds from Leith and Edinburgh, being positioned perfectly between the two. From wharf workers to nearby shop owners, all walks of life could be seen there sharing a pint and a story from the day. Breathing deeply, he pushed open the door.

"Well now, look who decided to make a pease-kill!" came Malone's deep voice over the laughter and noise.

Malone motioned for Chip to join him at the bar. Chip made his way past a band of pub goers, as they began to sing something that sounded like, "Bonny Sweet Lassie." Malone patted the stool next to him. Chip felt as though a bucket full of nails lay upon his chest as he sat down.

"Did no' come back for that pint, did ye?"

Chip stared at the bar, his heart lodged in his throat. "McClure stopped by me home today."

Malone sighed, "What did the blaggard want?"

"Parliament passed another tax levy."

"Aye, I heard wind of this new levy."

"Bleedin' Britons believe we be made of benders!" Jonah interjected, joining the two at the bar.

"Aye. Yet I hath not one sixpence to spare as it be. Sir," Chip breathed deeply to steady his resolve, "I need more hours."

"There be none to give." Malone wiped his face with his hand. "I wish I could, but trade hath slowed."

Jonah sat his pint down on the bar. "Sir, give a portion of me wages to Chip."

"Jonah McCullah! Ye shall not such a thing!"

"Listen, I know how ye feel," Jonah said seriously, "but I hath only me self and me whither to care for. Should it not hath been for ye, ol' Malone here would hath never a-kept me. In that I owe ye. Repay me later, should ye be stubborn about it."

Chip swallowed hard. While he hadn't known Jonah nearly as long as others he had called mate back in Balloch, Chip was sure he had found a faithful friend he could depend upon.

"I shall repay ye. That I so swear," Chip said as he stood and shook Jonah's hand.

"Now that be settled, how 'bout that pint?"

Chip conceded to a pint before heading back home. Though he now bore the burden of repaying his friend, his shoulders felt much lighter. As one pint became two, the conversation shifted away from the woes of the day.

"Tell me, Chip, what doth ye think of this new game where ye run while carrying a ball?" Jonah asked, sipping on his pint.

"Hath not seen it played."

"It be a right foul game," Malone interjected. "Carrying a football. Where be the challenge in that?"

"It looks to be quite difficult. Players be allowed to hit one another."

"Doth ye play in teams?" Chip asked.

"Aye. I've seen it played with as many as twenty on a team!"

"I'll gladly play supposing the other team be full of Britons," Malone said.

Two hours, several more pints and many laughs later, Chip said goodnight. He pulled his coat tight, preparing for the brisk night air and was almost to the door when he heard a man call to him.

"Excuse me, lad," the scratchy voice of an older gentleman

called out.

Chip turned back to see a stately fellow, who sat in a booth nearest the entrance to the pub. His appearance spoke of one not accustomed to hard labor.

"Sir, did ye call to me?"

"Aye, I did, lad. And what manners. Someone raised you well."

"Thank me mother for that." Chip nodded, smiling as he accepted the compliment.

"Would you join me for a short spell? What I ask shall not take long. I see that you are traveling with haste."

Chip took a seat across from the old man, wiping his eyes as the effects of one too many pints began to set in. "What might I for thee?"

"Forgive me. I could not help overhearing your conversation, as I fetched a pint from the bar. Are you in search of work?"

Chip shook his head. "Nay, sir. I hath work, just not enough. Making preparations for the new tax levy parliament passed."

"Good, lad. Always be prepared."

Chip was familiar with most in and about the area, but could not recall seeing the man before.

"Forgive my rudeness," the old man said. "I have not formally introduced myself. My name is Phosphorus Prose."

Chip shook the older gentleman's hand without hesitation.

"Mr. Prose, I be Christopher, Christopher MacDougall. Though most call me Chip."

"MacDougall," Mr. Prose repeated, rubbing his hands together slowly. "You would not happen to be relative to the MacDougalls of Balloch, would you now?"

"One and the same, sir." Chip's eyes widened, amazed anyone would know of his family. "Moved me family to Edinburgh not long after the—"

"The fire. Yes, I remember. It was truly dreadful. Consumed the entire town square, including your father's bakery."

Mr. Prose leaned back, folded his hands in his lap, and smiled. Chip frowned as he contemplated the man before him and the memories he rekindled. He could not ever remember the name Prose in or around the town of Balloch.

"It is Greek."

"What be, sir?"

"My name. You were wondering about my name. My father was from the Mediterranean."

Chip stared in disbelief, raising his eyebrows. "How did ye—"

"Expressions, Mr. MacDougall. Besides, I am used to answering the question by now."

"Pardon me, sir, but what might I for thee?"

"Mr. MacDougall, I have a task here in Edinburgh. However, I must take journey before its completion. Therefore, I came here tonight in search of someone to perform said task."

Chip leaned forward, his curiosity piqued. "What be this task?"

"I'd rather not discuss the task or terms here," Mr. Prose countered. "Be of the sensitive nature."

"Be it legal?"

"Absolutely, Mr. MacDougall. All that I do is perfectly legal and binding."

Chip studied the gentleman before him. "Might I ask how long it would be before I receive pay for this task, should I agree to it, sir?"

"The cautious lad," Mr. Prose said appreciatively. "Good to be as such in these times. Should you agree to assist me, you shall receive pay in three weeks' time, however, I did overhear your plight and am willing to pay you twelve shillings in good faith that you shall meet me tomorrow evening. Should you choose to accept the task, I shall deduct the good faith from your final pay. Should you choose not to accept my task, you may keep the shillings for your time."

Chip whispered, "Sir, that be a week's wages!"

"Then best not spend it in a single day. Now, do you agree to meet me tomorrow evening at the end of the wharf?"

"Ye hath me word, sir, and any here might be witness." Chip waved his hand, pointing to the men still sitting at the bar.

Mr. Prose shook his head. "No need, lad. I take you at your word, because I see it in your eyes."

Chip could have danced around the pub and all the way

home. He shook Mr. Prose's hand vigorously. They stood together and made their way out to the street. Mr. Prose handed Chip a leather pouch. Chip glanced inside, and his heart leapt for joy.

"Ye shall not be disappointed, sir."

"I am sure of that, Mr. MacDougall. I shall see you at sunset."

Chip shook Mr. Prose's hand once more before tipping his cap to him, then he bounded down the street like a child headed to the schoolyard. When Chip turned to tip his cap once more to Mr. Prose, he was nowhere to be seen. *"Moves fast for an older gent,"* thought Chip, as he stuffed the pouch inside his coat, patted the bulge it caused, and turned to begin the trip home.

———◦———

"Twelve shillings!" Mary shrieked before covering her mouth, glancing around at their sleeping children. "Whatever it be it shan't be honest labor."

"Should the work not be honest, or he not be forthcoming, I shall repay him and decline," Chip said reassuringly, rubbing her shoulders as he stared into her eyes. "Now, be there any stew left?"

Mary glanced over her shoulder. "I left ye a bit over the fire. I knew ye would still be hungry."

Chip kissed her on the forehead as he embraced her lovingly before fetching his stew and sitting down at the table to eat. Mary fetched a bowl and spoon then joined him. As he ate,

Chip told Mary all that had happened. He could tell that Mary was still uneasy about this, and she had good reason. Edinburgh and Leith were full of con-men, looking to take advantage of an unsuspecting bloke down on his luck. The trouble was, Chip could not see Mr. Prose as a con-man, for what could he possibly gain from Chip that was worth twelve shillings.

Though it wasn't the custom, Chip held Mary close that night as he drifted off to sleep. To preserve wood, they only lit the one fireplace nearest the children, Chip and Mary sleeping closer to the door. That night, Chip dreamed of what it would be like to not have to worry again as to whether tomorrow would bring starvation or something worse for his family.

TWO

———◆◆———

THE TASK

Filled with excitement, Chip rose early the next morning. Dressing for another day at the wharf, he picked up the pouch of coppers and stuffed it back into his coat pocket. The fire, that was hope, was rekindled inside his belly.

After a breakfast of grain and goat milk, Chip bid his family farewell and headed out into the bitterly freezing morning air to make his ritual trek to the wharf. His mind was so engrossed with what this Mr. Prose might have for him to do, that he was shocked at how quickly he arrived at the wharf.

Once at work, he did his best to focus upon the job at hand, but the day dragged and when the noon whistle sounded Chip swore loudly in disbelief. After midday break, Chip buried himself in his work, determined to not to think about the evening. Driven to escape his own thoughts, he accomplished his loads earlier than anyone else.

"Taken me praise a bit too far." Malone laughed, slapping Chip hard on the back.

Chip smirked, "Hath much on me mind."

"Best take a kip in an empty crate till shift's end, lest the wharf master see ye standing about and cuts yer hours."

Chip nodded before searching out an empty crate large enough and tucking himself inside till the evening whistle blew.

———◆———

The light dimmed in the western sky as Chip headed toward the end of the wharf. Brisk winds ripped across the pier as storm clouds rolled in, blanketing the waters and churning the sea. Chip tugged up his collar as he gazed across the harbor at Edinburgh Castle, set above Edinburgh and Leith, a symbol of Scottish pride.

"It is a magnificent structure."

Chip turned, startled to see Mr. Prose standing behind him holding a small cage in one hand and a walking cane in the other. He was dressed for traveling in a black tricorne hat, waistcoat, white ruffled long sleeve shirt, black breeches, red stockings, and black leather shoes with gold buckles.

"Aye, I look at it often, sir. I hope I hath not kept ye waiting." Chip said, wondering how he hadn't heard Mr. Prose approaching.

"Not at all, Mr. MacDougall." Mr. Prose waved his hand dismissively. "It is I who have kept you waiting. Please accept my apology. I was detained by a previous engagement. I suppose you are curious as to what my task might be."

Chip nodded. "Indeed, I am, sir."

"Good, lad. I believe you shall complete my task."

Chip frowned, contemplating the man before him. "Sir, how be ye certain? Ye hath not even told me what it be."

"I paid you a portion in advance and still you showed," Mr. Prose explained. "Most would have fled with the coppers."

"I would never pay me debt with the topsail."

"Which is exactly why I am being certain that you shall complete my task. Now, let us discuss the task at hand before we are stifled by the west winds."

Chip nodded then waited to hear the task which required such secrecy.

"Alas Mr. MacDougall, I must leave Britain immediately, and I shall be traveling deep into the heart of Europe. Because of this, I have two requests to make of thee. My first request pertains to my rat."

Mr. Prose held up the cage so that Chip could see the creature within, which looked to be sleeping.

"Plague and disease torture Europe and animals, such as my rat, have been banned. Should you would watch over him until I return, I would be most pleased."

While having a pet rodent wasn't a widespread practice, it wasn't unheard of either. Chip considered the task a bit odd to ask of a stranger, but listened on.

"He be old and doth not require more than to be fed and watered. Should he pass while I be gone, all I ask is a proper burial, lest he be tossed with the rubbish. As for my second request."

Here it be, Chip thought. *The true reason he be wishing to speak in private.*

"There is land that I would be selling to an Englishman in three weeks' time. I shall be gone, and I wish for you to represent me in my stead. I do not trust my counting house to make the transaction without scavenging a portion for themselves in my absence."

Chip stared at him in astonishment. "Sir, I know nothing of land trade. I hath not years of schooling. How shall I know that the Englishman not make a paper skull of me?"

"I trust the Englishman, Mr. MacDougall, and shall accept whatever he offers. My counting house doth not know you and shall be leery to swindle thee. I trust you because you have everything to gain from fair trade and nothing to lose."

"It be a risk ye be taking in me," Chip said, trying to understand the older gentleman's reasons.

"No risk, Mr. MacDougall. Think of yourself as the trade overseer. Only my counting house be able to seal the trade in my absence. Take six shillings of the good faith and purchase a proper formal Scottish attire. Present this contract with my seal at the bottom to the counting house as to verify that you represent me."

Mr. Prose withdrew a scroll of parchment and handed it to him. Chip unrolled the parchment, glancing over tight scrawl. The parchment bore a seal at the bottom, with the likeness of a serpent at its center.

"You shall take one third the value of the land as payment

for your time and for caring for my pet in my absence."

"Sir, I doth not know what the land be worth, yet ye be too generous. One tenth would be more than enough!"

Mr. Prose grinned, "Too late, lad. The portion be already set in the contract."

Chip considered the tasks. The rat would be easy to care for and he only needed to be a witness to the land trade.

"Sir, it would be me honor."

"Thank you, lad. I be most grateful, knowing my old friend shall be cared for." Mr. Prose handed the cage to Chip. "Now, I must be on my way. You shall find the address of the counting house and the date in which you must meet the Englishman at the bottom of the parchment. Come, let us make haste, for I have a ship to board and you need to be getting home."

Chip and Mr. Prose walked side-by-side, up the wharf and away from the harbor. When they reached the edge of town, Mr. Prose stopped.

"This is where we part ways, Mr. MacDougall. My way is to the south while your way is to the west." Mr. Prose turned to face him and placed a hand upon Chip's left shoulder. "We shall see each other again soon."

"Sir, I shall not fail ye."

"Fare-thee-well, Mr. MacDougall. Until we meet again."

Chip watched as Mr. Prose headed south, walking with poise. Chip then turned and headed west towards his home as he pondered the task set before him. He sheltered the cage under his coat against the brisk wind, lest the tiny animal froze to death before he reached his destination.

When he arrived home, Chip was greeted by Marcus and Anna in the usual fashion. Marcus immediately spotted the rat and began to ask a thousand questions. Mary also spied the rat and looked upon it with distaste. When the children finally settled down, Chip sat at the dinner table and explained what had happened.

"We shall be paid in three weeks' time and the rodent shall stay with us until Mr. Prose returns," Chip said, trying to decipher the look in Mary's eyes.

"And nothing seemed a wee bit off?"

"Nay, me love. I thought it through and not found a thing. Hath ye spied something amiss?"

"It be just that ye hath never held such a post," Mary said, biting her lower lip. "Suppose ye doth something wrong? Shall this Mr. Prose expect ye to pay him back?"

"All things he said be in this here contract." Chip handed her the parchment. "Ol' Malone knows agreements quite well and I trust him. I shall hath him look it over tomorrow."

"Ye best make sure he reads the whole of it, Christopher MacDougall." Her eyes fixed upon his. "Lest we be left with the devil dancing in our pockets."

"Aye, love, I shall."

Chip understood Mary's reservations. He would only be lying to himself if he said he had none. There were too many swindlers about those days. Being leery was being wise.

"We doth not hath to eat the rat?" Anna asked, staring at the small rodent in the cage.

Chip turned to face his daughter. "Oh, come now, Anna. Doth ye think yer father would feed ye a rat?"

"Ye hath brought strange things home for food before," Mary interjected playfully.

Marcus scrunched his nose. "There not be enough of him to season soup!"

Chip and Mary laughed at the look on their children's faces. He watched the small rat open its eyes, curled its tail beneath itself, then go back to sleep. As he did, his mind drifted back to the contract. *Was he being taken a fool?*

The next day at noon break, Chip showed the contract to Malone. Malone read over the parchment several times, before rolling it back up and handing it back.

"Chip, me lad, all be in order." Malone slapped Chip on the back. "Mr. Overseer, I pray ye deed brings three hundred pounds for ye client and a hundred pounds for thee."

"A hundred pounds!" Chip hissed, his eyebrows traveling up his forehead. "What would I with such?"

"Purchase a small cottage of ye own and save the rest. That be what I would."

"Surely, it not be worth much lest he would hath stayed."

Malone shrugged his massive shoulders. "Must be worth somethin', lad. Why else would he be needin' an overseer."

"All I ask sir, be that ye keep this matter between us."

"Course, lad! This be none other's business but ye own. All I ask be that ye spot me a pint at O'Gills when ye be around, seein' I be yer official adviser."

"Aye, sir!" Chip exclaimed, grinning broadly. "Ten-fold!"

That evening, Chip stopped by a local shreds he passed every day on his trip to and from the wharf. The tailor measured and fitted him according to Mr. Prose's request. Chip paid the tailor three shillings in advance before continuing on his way. The tailor assured him his garments would be ready in three days' time.

The first two weeks crept by. The children became quite fond of the small rat, while Mary was still reserved about feeding a rodent in her home. Chip became accustomed to having the small creature around. Marcus pointed out that the rat always perked up whenever his father was there. He didn't know if Mr. Prose's pet had ever been given a name, however Anna named him Tiny upon the second day of his arrival.

The morning of his appointment, Chip was a bundle of nerves. He hadn't slept much the night before and fidgeted constantly while Mary helped him dress, the new attire being a snug fit. Chip stood before a long piece of reflective metal he had salvaged from the destroyed blacksmith's shop in Balloch and did not recognize the man staring back at him. He hadn't worn his formal attire since the day he tried it on at the shreds. He wore a soft brown hat, white ruffled shirt, black coat with red threads, Clan MacDougall tartan kilt, leather sporran pouch, kilt stockings, and brown leather shoes with clasps.

"Ye be a handsome sight, Christopher MacDougall," Mary said, straightening his collar.

Chip tugged at his sleeves. "I feel like a mule wearing breeks."

"Oh Chip, me love." Mary caressed his cheek and hugged him tightly. "Ye shall be fine."

"I would ask for a wish of good fortune, but ye hath given it to me already." Chip kissed her then said goodbye to Marcus and Anna.

Malone was covering for Chip today, having claimed he was ill. Chip arrived at the address on the parchment and tugged a few more times on his sleeves before entering. He was greeted by a middle-aged man in similar attire, sporting the tartan of Clan Wallace.

"How might I assist thee, sir?"

Chip breathed deeply, mustering all of his confidence. "I be here to oversee a trade on behalf of Mr. Prose."

"Aye. Ye be early. Right this way, sir."

The man did not introduce himself, but motioned for Chip to follow him into a back room. "Please wait here, sir." The man motioned for Chip to one of the four high back chairs which sat in front of an ornate looking desk. "Mr. Moor, Mr. Prose's accountant, shall join ye shortly once Mr. Tomlin arrives."

Once the man left the room, Chip reached out and ran his fingers along the grain of the desk. It was made of a wood that Chip did not recognize, and it was covered by pictures of animals that had been painstakingly carved into its side. The chair that Chip sat in was softer than anything he had ever sat upon before and the room was what he imagined one of the rooms in Edinburgh Castle would look like. The creaking of the door drew him from his musings.

"Well good morning," a man greeted Chip with a strong Highland accent.

Chip rose at once to greet the newcomer. He was another middle-aged man of similar attire, sporting the tartan of Clan Campbell.

"Me name be Jeffrey Moor," the man said as he shook Chip's hand.

"Mr. Moor, I be Christopher MacDougall. I be here today to represent Mr. Prose."

"Excellent, Mr. MacDougall. It be a pleasure to meet ye. Mr. Tomlin, the Englishman, hath just arrived and shall be joining us in a moment. I be glad to see a fellow Scot to represent Mr. Prose. He be … dare I say, odd sometimes."

Chip knew not what to say. He did not know Mr. Prose well enough to comment on the man's behavior. The door opened again and in walked a man in a long black waistcoat and ghostly white breeches, wearing a tricorne hat.

Mr. Moor inclined his head to the newcomer. "Mr. Tomlin, please allow me to introduce Mr. MacDougall. He shall be representing Mr. Prose in his absence."

As Chip shook Mr. Tomlin's hand, he noticed the man had an odd scar on his wrist in the shape of a star, as though someone had etched it into his skin.

Mr. Moor gestured to the chairs in front of his desk. "Gentleman, shall we begin?"

Mr. Tomlin and Chip each took a seat while Mr. Moor walked around the desk, placing a pair of reading spectacles on the bridge of his nose. He picked up several stacks of parchment from his desk, which he began to sort through.

"Now, to begin we must revisit the deeds that be a part of today's transaction."

Chip stared blankly at Mr. Moor for a moment, as he processed what had been said. There was more than one deed to be sold. When Mr. Prose said land, Chip presumed it would be only one deed and not many.

"Ah, here be the deeds," said Mr. Moor, snapping Chip back to the present. "There be seven in all. Would ye care to look over the deeds, Mr. MacDougall?"

Chip took the deeds, not certain what to do. His reading and writing skills were not the best, but he could read a little. He skimmed over each parchment. None of the deeds were for large plots, though he did notice that they were spread out across Scotland.

"Everything be in order, Mr. MacDougall?" Mr. Moor stared at Chip over the top of his spectacles.

Chip felt as though his throat was filled with sawdust. "Everything seems to be as needed."

"I must say, Mr. MacDougall, as pleasant as you be, I had hoped to meet Mr. Prose."

"Had Mr. Prose not been committed in Europe on business, I be sure that he would be here," Chip said stiffly, mimicking the memories of his wharf master.

Mr. Tomlin nodded. "Another time then. As for the deeds. What does Mr. Prose wish for them?"

"What doth ye wish to pay for them?"

At first Mr. Tomlin looked cross, but then his face broke into a small smile. He leaned forward, placing a hand on the desk and looking between Mr. Moor and Chip.

"Very well. I shall pay twenty for the lot."

Chip felt crestfallen. Twenty pounds was far less than he had dreamed, but one third of twenty pounds was more than enough for him. Mr. Moor raised an eyebrow, staring at him.

"Doth ye accept Mr. Tomlin's offer, Mr. MacDougall?"

Before Chip could answer, Mr. Tomlin interjected, "Twenty and four, but I shall pay no more!"

Chip glanced at Mr. Moor, whose eyebrows had disappeared completely into his hairline. He knew his response had been noticed and completely misunderstood.

"On behalf of Mr. Prose, I accept yer offer for the seven

deeds." Chip shook Mr. Tomlin's hand.

"Excellent." Mr. Moor picked up a quill from his desk and scratched something onto a parchment in front of him. "Mr. Tomlin, please sign here, accepting the terms. I shall be needing a note from thee authorizing the transfer of funds."

Mr. Moor passed the parchment and quill to Mr. Tomlin, who signed the bottom. Mr. Moor passed him a note for the authorization of the transfer of funds. Once all the parchments were in order and signed by Chip, Mr. Moor and Mr. Tomlin, the latter shook Chip's hand once more then left the office, his receipts of trade in hand. Once they heard the outer door shut, Mr. Moor broke the silence.

"I be thinking Mr. Tomlin changed his mind about ye being pleasant!" Mr. Moor laughed, pounding his fist upon the desk.

"I be going to accept the twenty, but Mr. Tomlin not give me the chance."

Mr. Moor looked as though he might get up and dance. "Course ye were, but the look upon yer face was brilliant! Mr. Prose had advised me to accept no less than eighteen, but to get an extra two and four! He sure be selecting the right man for the post!"

Guilt churned inside Chip's stomach. He was told to accept whatever the Englishman offered, yet something just didn't feel quite right.

"Mr. Prose not advise me how much to accept. I doth not wish to leave a man-a-hanging."

Mr. Moor sighed, "Doth ye wish to search out Mr. Tomlin

and inform him ye shall accept less? I shall tell ye now, it would be to eat yer nails."

"Nay," Chip replied, ignoring the continual nagging feeling.

"Good, good." Mr. Moor tossed his reading spectacles onto the desk, looking thoroughly relieved. "Now, doth ye have an account with the Bank of Scotland?"

"Nay, sir."

Chip barely registered his own response. He was still contemplating what had just transpired. He could hear Mary's warning ringing in his head. *What was he missing? Surely these men knew their craft.*

"Then ye shall be needing one. Let us see. Ye be to receive one-third, as payment for this and another unspecified task. That shall be six and eight."

Mr. Moor rang a small bell that sat on his desk. As he filled in another note, the office door opened once more.

"Ye rang, sir?" asked the middle-aged man who greeted Chip earlier.

"Aye, I did. Please take these notes to the Bank of Scotland. Tell them the first be transferred to Mr. Prose's account, while the second be for transfer into a new account under Mr. MacDougall's name. Also tell them that Mr. MacDougall shall be by later to complete the necessary parchments."

"Right away, sir." The man took the notes from Mr. Moor then left the room with haste.

Chip frowned at Mr. Prose's accountant. "I could hath

taken the note with me and saved ye the trouble."

"Mr. MacDougall, this counting house hath been here for many a year, because we doth not leave anything to chance. Now, here be yer receipt. Hold it tight for ye shall need to present it to the bank."

Chip glanced down and his mind became as empty as a church on Monday. The receipt nearly slipped from his hand as he slouched. The note within his grasp marked the sum of six thousand, eight hundred pounds sterling to be paid to one Christopher MacDougall.

Mr. Moor chuckled, "Just now be hitting ye, aye?"

"I doth not understand."

"Doth not be questioning me abilities with numbers, Mr. MacDougall," Mr. Moor said sternly. "I hath been in a counting house since me youth, and besides, it be easy to comprehend a third of twenty thousand and four hundred pounds sterling be six thousand and eight hundred pounds sterling."

"Nay sir, I not be questioning ye concerning ye trade. It be just that I wasn't expecting … I mean, six thousand, it be far more than—"

"Ah, so ye thought it be fiddler's money that ye be negotiating!" Mr. Moor interrupted, laughing in good spirit. "Lad, I did wonder why ye were so crestfallen. I for one was ready break out me fiddle and dance the side."

"Why would Mr. Prose agree then to pay me such a lumping pennyworth?" Chip's concern etching his face.

Mr. Moor became still as death, staring at him for a long moment.

"Lad, Mr. Prose be a topping man. Being he made such an investment in ye, then he shall be expecting a lumping pennyworth in return."

Chip leaned back into his chair. "There be another task that I be performing for Mr. Prose."

"None of me business, Mr. MacDougall, but whatever ye be doing for him must be important. Now, might I be so bold as to request that ye consider this counting house for any financial needs ye might have in the future?"

"It would be me honor."

Mr. Moor rose to his feet, as did Chip.

"Now then, Mr. MacDougall, ye need be off to the bank to secure yer funds. I shall be sending a message to Mr. Prose to inform him that the trade be successful."

Chip smiled and shook Mr. Moor's hand before bidding him farewell, then left the counting house for the bank. As he exited onto the street, that the air smelt fresher and the day looked brighter. While he still could not comprehend how his life had just changed, he knew it had.

Chip had passed the Bank of Scotland many times since he'd come to live in Edinburgh. Until then, the building had never earned more than a passing thought. Now, standing before it, the massive structure was quite intimidating. He decided that the best thing to do was to follow a gentleman entering the bank and go wherever he went. This was a mistake, as the gentleman turned out to be a teller.

"What doth ye think ye be doing?" an officer of the bank demanded.

"I be here to open an account, sir." Chip could feel his face begin to burn.

"Why were ye following me teller?"

"I knew not where to go, sir. This be me first visit."

"Aye. Follow me then."

The officer led him into a room and asked him to wait. Chip was sure they were fetching the constable, thinking him an impostor, but moments later, a man entered the room wearing a long blue waistcoat and brown breeches.

"Mr. MacDougall, me name be Jefferson Wallace, and I am the bank manager. Me apologies for yer wait." The man shook Chip's hand. "Mr. Prose informed me before his departure that ye and he would be conducting a substantial land trade, which would require ye opening an account here."

"Mr. Prose be a thorough man, indeed."

Mr. Wallace nodded in agreement. "Aye, Mr. Prose never be missing a detail. Now, we have several matters to cover this fine morning, however before we begin Mr. Prose asked me to ask ye one question. Doth ye believe that the trade and the payment be fair?"

Chip considered the question for a moment, as the same nagging feeling in his chest returned. While the payment was more than fair, the thought of costing Mr. Tomlin that much money bothered him. Then Chip thought of his family and what this meant for them. His eyes dropped to the floor. "Aye."

"Very good, indeed, Mr. MacDougall. I shall send a message to Mr. Prose informing him that ye were satisfied with the trade and payment."

"I believe Mr. Moor be sending one as well."

"Again, Mr. Prose never be missing a detail. Now, on to the business at hand."

Mr. Wallace guided Chip through all the necessary proceedings to establish his account and the many ways he could access his funds for purchases, including a seal that was assigned to him. He could use the seal to approve transfers of substantial amounts without having to be present at the bank. All transfers from then on would require both his signature and his seal.

Chip was fitted with a leather money belt that sat snugly under his waistcoat and kilt before leaving the bank. The belt alone contained more money than he had ever possessed at one time in his life. As he left, he turned to stare up at the impressive structure. The thought that six thousand pounds sat in the bank at his disposal was more than he could fathom. He swore then and there that he would one day find a way to repay Mr. Prose for what he had done and make things right with Mr. Tomlin.

———•———

Mr. Wallace was looking over some papers at his desk, remembering how he once loathed the endless stacks of parchment he sorted as a young teller, when there was a knock at his office door.

"Enter," commanded Mr. Wallace.

The door crept open, and one of the younger bank tellers entered the room.

"Sir, yer next appointment hath arrived."

"Very good. Please send him in."

"Right away, sir." The young man nodded, excusing himself from the room.

Mr. Wallace rose to his feet then made his way over to a small elegant liquor cabinet to pour himself a glass of Scotch. He breathed in the aroma of the vintage amber liquid as he uncorked the bottle. It was a scent that reminded him how far he had come. He returned to his desk, just as there was another knock at his office door.

"Enter," commanded Mr. Wallace yet again.

A man in a long waistcoat, carrying a tricorne hat pressed between his left arm and his torso entered the room, closing the door. The man inclined his head and Mr. Wallace returned the gesture.

"Evening, Mr. Tomlin." Mr. Wallace lifted his glass and motioned to the liquor cabinet. "Please, indulge yer self."

Mr. Tomlin smiled then poured himself a glass as well before seating himself in one of the chairs in front of Mr. Wallace's desk.

"Thank you, Mr. Wallace." Mr. Tomlin lifted the glass to his nose and inhaled deeply. "Fine year."

"I take it ye had no trouble with Mr. MacDougall?"

"No trouble whatsoever. You believe the wharf rat actually had the courage to hold out for more?"

"I believe there be more to this Mr. MacDougall than we see." Mr. Wallace silently contemplated the man who had visited his office. "For today, it matters not. A toast … to Mr. MacDougall and to another successful deal."

The two men reached across the desk to clink their glasses together, laughing as they did.

"I do wonder … what interest does Mr. Prose have in the wharf rat?"

From the dark shadowy corner of the room, behind Mr. Wallace's desk, stepped a figure into the light.

"What I wish with Mr. MacDougall is my business, Mr. Tomlin," said Mr. Prose sternly, his eyes hard and focused.

Mr. Wallace stiffened, and the sound of Mr. Tomlin's glass shattering on the hard floor echoed throughout the room.

THREE

———◆———

WHISPERS IN THE WIND

When Chip returned home to his anxious wife, he tried hard to gently break the news to her. Unfortunately, this did not work, and it took several hours and much fanning before Mary was able to come to grips with what her husband had told her.

"It not be any wonder Mr. Prose be not concerned over twelve shillings!" Mary exclaimed, as she drank her forth cup of water, whiskey being unavailable. Mary would not allow strong liquor inside their home.

"I forgot," Chip mused aloud, just above a whisper.

Mary's smile faded. "What hath ye forgotten?"

"I forgot to hath the counting house deduct the shillings from the wages."

"Oh, Christopher," Mary sighed, her smile returning "it be less than a pound that ye be worrying over. Ye shall settle up with the counting house another day. Ye be a topping man now!"

"We shall not go about making a pease-kill. Remember, we be simple people."

"At least let us buy ourselves a better place to live!" Mary scoffed, smirking and crossing her arms.

Chip laughed, looking about the small cottage. "That we shall! And more than that, I be sure! As soon as we hear back from Mr. Prose."

"What be yer concern?"

"I want to be sure that nothing be amiss. That be all."

"Ye be a wise man, Christopher MacDougall." Mary wrapped her arms around him.

"Only in yer eyes, me love."

"Aye, but does any other's matter?" Mary retorted, laughing at her own wit.

"None, me love." Chip lifted her chin up, kissing her softly.

————◆————

Several months passed before Chip and Mary could come to grips with the idea that their family needn't worry for money. Chip continued to work at the wharf for several weeks. His concern that there had been a mistake and the money in the bank might disappear wouldn't let him rest. Finally, upon receiving a message from Mr. Prose via Mr. Moor, thanking him for his diligence, did he come to the realization that the money was indeed his to keep.

As a surprise for Mary, Chip arranged with the bank to purchase a manor home in the heart of Edinburgh. He then met up with Gregor Malone at O'Gills to inform him that he would no longer be returning to the wharf. Malone was happy for him, yet sad to lose his best docker.

Upon leaving, Chip handed Malone a sealed envelope. "Doth not open it here."

Malone eyed him with suspicion, but agreed to wait to open the envelope. Later Malone found a promissory note for fifty pounds and a piece of parchment bearing the words, *For hard times*. He did the same for Jonah, who refused to accept the note unless Chip allowed him to be present when he informed his landlord, Mr. McClure, that the cottage would be vacant again.

———◆———

One morning, Chip was walking down the upstairs hallway of their new home when he heard a muffled crying coming from Anna's room. He quietly stepped inside to find his little girl curled up in the corner sobbing.

"Why be ye crying, Angel?"

Her only response was a soft muffled sound. He crouched down next to her and brushed the back of her head.

"Where be Marcus?"

"In his room, staring out his window at his castle," Anna sniffed. "He not want to play with me."

"It be new to him, having his own room." Chip rubbed his angel's back, hoping to calm her.

"Be that why he saith I hath to stay in mine?"

"When did he say this?"

"Last night."

"Be that why ye joined me and yer mother last night?"

"I be scared when I be alone." Anna looked up at him through watery eyes. "This house be too big, Papa."

"Ye say this now, but ye shall be happy here. Ye hath me oath."

Anna wiped the tears from her eyes. "Aye, Papa."

Chip pulled her into his arms and held her for a while before heading downstairs to the kitchen where he found Mary baking. He poured himself some water and sat down at the table.

"Something troubling ye?"

"I found Anna sobbing in her room."

Mary wiped her hands on her apron before joining him at the table. "Hath Marcus done something to her?"

"Aye. He be enjoying his new room."

Mary sighed, "This move be difficult for all of us."

"We knew the measures that lied before us when we moved here, love."

"Aye, but did ye foretell such a welcome?" she countered, her tone icy.

"Aye, I did. We hath invaded the blood-borns. They know not our ways, nor doth they wish to. They believe that I should be a lay about while ye clean, cook and make faces."

"Be that what ye wish for me to become?"

"Nay!" he replied, grasping her hands. "I told ye before. We be simple people. Besides, we hath enough faces about."

Chip received a playful smack for his cheekiness. He truly loved to make her smile.

"How doth ye plan to help Anna?"

"She needs a companion to get her through."

"I shall not allow that beast to sleep in her room, cage or not!"

Chip patted his wife's arm. "The rat shall remain in the sitting room. I be more thinking of the lifeless sort. There be a tiny porcelain doll in a window on Toppum Street. I think it shall be up to the task."

Mary agreed, and Chip set out the next morning to retrieve the tiny toy. Though he didn't tell his wife, there was more than just a trinket of porcelain drawing him to Toppum Street.

Anna shrieked with glee when she saw the tiny figurine in her father's hands. "She's beautiful!"

"What shall ye name her?" Chip asked, as he watched his angel dance about the room with her new doll.

Anna ran to hug her father, her bare feet slapping against the polished floor. "I shall name her Angel. Thank ye, Papa!"

Chip patted her softly on the back. "We'll be happy here, me angel. Give it time."

"I love the house, Papa. Really I do."

"Especially the fireplaces," Mary interjected, entering the room. "I shoo her out from inside them once a day."

"They be so big! I stand beneath without touching."

"Might it be that ye be so small?" Chip retorted playfully.

Anna only smiled as she danced out of the room with her new doll, her blue dress swishing about her. He knew that soon enough, life would return to a form of normal.

———◆———

Chip knew he wasn't suited to stay at home with his feet propped up, like his blood-born elitist neighbors. He needed to work to feel useful. It didn't take him much effort to decide what he wanted to do. He wanted to reopen his father's bakery.

He had spent quite a bit of time walking the west side market streets, looking for the right place. Within a fortnight though, he knew he had found the perfect spot.

"It be a bit shabby," Chip explained, while ladling the soup Mary had just prepared into his bowl. "The previous tenant be an old peddler and he left much behind."

"Be there not another store that ye might want?" she asked, joining him at the table.

"Not with such an arching window front and not on Toppum Street Road. It shall need some work, but I believe it be the one. Even now I see fresh bread on display for passersby."

Mary sighed, "Me husband, the baker. I never thought I'd hear me self utter those words again. God be gracious."

"Aye, for He gave me ye."

"How long doth ye think it shall take ye to wax and prepare?" she asked, rubbing his arm lovingly.

39

"Lest I move at a snail's gallop, the store shall become a bakery in a fortnight. Never know. I may hath been a lay about too long to complete a sensible day's work."

"All I ask be that ye don't work yer self into a dustman. I doth not wish to place ye in Greyfriar's Kirkyard."

"Supposing I do, ye shall slap me back to life."

Chip moved quickly to avoid a slap to the back of the head, laughing as he did. As he sat there sipping the sweet broth, he envisioned himself a baker once more. He knew that challenging work laid ahead for him and it only added to his excitement.

The task did prove to be harder than he had anticipated, but he was more than ready for the task. He installed a large brick oven, re-purposed a back room into an office, and placed shelves in front of the window to display his daily creations. He had just finished his first round of baking when he spied a young man lingering in the doorway.

"What might I for ye?" Chip asked, approaching the newcomer cautiously.

"Forgive me sir, but I smelled yer delicious bread and wondered whether ye might spare a pone."

Chip folded his arms while he appraised the young man. "What be ye name, lad?"

"Spencer Thomas, sir."

"Well, Mr. Thomas, I hath a proposition for ye. Opening day for me shop be tomorrow and I hath much to do. Sweep me floors and I shall consider yer request."

"Right away, sir!"

Chip smiled as he watched the young man eagerly complete the task. His dream of owning a bakery again was almost a reality and he knew there was only one thing he lacked. He pulled a fresh pone from the cooling rack and waited until Mr. Thomas was finished.

"Well done, lad," Chip said, handing him a pone of bread. "Tell me, where doth ye work?"

"Where I find it. Honest work be hard to come by, sir."

"Meet me here tomorrow at dawn and ye shall hath work."

Spencer stood motionless, gaping at him. The only response he could muster was, "Sir?"

"I need hands and ye need work. I be willing to pay thee two schillings a day."

"Thank ye, sir!" Spencer exclaimed, shaking Chip's hand.

"Call me Mr. MacDougall."

"Thank ye, Mr. MacDougall! Thank ye!"

The following morning was one of mixed emotions for Chip. He arrived early at the bakery and was pleased to find Spencer waiting for him. As they opened the doors and began to welcome morning shoppers, he felt he was finally where he belonged.

Chip woke one morning to a dark, turbulent setting. Storm clouds had gathered in from the sea and the wind whipped hard. He shivered, as he slipped out of bed and made his way downstairs to the kitchen to prepare breakfast for Mary and the children.

Per the usual, he scraped the bottom of the skillet into a small bowl, then covered it in shredded bits of leftover cheese. He made his way to the sitting room where a small cage sat perched atop a cedar table. Inside, laid Mr. Prose's pet.

Mary said that he wasted decent food on the rodent, but he did not care. This small creature had grown on him, and he often marveled at its intelligence. When she wasn't around, he would leave the rat out of its cage for extended periods of time, watching as it explored the house. It had become keen to his voice, and when he was ready to put the rat back in its cage, he would merely call for it.

Normally, the little rat would rouse at the sound of his footsteps, but this morning the tiny creature remained still. He opened the cage and with a pang in his chest, he realized that his little friend was dead. He never believed he would ever shed a tear for a rodent, yet he had to wipe his eyes as he closed the cage door.

After breakfast, he dug a small hole behind the house and buried the rodent inside a cigar box. The box had been gifted to him by one of his neighbors as a welcome present. Anna placed some heather bells she had picked from around the fence line atop the tiny grave.

"Mr. Prose could not hath asked more of ye than this, Christopher." Mary patted her husband on the shoulder. "Now, off with ye to the bakery. I shall see the children to school."

"Trying to be rid of me, Mrs MacDougall?"

"Aye, I be looking forward to a quiet day. Might even finish me quilt for Anna's bed."

Chip kissed his wife and children goodbye before placing the shovel back in the cellar and heading off. He tugged up the collar of his coat, as the morning wind was brisk, the smell of rain in the air.

Upon arriving at the bakery, Chip was pleased, as always, to see Spencer already there preparing for a morning of baking.

"Mornin', Mr. MacDougall. All the counters be clean an' the oven be warmin'."

"Good lad, Spencer. We hath orders to fill and not any time to be wasted."

As the morning sped along, Chip's thoughts of the tiny rat's passing were quickly burned away by the repetition of the day. Like his father, he could always lose his problems in his baking.

"Where be me singing bakers?"

"Ah, good morning, Constable O'Malley. Yer order of rolls be a coolin'." Spencer slid another tray of bread into the oven. "As for the singing, I not be so good a solo."

Chip chuckled. Of all the things in life that he had ever aspired to be, a singing baker was not one of them. Yet he had become just that. His father had always sung as he baked, and Chip had picked up the habit as a boy working alongside him.

Now, Spencer had picked up the same habit while working alongside him. All their patrons had come to know them as the singing bakers.

Chip sighed as he bagged the order. "Not in much of a singing mood this morning, sir."

The Constable paid Spencer for the rolls then accepted the bag of fresh baked bread from Chip. He opened the bag and breathed deeply.

"Whatever it be that hath ye down, Mr. MacDougall, at least it not be affecting yer baking."

"This batch be baked by Mr. Thomas here," he chuckled, slapping Spencer on the back.

"It does me heart well to see young Mr. Thomas prosper so. Not too long ago, me remembers seeing him beg for handouts."

"It be fortune the day I asked Mr. MacDougall to spare a pone."

Chip nodded in agreement. "Indeed, it be."

"Well, I shall leave ye to yer orders." Constable O'Malley tipped his cap. "Worry not. Singing or not, I shall be back tomorrow for more and the day after."

"Ye orders shall be waiting," Spencer called, waving to the Constable's retreating back.

"Constable O'Malley be a good man," Chip sighed, wiping the counter.

"So be ye."

Chip chuckled, "There not be more schillings earned by praise, Spencer me lad. Let us keep those orders coming."

The day continued on and soon Chip was humming and singing once more. Work was often the cure for whatever ailed him. Before he knew it, the day had flown by.

"Good day's work, Spencer," he said, cleaning one of the heavier iron trays.

"Thank ye, sir. I pray thee, what be ailing ye this morn?"

"Oh, 'twas nothing. Just be a fool pining over the loss of me pet."

"There be days when ye pet be all ye hath. Would be lost without me mutt."

"Go on then. Enjoy the rest of the day with 'em. Maybe make time for ye lass as well."

Spencer laughed. "Hath not found a lass that might stand the mutt!"

"Priorities, lad!" Chip chuckled, shaking his head in amusement. "A mutt only ever be a mutt, but a lass might become ye wife!"

Spencer laughed again, waving merrily as he bid Chip farewell for the evening. Chip decided that before he left, he would sort through some things. The county tax was almost due, and he wanted to make sure he hadn't overlooked anything.

He was in his small office when he heard a sound that caught his attention. He grabbed a broom that laid against the wall of his office and slowly made his way out into the front of the bakery.

"Hello? The bakery be closed."

"Hurry! Danger!" came a whispered cry in Gaelic.

"Ye need not be afraid. I shall not hurt thee. The bakery be closed, though. Come back in the morning."

There was no answer and Chip saw no one moving about. He gripped the broom tighter, fearing that thieves had entered the bakery, preparing to attack him from behind the counter.

"Danger!" came another whispered cry.

"There not be danger here."

Chip waited, but still no reply. He searched the entire bakery, but he could not find the source of the voice. Not certain what to think, he secured the shop for the night and quickly made his way back home. He resolved to search the bakery again in the morning for signs of where the unseen intruder might have been hiding.

Arriving home, Mary greeted her husband warmly. Chip brushed away the incident and told her all about the wonderful day he had while he ate. He nearly spilled his stew as Anna and Marcus raced each other to the kitchen table to hug him. Mary scolded them lightly for entering the kitchen in such a ruckus and interrupting their father. As they shared stories of the day, Chip knew that this was the best life that he could ever hope for.

"Papa?" Marcus asked hesitantly.

Chip knew by the look upon his son's face, he was about to

hear some sort of confession. "Aye, Marcus. What be it, me boy?"

"Papa, I lost me ball in the cellar." Marcus stared at the table, refusing to meet his father's eyes.

"Marcus William MacDougall, how did ye lose yer ball in the cellar when ye should not be down there?"

Marcus melted under the gaze of his mother's wrath. "Me an' Anna were playing near the steps to the cellar when we thought it be fun to kick the ball down the stairs!" he pleaded. "We meant no harm, Mama."

"It be okay, Mary," Chip said, attempting to bring calm to the moment. "I shall fetch the ball tonight. Though I shall be deciding when our children shall play with their ball again."

"But Papa—"

"Up with ye!" Mary snapped. "Chores, then prepare for bed!"

"Aye, Mama," the children said in unison as they rose quickly from the kitchen table.

"Doth ye believe?" Mary muttered, watching her children's receding backs.

"They be children, Mary. Supposing they be perfect, then what would become of us?" Chip took her hand in his, bringing a smile to her face.

Later that evening, Chip made his way down into the cellar to retrieve the lost ball, laughing to himself as he thought of all the mischievous things his children could get up to. The cellar was nearly as large as the cottage they once lived in with numerous places to hide. He could see the attraction it must present to Marcus. He finally spotted the small leather ball next to some jars of fruit that Mary had canned.

From out of nowhere came a whispered cry. *"Danger!"*

Chip nearly fell as he spun around, his heart hammering in his chest. He frowned as his eyes fell upon Marcus, standing at the bottom of the steps.

"Marcus! What be the meaning of this?"

"I came to help thee, Papa. Please doth not tell mother I be down here again."

"Why doth ye whisper danger?"

"What doth ye mean, Papa? I saith not a word."

Realizing his son was telling the truth, he forced a smile. "Go on up, Marcus. I be up in a moment."

"Aye, Papa." Marcus hurried up the stairs without a second glance.

Chip slowly walked around the cellar, looking around every corner. Nothing moved, except he and his shadow. *Could this be spirits?* he pondered silently. He rubbed his temples with his fingers to ease the nervous tension. *Nay, Chip. Pull yer self together!* He wearily made his way to the stairs and out of the cellar, forgetting the reason for his visit on a shelf next to some of Mary's canning.

He continued to reason with himself as he prepared for bed. He tried to shake off the entirety of the day, but his nerves and exhaustion toyed with him. He finally convinced himself the intruder from earlier must have still been on his mind.

Mary eyed him suspiciously as he climbed into bed. "What be troubling ye?"

He was so engrossed in his own thoughts that he hadn't even noticed that his wife was still awake. She was sitting up in bed and he now recognized that she was reading her nightly devotion by candlelight before turning in.

"Oh, it be nothing. Just the end of a long day."

"Christopher MacDougall, I hath seen ye at the end of long days before, yet ye never passed me by without even a word."

"Nothing to worry over. Me mind just be unsettled. Had unseen guests at the bakery today."

"Unseen guests?" Mary repeated, her brow furrowing.

"They came in late, but would not show themselves to me. Remained hidden amongst the counters."

Mary nodded her head in comprehension. "Aye, and ye be afraid they might be conveyancers, waiting for ye to close. Tell me then, Christopher, why did ye not go back tonight?"

"I believe I scared them away," he replied, as convincingly as possible.

Mary smirked, "I believe then, ye shall know in the

morning."

He laid down, then turned onto his side as he tried to forget the day. He hoped that a good night's rest would clear his mind. Though he knew fate was rarely so kind.

Thunder rumbled ominously, stirring Chip from his slumber. He opened his eyes to see lightning flash through the shuttered window. He rolled over to alert Mary, but she was nowhere to be seen. Realizing she must have went to check on the children, he decided to make sure the rest of the manor shutters were closed and secure.

He had just entered the kitchen, when he heard a knock upon the front door. Chip wondered who it could be at this time of night and in this weather. He made his way to the front door and opened it to find a soaking wet Mr. Prose.

"Mr. Prose!" Chip exclaimed, extending his hand in greeting.

Mr. Prose ignored Chip's outstretched hand. "I have come for my pet, Mr. MacDougall."

"Mr. Prose, I sorry to say that ye pet passed but yesterday."

Mr. Prose folded his arms, his eyes narrowing. "Did it now. Or did you grow tired of caring for it and do it in, thinking I would not return?"

"Nay," Chip retorted, taking a step back from the doorway. "We took good care of yer pet. Mary and the children cared for it, as though it be their own! As did I!"

"Tell me, Mr. MacDougall, did you suffocate the

unfortunate thing, or did you wait for it to die of starvation?" Mr. Prose asked darkly, a hint of danger in his tone.

"I swear to ye, Mr. Prose, I did nothing to harm yer pet! It twas old, as ye hath said. The small rodent passed while it slept."

"Why should I believe you? Why should I trust a man as greedy as you?"

Chip felt thoroughly confused. "Greedy? I hath never—"

"You cheated a man two and four to gain eight," Mr. Prose interrupted, advancing on him. "Be the eight you gained worth the shame?"

"Ye never told me a price!" Chip pleaded, backing away from Mr. Prose. "I tried to be honest! I asked the man his price!"

Mr. Prose pursued him into the kitchen, his eyes alight with malice. "When you knew you were wrong, did you try to make it right?"

"I—I—" Chip stuttered, his back slamming into the kitchen counter.

"No! You let the counting clerk make the decision for you! I hired you to keep him honest, yet you failed. You broke my trust for the sum of eight hundred pounds! Tell me Mr. MacDougall, why should I believe thee when you say my pet died of old age?"

"It be the truth. Yet ... I understand why ye doth not believe me." Chip lowered his eyes, feeling the sting of guilt.

Mr. Prose's mouth curved into a vicious smile. "Prove it. Take the rat's place!"

"What?"

When Chip looked up he was no longer in the kitchen. He was lying in a deep hole, looking up at Mr. Prose, who stood high above him, rain pouring down.

Mr. Prose laughed sadistically, as the small rat climbed up onto his shoulder. "Take his place, Mr. MacDougall!"

"Nay!" Chip shouted, as a large scoop of dirt struck him in the face. "Wait! Please!"

Mr. Prose stepped out of sight as showers of dirt fell into the hole, burying him alive. "Goodbye, Mr. MacDougall."

Through the thunder and the showers of dirt, Mr. Prose's sick laughter echoed in his ears.

"Nay! Nay! Nay!"

"Christopher!" Mary cried, sitting up in bed to embrace her husband. "Ye be having a bad dream!"

Chip was breathing hard, sweat pouring from his body. He leaned his head on Mary's shoulder. *It hath been just a dream. A terrifically horrible dream, yet it be just a dream.* He laid back down and tried to relax. Mary continued to hold him, stroking his hair and humming softly.

"Thank ye, me love." he sighed, patting her arm.

"Shush now and get some rest," she whispered, continuing to stroke his hair.

Slowly, he drifted off to sleep and dreamed no more that night.

FOUR

———◆———

SERENITY GONE

The next day, Chip returned to the bakery and searched every nook and cranny for any clues as to whom the unseen intruder had been. Spencer offered to spend the night at the bakery and lay in wait for any that should return. He declined the offer and assured him that it was not worth risking his most valued employee over a few rolls and pans.

"Sir, me be yer only employee!" Spencer exclaimed, his eyebrows raised.

Chip laughed, slapping the young man on the back. "That be what makes ye so valuable!"

Spencer shook his head laughing at his employer's humor, as he seasoned the pans. As the day hummed along, the events of the previous night faded from Chip's mind.

It was near closing, and Chip was wiping down the oven when he heard whispering coming from the grain closet.

"In here. In here. It be warm and there be food."

Chip's heart failed to beat. He looked around the bakery to find Spencer wiping down the window. He didn't bother his faithful employee, but crept slowly to the back of the bakery to investigate. Slowly, he entered the grain closet, peering around for any signs of movement.

"Sir?"

Startled by Spencer's sudden appearance, Chip's feet literally left the ground. "Ye gave me a fright!"

The whispered cries of, *"Danger! Danger!"* came from all around the closet.

Spencer frowned as Chip wiped away the beads of sweat that were forming on his brow. "Sir, be ye okay?"

"A-Aye lad, I be fine. Just thought I heard something coming from the closet. It be nothing."

"Danger! Danger! Danger! Danger!" The whispers were coming louder and louder.

"Sure ye okay? I shall close up, should ye need to go home and rest."

He pushed past Spencer, out of the closet and back into the small office area. "I accept ye offer."

"Go ye home, sir. Doth no' worry about me."

"Ye be a good lad, Spencer."

Chip patted Spencer on the shoulder, gathered up his things and bid him good night. He considered hailing a hackney, but chose to walk to clear his mind.

He was waiting to cross the usually busy High Street when he heard a voice behind him call out, *"Danger!"*

Chip whirled about to face a man standing extremely close

to him on the crowded city street. The man looked up at him, startled by his quick movements.

"Might I help ye, sir?"

Chip tipped his hat, "Sorry, did ye say something?"

"Nay sir," the man replied, shaking his head.

Chip tipped his hat again, then turned back to face High Street. Immediately he heard the voice again and again, repeating the same thing over and over—*Danger*. He glanced around at the people next to him, but none were speaking.

When the opportunity finally came to cross the street, Chip walked swiftly across. He was beginning to believe that whatever it was he was hearing was something supernatural. As the street crested, dipping down the hillside that led toward home, he broke into a jog. He fought the urge to run, for fear a gentleman in red might see him do so. Acting unusual or suspicious would only give the soldiers who patrolled Edinburgh an excuse to detain him.

"Evening, Mr. MacDougall."

He glanced round to see his neighbor, Mr. Farley, bustling about with something.

"Ye seem to be in a wee bit of a hurry. Anything be the matter?"

"Not feeling well, Mr. Farley."

"Should there be anything ye need, only let me or the misses know."

"That I shall," Chip said, waving as he reached the front door, entering quickly.

He hated to be less than friendly with Mr. Farley, for he truly was his only neighbor willing to accept him for who he was.

"Christopher! What in Heaven's name be ye doing here so early?"

Chip hung his cap and coat on one of the hooks. "Not feeling well."

"Go rest yer self by the fire," she ordered, pointing towards the sitting room. "I shall fetch the hot water bottle and a blanket."

Chip wanted to tell her that he wasn't ill in that way, but he knew better than to argue when she was so focused. His dear wife believed everything could be cured with a hot water bottle and a blanket. Before he knew it, he was sitting in front of the fireplace, his boots off, his feet propped up on a hot water bottle, and a blanket wrapping him from his neck to his waist.

Mary pulled up a chair beside her husband, taking his hand in hers. "Tell me love, what ills ye?"

"Not quite sure. I fear I might be coming down with fever."

She felt his brow and cheek with her hand. "Ye face not be burning. Ye be cold and sweaty. Hath someone or something given ye the fright?"

Dare he tell her? he pondered. *Supposing I be going mad, then should not she hath earned the right to know?*

"Given me the fright?" he repeated, feigning surprise. "What would give me the fright?"

Mary frowned, knowing he was avoiding the question. "Something be wrong. I hath not seen ye like this since we up and

56

moved here to Edinburgh after the fire."

"I … I need to lie down a bit."

"Aye, ye do. Go up and lie. I shall fetch ye when supper be ready."

As he made his way upstairs and to his room, he convinced himself he had done the right thing. *It would be foolish to trouble her over such nonsense*, he reasoned.

Within the safe confides of his and Mary's room, Chip found it easy to relax. He closed his eyes and focused on the peaceful rhythmic sound of the wind blowing past the shutters.

Suddenly, the wind began to blow harder. The shutters creaked and groaned under the strain. The sounds of thunder filled the room. Chip opened his eyes just as a flash of lightning illuminated the sky. He rolled out of bed and wandered out of his room and down the stairs, feeling disorientated by the sudden change of weather. He wondered why Mary had not come to wake him.

He entered the kitchen looking for his wife, however a knock at the front door caused him to cease his searching. He answered the door before taking three steps back.

"Where's my pet, Mr. MacDougall?" a soaking wet Mr. Prose demanded.

"Mr. Prose! I'm sorry sir, but yer pet passed."

Mr. Prose stepped inside, slamming the door behind him. "At your hand, no doubt!"

"Sir, I understand that ye be upset—"

"Upset? You think that I be upset? You have yet to see me upset, Mr. MacDougall!"

Suddenly, Chip was outside in the pouring rain, being held over top an empty grave by the neck, Mr. Prose choking the life out of him. Chip struck at the man's arms with his own, but the strength of Mr. Prose was almost inhuman.

"Be this how you offed my pet, Mr. MacDougall?" Mr. Prose growled. "Do you feel the life leaving your body? You shan't escape me, Mr. MacDougall."

"Christopher! Wake up!"

Chip's eyes flew open to see Mary staring at him. A small gasp caught his attention and he looked over to see Anna standing near the bedroom door in a pale pink dress. He rubbed his face with both hands, wiping away the sweat.

"Christopher, be ye okay?"

"Aye, love." He swung his legs off the bed to sit up. "A bad dream. Nothing more."

Mary rubbed his forehead with her hand. "I heard ye screaming from the kitchen."

Chip looked up at the window to see the dusk peeking through the shutters. Footsteps caught his attention, as he looked over to see Marcus entering the room.

"Marcus, take yer sister downstairs," Mary said. "Be quick about it!"

"Come, Anna." Marcus tugged his sister's arm for her to follow him.

58

Mary waited until the children left the room before kneeling in front of her husband, so she could look him directly in the eyes.

"Christopher, what be this dream? Please, I need to know."

Chip looked into her eyes and decided it was time to tell her. He placed his hand on her shoulder. "I dreamt Mr. Prose hath come for his pet. When I told him his pet hath passed, he became angry ... violent even and accused me of offing his pet. He would not listen. He began to choke the life from me while holding me off me feet above an empty grave."

Mary covered her mouth with her hand.

"I couldn't break free."

"Christopher, me love," she rubbed his hand in hers, "ye be still worrying over Mr. Prose's pet. Mr. Prose shall not be angry with thee. Ye did all that ye could for the tiny creature."

This would have been soothing to hear, if it wasn't for the voices—those bodiless voices calling—no, warning him of danger. He wondered if they were warning him of Mr. Prose and the danger he imposed. He rubbed his eyes with his free hand.

"Suppose these dreams be warnings ... of ... of danger?" Chip shook as he uttered the word that filled him with fear.

"Christopher, me father told me when I be little that ye need not fear tomorrow. Tomorrow shall come, lest we perish in the night."

"I doth not deserve thee."

"I agree," she said with a hint of laughter, kissing him softly. "Come, supper awaits. I am sure our children be waiting ...

patiently."

Chip wished tomorrow held nothing for him to fear. He wished he could stay within the safe confides of his warm home, but he knew better. He knew that tomorrow would come, and it did.

The next morning, after another restless night, Chip awoke to the fading images of Mr. Prose demanding his life in exchange for his pet's. He splashed cold water upon his face from the taps in the water closet to clear his thoughts. Though no amount of water could wash away his nightmares.

Day after day this continued. Mysterious voices tormented him by day and chilling nightmares haunted him at night. It was maddening, and Chip felt as though he was starting to take leave of his senses. Mary and the children could only watch helplessly, as he slowly tried to shut out the entire world.

The third week of Chip's refusal to leave the house saw Mary's patience of gold begin to crack.

"Christopher MacDougall!" She stomped her foot, her auburn dress swaying madly. "I be fetching the beaton tomorrow if ye continue to refuse to leave this house!"

"I tell ye, me love, I need not any healer. I just doth not wish to go with thee."

"Surely ye not be afraid to go to church!"

"It not be the church I be avoiding. I swear to ye!"

"Tell me, Christopher MacDougall! Tell me now! Ye hath terrible dreams every night and hath abandoned the bakery! Poor

Spencer runs it in yer absence, but for how much longer? Supposing ye not be ill in yer body. Come pray for yer soul."

"Ye pray for me." His eyes fell to the floor, unwilling to see the look her in the eyes. "I hear thee at night."

"I pray for thee because I love thee!"

"I know." He looked up and wiped a tear from her cheek with his hand. "I shall go with thee today."

She threw herself into his arms, sobbing into his shoulder. He would face anything for her, even the torture that waited for him outside their front door.

Chip hummed loudly, as they walked down the High Street, their destination only a few more blocks away. Passersby looked oddly upon him, but he did not care. The humming helped drown out the whispers of the bodiless voices. Mary didn't mind too much, for he was finally out of the house.

When the morning service was over, Mary pressed Bishop Seamus for a moment of conference. He graciously invited them into his quarters, while his wife entertained Marcus and Anna by introducing them to her Scottish terrier pup. He listened as Chip reluctantly told him about his nightmares, omitting the true source of his torment.

"Mr. MacDougall, yer dreams be troubling. I not help but feel there be more that ye not be telling me."

"I hath done nothing to Mr. Prose, should ye be suggesting such!" Chip exclaimed, gripping the arms of the wooden chair that he was sitting in. "I hath done all he asked of me."

Mary gripped Chip's arm tightly.

"I be not accusing ye of misgivings, Mr. MacDougall," Bishop Seamus said calmly, rubbing his chin. "I be simply wondering, whether there be more."

"I be truly sorry for me outburst, Bishop. Unfortunately, there be nothing more for me to tell."

Chip shifted uncomfortably in his chair. He hated to lie to the Bishop, but he could not even comprehend what he might say to the response. "I be hearing voices."

"Supposing that be all, then I would say ye be suffering from plate-fleet remorse."

"Plate-fleet remorse?" Chip repeated, looking confused.

Bishop Seamus folded his hands upon his desk. "Over the past year, ye hath gone from a man-a-hanging to a topping man. While this be a grand thing indeed, ye feel as though ye now be merely flashing the gentleman and whether it be a mistake that shall eventually right itself."

"What doth I do?"

"Ye must come to realize ye be deserving of good fortune and hath done nothing wrong. I believe that once ye come to this understanding, then ye shall be able to rest and enjoy life again."

Mary and Chip thanked the Bishop for his time before collecting the children. Upon arriving home, Mary sent the children to their rooms then went right to the task of fixing the meal. Chip could not ignore the icy presence that surrounded her as he entered the kitchen.

"Mary?"

"Hmm?"

"Be ye upset with me?" he asked, knowing full well the answer.

"Why did ye agree to go knowing ye were not going to be truthful?"

"I agreed to go with ye to church," Chip replied, biting back his frustration. "I did not agree to meet with the Bishop. That be ye own doing. Tell me, when be I untruthful to the Bishop?"

Mary rounded on him, a fire burning in her eyes. "I know ye, Christopher MacDougall. I know when ye be hiding something and ye were not truthful today."

"Me word shall not be challenged in me own home!" Chip's anger vanished, as quickly as it had come the moment he spied the hurt in her eyes. He reached for her shoulder. "Mary, please forgive me—"

Mary retreated from his touch. "Nay, Christopher, I shall not. Ye hath been untruthful already on the Lord's day. I shall not accept another. Supper shall be ready shortly."

Mary turned away from him and returned to fixing the meal. He fought back his anger, knowing it was best not to press his wife on the matter. She did not understand. How could she. How could anyone understand what he was going through.

The next day he awoke from yet another tormenting dream, determined to find a way past all this unrest. He quickly dressed and headed out. Prim Street was still slumbering, as the morning light had yet to break across the distant hills. The street lamps gave stark contrast between light and dark, casting long dark shadows into areas their light could not reach.

Chip always loved the serenity the morning gave. He could still feel the serenity, but now it was marred by the fear of unseen forces that tormented his soul.

"Pardon me, sir."

Chip nearly jumped into the air, as he turned to see a young man standing near him with a ladder propped up on one arm.

"Forgive me, sir," the young man said, removing his cap and holding it in his hands. "I not wish to give thee a start."

Chip steadied himself, regaining his composure. "Not to worry, lad."

"Sir, would ye steady me ladder? Me help hath run off, and this be the last lamp that needs filled." The young man pointed up to the nearby street lamp.

"Aye, I shall help thee."

"Thank ye, sir! I shall hurry."

"Take yer time, and doth a respectable work."

The young man smiled as he propped the ladder up against the lamp pole. Chip held the bottom of the ladder as the young man climbed up to the top with a pitcher of oil. A few minutes later, the task complete, he climbed back down.

"Again sir, thank ye."

Chip appraised the young man before him. "What be yer name, lad?"

"Donovan, sir. Donovan Wood."

"How much does this job pay ye, Donovan?"

"A schilling a day, sir," Donovan replied proudly.

"How many days a week doth ye fill the lamps?"

"Two days, sir."

"Ye make two schillings a week then. Be this ye only post?"

Donovan nodded. "Aye, sir. Work be tough to come by."

"Aye, it be. Suppose ye had the chance to earn more, would ye take it?"

"Should the work be legal." The young man's eyes widened with excitement. "Doth ye hath work for me?"

"I hath a bakery on Toppum Street Road that be in need of hands. The post would require that ye work six days a week. I would pay thee seven schillings a week supposing ye doth well."

"Sir, I thank thee, yet why would ye offer the post to me?"

"Ye could hath claimed the task the same as milkin' a pigeon with the loss of yer help or lied and said that ye filled it. Ye did neither. Ye showed a willingness to complete the task."

Donovan shook his head. "Not a willingness, sir. It would be dishonest to accept an unearned copper."

Chip admired the attitude of the young man before him. Hard times often caused even the most honest people to contemplate less than savory ideas.

"Well, let us see whether ye might earn more coppers. Go tomorrow to MacDougall's Bakery on Toppum. See Mr. Thomas. Tell him Mr. MacDougall sent ye and that ye be to work there as a hand for seven schillings a week."

"Aye, sir! Thank ye, sir!"

"Doth an honest job, lad. That be all I ask."

Donovan shook his hand vigorously. "I shall, sir! I shall!"

He sprinted off down the road before remembering his ladder and running back to get it, tipping his cap as he did. Chip chuckled at the excitement of the young man, only to be stirred from his musings by the sound of someone clearing their throat behind him. He turned to see Mary, standing on the front stoop and smiling softly. He walked back up the steps to greet his wife.

"Did I wake ye?"

"Ye could never slip away without waking me. Ye hath made that young lad happy."

Chip glanced back up the road. The young man having already disappeared from view. "He seemed honest and Spencer could use the help."

"Spencer could use ye there as well."

Chip took her hand in his. "Mary, there be something else that I hath not told ye. Let us go into the kitchen and—"

His words were cut off by the sound of their daughter, Anna, screaming from within the house. He and Mary raced inside, his chest tightening with fear.

Spencer heard the shop door open and close behind him as he kneaded dough for the following day.

"Be with ye in a moment."

"Take your time," a pleasant voice replied. "I shall wait."

Spencer finished prepping the dough then wiped his hands on his apron as he turned to face a well-dressed man, looking about the bakery with mild interest.

Spencer greeted the man, smiling brightly as Mr. MacDougall had taught him. "What shall I fetch for thee?"

"Where be Mr. MacDougall?"

"Mr. MacDougall not be in today," Spencer replied, his response well-rehearsed over the last few months. "Be there something I might for thee? Doth ye wish supply trade?"

"Mr. Thomas, I have always admired you," the man said, ignoring Spencer's questions. "Never let your situation define your worth. Once a lily white and now a baker's understrapper."

"Doth I know thee?"

"We have never met, but I know thee. Never let being gutfoundered trouble you."

"Sir, being ye hath not come with a request then I bid ye good day," Spencer said firmly, feeling uncomfortable.

"Ah, but I have come to make a request."

The man extended his right hand, before rotating it to the right, causing his sleeve to rise up his arm. Spencer glanced at the man's wrist before taking several steps backwards, eyes wide with fear at what he saw.

FIVE

LOST

Chip and Mary found Anna at the top of the steps to the cellar, screaming uncontrollably.

"Anna!" Mary shouted, wrapping her arms about her. "What be it child?"

"Marcus!"

Chip darted down the steps to the still form that laid at the bottom. He cupped Marcus' head and felt his son's breath upon his palms. Joy filled his heart as tears streaked his cheeks.

"He be alive!"

Chip carried his son up the stairs and to the sitting room, laying him gently on the long sofa. Mary followed, holding Anna as she tried to calm her. Without hesitation he set off, racing to fetch Dr. Brown. If the voices that haunted him yowled along the way, he could not recall. All that filled him was that his son needed him.

When he returned with the doctor, he found Mary sitting on the floor next to the sofa, Anna at her side. His two ladies were tending to Marcus who remained unconscious. Chip took Anna into his lap while they waited for the doctor to examine Marcus.

"Tell me, what befell Marcus, Angel?" he whispered.

"His ball fell down the steps. He not want to anger ye, Papa. He went to fetch the—"

Unable to continue, Anna succumbed to sobs. Chip handed his little girl to Mary as the doctor crossed the room to join them.

"Yer boy be a stout lad."

"Be he well?"

The doctor gave them a look which made his stomach fall away. "He still refuses to wake. There be much swelling to the back of the head."

"What doth this mean?" he asked as Mary cupped her mouth.

"We shall have to wait until he awakes. I be truly sorry. Only wish I knew more."

"Thank ye healer. I shall show thee out."

"I shall be back round tomorrow. Fetch me should he wake."

"We shall."

———◆———

Three days passed and Marcus' condition remained unchanged. The doctor had come and gone every day—checking the swelling where Marcus had hit his head, his heartbeat, and breathing. The bruising was getting worse, and even though the doctor had said it would, Chip was still shocked by the amount of deep blue that covered his son's face.

He pounded his fist on the kitchen table. "I not bear this any longer! Another day and I shall be off me hooks!"

"Christopher, it matters not what we be going through as long as we keep the faith." Mary said softly, unable to keep the pleading from her voice.

"Faith?" he repeated bitterly. "Faith that God shall what … help me? Help Marcus?"

"Aye, me love. He be help to all, should ye trust in Him. Hath ye told Him what troubles ye? Ye hath yet to tell me."

"I thought God knew all! Supposing He already knows, why must I tell Him?"

"Ye must not be this way."

Chip growled, "Where be He when me father passed? Where be He when me brother died and me father's bakery burnt? Where be He when we be forced to move to Edinburgh? When I be forced to work as a wharf rat? Where be He now, when our son lies before us?"

She grasped his hand. "He be always with us. We must be willing to accept His will. He hath blessed us in many ways."

Chip yanked his hand from her grasp before striding to the kitchen window. He could not bear to look at her. He knew not how she could keep her faith in a God that allowed so much to go wrong. It was unimaginable to him.

"Christopher, Bishop Seamus said yesterday when he visited that we must stay strong and pray."

Chip refused to look at her. "Ye pray to God then. Let me know what He saith to thee."

"Anna shall be home soon," she said, her tone penetrating his skin like shards of ice. "Please doth not speak this way. She be already tormented by her brother's condition."

"Then ye be here when she comes home. I hath need to walk."

Without another word, Chip exited through the backdoor, slamming it as he did. He did not want to listen to any more of his wife's excuses for her faith. He had once been a religious man, attending church with his mother every Sunday. After the loss of his father, Chip's faith had begun to waver. He had been tolerant of Mary's beliefs, but he could no longer pretend to share her level of devotion.

He walked without thinking until he found himself at the wharf. The voices that tormented him echoed all about, but he would not give into the madness they induced. Not today. He stared out into the harbor, desperately searching for the peace he once found in those clear waters.

As he stood there, his mind drifted to the day he first met Mary. Her father had sent her to the bakery to purchase some bread. She was the most beautiful thing that he had ever laid eyes upon. He remembered wondering if she would ever return, and how delighted he was when she began making the rounds to town for food and supplies once a month for her family. He remembered how nervous he was the first time he visited her father's homestead to ask permission to begin their courtship. The day she became his wife, he remembered thinking how he couldn't possibly be any happier.

Then, happiness beyond his own imagination arrived in the form of his newborn son. He remembered holding him and thinking what joy it was to hold a human so small in his arms. He wished his father had been alive to share in his joy.

He contemplated how time was a cruel master, taking his payments when you least expected. His father had not known Marcus, and his mother had not known Anna. Both had died before their time, leaving him to raise his children with his wife, without the wisdom of his parents to guide him. Mary's parents had filled the void to some extent. Though now her parents lived too far away to look to for wisdom.

"Ye lost?"

Chip was torn from his brooding by a familiar voice. He turned to see Jonah McCullah standing behind him, his arm extended in greeting. "That I be, me friend."

Jonah chuckled, "I had to look upon ye for an eternity before I be sure that it be thee! Ye not look the wharf rat anymore—dressed in such!"

"I feel like one today."

"What be wrong?" Jonah asked, his demeanor sobering at once. "Ye look troubled."

Chip's gaze fell. "It be me son, Marcus. He suffered a terrible fall and hath not awakened for days."

"Hath a beaton been roun' to tend to him?"

"Aye, but he hath no answers." His chest heaved with emotion.

"Doth not lose hope. He shall be well."

"I wish I be as confident as thee." Chip grimaced as he tried to ignore the sudden shouts of "Danger!" from behind him.

"It not be confidence. It be faith."

"Ye double me wife."

"For most, faith be all we hath left. Ye hath received ye plate-fleet, Chip. Doth not let misfortune bring ye low. Ye son shall be well. Hath faith."

"I hath not yer sanguine or yer faith." Chip looked around to make sure that there was no one else about. "Suppose what befell to me not be a plate-fleet? Suppose ... suppose I be cursed?"

"Yer off ye hooks!" Jonah exclaimed. "Ye hath a radiant family, toppings, and a beautiful homestead. How doth ye call such a curse?"

"What about me health?"

"Ye be ill?" Jonah squinted, as though examining him.

"I—I believe ... I believe I be losing me mind." For the first time, Chip voiced his true fear.

"Why doth ye hold to this?"

"Me dreams be tormented—"

"Ye be worryin' over ye boy, be it all."

"Let me finish!" Chip snapped, the tension in his body reaching unbearable levels. He lowered his eyes to the ground.

"Forgive me, Jonah."

"It be alright. Ye helped me when we worked together here. Me and the whither hath enough for a larger homestead thanks to ye."

"Ye be needing a larger place?" Chip asked, looking up at his friend.

"I soon be a father!"

"Well fetch me a calf-skin fiddle!" he exclaimed, grabbing Jonah by the shoulders and smiling. "A soldier's bottle be in order! Shall we retire to O'Gills for a round?"

"Supposing ye tells me what be troubling thee."

Chip frowned and nodded. "I shall."

The two walked together down the old familiar street towards the tiny tavern where he once frequented on a weekly basis. Weaving their way past other pub-goers, they took a booth nearest the back.

"Two pints," Chip called to the barmaid as she passed by.

Jonah stared oddly at him. "Ye drink only like a beast unless ol' Malone be pestering ye."

"I be sipping today supposing I be telling ye what be troubling me."

He waited for the pints to arrive before telling Jonah his problems. Jonah sat quietly, allowing for his friend to finish before speaking.

"Hath ye told yer whither?" Jonah asked, taking a sip from his pint.

"I be about to when me son ..." Chip's eyes drifted towards the tavern door. "How doth I tell her now? She be a strong woman, but I doth not think she could bear this."

As his eyes traveled back from the doorway, they rested on the booth where he first met Mr. Prose. *Be their meeting by chance, fate, or be something direr at hand?* His eyes started to leave the booth, but snapped back when he caught sight of movement.

"Chip?"

His attention snapped back to Jonah's intent face.

"What be ye starin' at so fiercely?"

Chip squinted again at the booth. "There be something moving in that booth near the door."

"Be only a wharf rat," Jonah said dismissively. "They wander in and out of the tavern doorway, lookin' for scraps."

He shivered at the thought of a rat sitting in the booth where he first met Mr. Prose. *Be this a dire omen?*

"Be ye hearin' voices again?"

"Nay. Just a bad thought."

"Hath ye considered that all these voices and bad dreams be nothin' more than bad thoughts gettin' the better of thee?"

"Suppose they be, then how doth I be rid of them?"

Jonah sighed, "That I not know. Ye saith ye spoke with yer Bishop. What doth he say?"

"Ye be the only soul I hath told of the voices."

"Would say I be honored, 'cept now I worry I may suffer dreams n' thoughts as ye, now that I hath heard them."

"Should not hath troubled thee with me burdens." Chip rose from their booth to leave.

"Sit thee back down," Jonah growled, smacking the table with his hand. "I worked with thee for four years on these here docks, an' one thing I know be that ye doth not wallow in self-pity."

"Self-pity? Ye think this be self-pity?"

"I think Chip MacDougall shall find a way about this problem." Jonah stared hard at him while gripping his pint of ale. "When we first did meet, ye had lost all that belonged to thee, save yer wife and children. Ye were down, but ye kept yer pride and started anew. Ye helped me deal with me losses as well."

"This be different, Jonah."

"Aye, that it be. But I be tellin' ye now what ye told me then. Keep yer pride and faith, cause we Scots shall always press on."

"Be what me father always cited," Chip said, remembering the last time his father spoke those words to him.

"Then yer father be a wise man."

"I hath me pride, Jonah, but me faith be gone. How doth I keep the faith when torment and suffering be waiting for me each day?"

"For the sake of yer family, Chip, find yer faith." Jonah hissed. "Be strong for yer wife and children. Doth not let the devils win."

"I shall try."

"I wish I hath the answer ye seek, me friend. I be sure that ye shall find a way past this an' that yer son shall recover."

Chip took another sip from his pint before standing up. "I must go. Please keep what I hath told ye in confidence."

"Aye, I shall," Jonah said, standing up and shaking his hand. "Be strong for yer family, Chip."

"And ye for thine."

The two parted ways outside the tavern. He knew that Jonah was trying to encourage him, but no words could be said that could drown out the tormenting voices that yowled out all about, *"Danger!"*

Chip tried to find strength for his family, like he swore to Jonah. However, the days that passed proved too much for him to weather. Marcus was still ill and had not awoken since his fall. The doctor was becoming more concerned with each examination. Marcus showed no signs of life, other than the ragged breaths he took. Mary read to him each night, praying by his bedside before retiring to hers. Though he wished his son well again, he could not join her in praying to a God who either did not exist or did not care.

The one who suffered the most was Anna. Mary comforted her and he tried his best to do the same. The heaviness in the house was nearly unbearable, and it shone upon their faces.

It wasn't until the sixth morning that there was a change in Marcus's condition. Mary recognized it first, faint but defining—a cough.

"Christopher!"

Chip raced from the kitchen, scattering biscuits across the floor, as he made his way up to Marcus's room. Anna stood just inside the doorway, staring at her mother who held Marcus in her arms. His eyes were definitely open. He slid across the floor to his son's bedside, and fell to his knees. Reaching out, he cupped his son's face with his hand.

"Marcus?"

"Papa," Marcus replied in a hoarse whisper, "may I hath some water?"

Mary sobbed tears of relief as she hugged her son tightly.

"Aye, son." Chip choked back his tears, smiling at his boy.

He leaped to his feet and turned to see, a smiling yet hesitant, Anna still standing near the doorway. He smiled and Anna flew to her father, hugging him around the legs.

"Marcus be alright now?" she asked, looking up at him hopefully.

"Aye, me sweet girl. Go and fetch Marcus some water while I fetch the beaton."

Anna nodded and darted off. Chip made to follow, his purpose clear, when he felt a hand grasp his wrist. He turned to see Mary smiling up at him, tears covering her cheeks.

"Ye shall fetch the beaton later."

Dropping to one knee, he wrapped his arms about her and Marcus. Anna squeezed herself under his arm after returning with the water, resting her head on Marcus's shoulder.

Once he was able to tear himself away from his family, Chip sprinted into town, ignoring the torment that followed him. Arriving at the beaton's home, he pounded upon the door.

"What be the meaning ..."

"Marcus be awake," was all the response that Chip could muster.

"Hail a hackney, Mr. MacDougall, while I fetch me bag and me cap."

During the examination, it became apparent that Marcus could not feel anything below his waist. He could move his legs and feet, but was completely incapable of standing.

Dr. Brown ruffled Marcus' hair. "Young lad, ye gave us a start. Now, ye must rest."

Marcus nodded and closed his eyes. Anna sat with him while the adults retired to the sitting room to discuss the matter in private.

"What of his legs?"

"Mrs. MacDougall, I believe that with rest he shall regain the feeling within his legs. We must be patient."

"Thank ye, healer, for all that ye hath done," Chip said, shaking his hand.

"He be a fortunate lad, Mr. MacDougall."

"God be good to us," Mary interjected.

Chip frowned, but hid his face from her sight.

Dr. Brown smiled and nodded. "Well, I best be going. Fetch me should his condition change."

"Aye, we shall." Chip shook the doctor's hand once more.

He walked the doctor to the front door as Mary made her way back upstairs. As he opened the front door, he heard something that made his blood run cold. The cry of *"Danger!"* reached his ears from just beyond the front stoop.

"Something wrong, Mr. MacDougall?"

"N-Nay."

"Be ye sure? Ye have been through a lot these last few days. It doth take a toll on a body when yer child be ill."

"Aye, I be sure," Chip replied dismissively. "I be just remembering something."

"Well then, good day, Mr. MacDougall. Be sure to fetch me again should ye son's condition change."

"Aye, I shall." he said, nodding and closing the door behind the doctor, fear gripping his mind.

It all be in me head, he thought, slowly backing away from the front door. *It all just be in me head. A warm cup of tea might sooth me nerves.* He made his way towards the kitchen, but stopped dead in his tracks. The chilling cry of *"Danger!"* echoed from just inside the thick wooden doorway. Shoving his knuckles into his mouth to keep from shouting, he quickly backed away. Before he could decide what to do, he felt a tug on his shirt from behind. He spun round on the spot, not certain what horror to expect.

"Papa? Be ye okay?" Anna stared up at him, looking worried.

"Aye, me darling girl," he replied, breathing hard. "Ye just

81

startled me."

"Momma sent me to see whether ye were coming back upstairs."

"Tell yer mother that I shall be up in a bit."

"Papa, when shall Marcus be well enough to play?"

Chip forced a smile as he stared down at his innocent little girl. "Soon, me darling. Now, run along upstairs."

Anna smiled, then hurried back upstairs to her brother's room. Chip sighed and rubbed his chest, trying to calm his racing heart. He closed his eyes and tried to regain his composure. He refused to allow whatever was tormenting him to have its way today.

A week later, Dr. Brown returned to check on Marcus. He was concerned to hear that Marcus was still unable to feel anything below his knees. After conducting another examination, he requested to speak with Chip and Mary in private.

"I be quite concerned that yer lad hath been severely hurt. It be far worse than I once believed."

Mary took hold of Chip's hand for comfort as they sat in the sitting room. "What does this mean?"

"Mrs. MacDougall, I wish I knew. The body be a complex thing. The mind be even more. Ye son may still fully recover. We shall know in time."

"Thank ye for yer efforts," Chip said, forcing his grimace into a smile. "We be truly grateful."

"He needs to continue to rest."

Chip nodded. "Aye, we shall see to it. When shall ye be by again?"

Dr. Brown folded his spectacles and placed them inside his coat pocket. "I shall come by in a week's time. Doth not fret—"

Chip was distracted from what the doctor was saying by a voice coming from across the way. *"Why be she up so high? She be going to fall for sure."*

He leaped to his feet and ran towards the kitchen, not caring about the way Dr. Brown and Mary stared after him. He entered the kitchen just in time to see Anna's foot slip off the third shelf in the cupboard and fall backwards, screaming as she went. He reached out and caught her just before she hit the floor.

"What happened?" Mary shouted as she ran into the kitchen, the doctor close behind.

"Me word. What in Heaven's name be going on here?"

Anna's voice shook. "M-Marcus wanted a cracker."

"Why did ye not ask yer mother or father?" the doctor questioned her disapprovingly. "Ye could hath been seriously injured, lassie."

Anna looked up into her father's face. "I not want to bother thee. I just be trying to help."

Chip pulled Anna close to his chest. He felt her small arms wrap around his neck. As he lowered her to her feet, Mary drew her up into a smothering hug.

"Doth not ever tempt this again," she said, half-scolding, half-pleading.

"Aye, Mama."

"Mr. MacDougall, how did ye know she be in here?" Dr. Brown asked, looking totally astounded.

"I heard a noise," he lied, glancing back at his wife and daughter.

"That be incredible! Yer hearing must be exceptional."

Chip smiled briefly, as he glanced about the kitchen, wondering what he had heard. *Be this in me head or be this something more?* He continued to ponder the thought, as he went throughout the rest of the day.

That evening, Spencer stopped by to inform Chip that the farm which supplied them grain had been late twice the week before and failed to deliver that morning.

"Well Spencer, supposing this continues, we shall need to find another farm. It be a shame though. The O'Neil family hath done well. I wonder whether they be fallen on hard times."

"Sir, a gent stopped by the bakery offering the services of his farm," Spencer said, his voice sounding a bit strained. "Should the O'Neil farm not supply, maybe we should consider his offer."

Chip noted the change in Spencer's attitude. "Who be this gent?"

"He not give his name. Only that he represented the Douglas farm."

"Should he stop by again, request his name and how much he shall charge for grain supplies."

"When shall ye be returning to the bakery?" Spencer asked

hopefully. "Donovan be right helpful, but he not be a baker."

"Spencer, I doth not yet know. Be the load too much for thee?"

"Nay, sir! I enjoy the work immensely, but I enjoyed it more with ye there."

Spencer gave him the earning tallies from the previous month before hurrying on his way. Chip noted a slight decline in sales from the month before, but the bakery was still quite profitable.

"I be asking thee the same question," Mary said, striding quietly up behind him. "When shall ye return to the bakery?"

He rubbed his forehead. "Must we?"

"Aye, we must," she replied, folding her arms. "And we shall until ye tell me what be troubling thee."

"Ye know of me dreams."

"Aye," she agreed, placing a hand on his cheek. "But I also know me husband. Ye hath never been a lay-about or slighted honest work. Ye look for the challenge, not run from it. That be why ye started the bakery. We hath no need of the money. Now, something more be going on with thee than just tormenting dreams."

"Aye, there be. Our son lies upstairs, unable to walk, because of me."

"How shall ye blame yer self for this?"

Chip turned away from her, unable to look his wife in the face. "Me torment be no longer enough. Now, it passes to me family."

"What be ye on about?"

"Mary, I be afraid that I … I may be a cursed," he choked out. "Me mind be leaving me, and now me family be in danger."

Mary forced him to face her. "Ye would never harm this family. I know this."

"First Marcus … then Anna nearly …"

"Those be accidents, Christopher, and ye saved Anna from harm."

His voice cracked. "Were they? The only reason I be there to catch Anna be because I heard … something."

"What did ye hear?" she asked softly, taking a step closer.

"Voices, Mary," he whispered. "They be in me head, in me ears, calling to me from everywhere." He took hold of his hair with both hands as the maddening feeling overwhelmed him again.

Mary gasped, "What doth these voices say?"

"They warn of danger." Chip closed his eyes, unable to bear to see her reaction.

"Why hath ye waited so long to tell me?" she asked calmly, her voice laced with fear.

"How doth ye tell yer whither that ye hath lost yer senses?"

She rubbed his arms, attempting to relax him. "Ye hath not lost yer mind."

"Aye, I hath!" he shouted, his eyes still tightly shut. "How saith ye other?"

"I keep the faith."

Chip's eyes flew open. "I hath none left to keep! Not anymore!"

He froze at the sight of his wife's tear-streaked face. His heart tore in two at the heartache in her eyes. He watched helplessly as she slowly backed away, unable to comprehend what to say. In a move that he would one-day regret, he turned and left the room without another word.

The days and weeks that followed passed by with barely a word spoken between the two. He regretted having told Mary and resented her for telling him to keep the faith, as though this was the answer to everything. He no longer retired to their room at night to sleep, for he could not bear to listen to her pray for him when she thought he was asleep. Instead, he resigned to sleeping on the sofa in the sitting room downstairs.

"I shall not lie the thee, lad." Dr. Brown said, sitting in front of Marcus one morning, having just finished another examination. "It hath been four weeks now since yer fall and I doth not foresee thee walking ever again."

Mary moved swiftly to Marcus's side to console him while Chip faced the mantle lest anyone spied a tear streaking his cheek.

"Sir, ever be long," Marcus said. "I shall walk again."

"Lad … it be best ye learned to accept yer condition."

"Sir, I not wish to protest, but I shall walk again."

Chip turned and marveled at his son's words. Mary hugged him tightly as the doctor sat amazed by the young lad before him.

Anna gently tugged on the doctor's coat. "Sir, doth me

brother keep the chair with wheels until he be well again?"

"Aye, child," the doctor replied, tearing his gaze from Marcus's face. "Ye shall continue to help him?"

"Until he be well."

Chip bent down and hugged his angel, wishing he had half the faith his children possessed. That night, after the house was asleep, he lost control of his emotions. Running into the cellar, he began smashing everything in sight. Cries of *"Danger!"* rang out from every corner of the cellar. Shouting at the top of his lungs and swearing like a cutter, Chip raged at the voices which were shoving him to the brink.

Heaving one last glass jar against the wall, he sighed as his shoulders slumped. He felt no better than before he started and now thanks to his temper, he had an almighty mess to clean up. A noise behind him caught his attention and his heart failed him. Mary stood at the top of the cellar stairs, a ferocity in her eyes.

"How ye managed not to wake the children, I know not!"

"Forgive—"

"Nay Christopher," she snapped. "I forgive much, but this I cannot. Now ye hath brought violence into our home. Shall ye harm me or the children next when ye hath nothing left to break?"

"I would never harm ye or the children."

"Ye saith, but the Christopher I know wouldn't hath thrashed our cellar. Nay … ye I know not."

Mary stormed back into the house with the force of a hurricane. Chip pursued her into the kitchen.

"What would ye hath me do?" he demanded. "Shall I keep it in and go mad in the way?"

"Maybe it be best if me and the children found another place to stay."

"Stay?" he repeated, rage threatening to overcome him. "This be me children's home and Marcus needn't be moved about. If ye wish not to be under the same roof as me, then I shall leave. Be this what ye wish?"

"Only till ye find help," she whispered, tears tracing her face.

Chip turned and left the kitchen without another word. He did not have to leave, but would do so out of respect for his wife and children. *They did not need to suffer because of him*, he reasoned.

The next morning, he found a small room in Leith, near the wharf where he once worked. When the day came to leave, he vowed to Marcus and Anna he would come and see them as often as he could. Marcus held strong and refused to cry, while Anna clung to him for dear life. Mary had come to grips with his departure, so she was able to help with Anna.

Chip glanced back as he walked away from his home, his heart crumbling. Cries of "*Danger!*" chorused about him, taunting him. If he had only known that by leaving, he was destroying the family he sought to protect.

———◆———

It was another fine morning on Toppum Street Road. Spencer worked away, baking and humming to himself while Donovan wiped down the counters. The bell atop the door rang, alerting them that a customer had arrived.

"May I help ye?" Donovan asked, greeting the customer.

"I wish to speak with Mr. MacDougall."

Spencer spun round at the sound of the man's voice. "Donovan, go tend to straighten the cupboard in the back. I shall tend to this customer."

Donovan frowned at Spencer, then proceeded to the back.

"Good to see that Mr. MacDougall provides ye with quality help in his absence. It has been a month since I last saw ye. Still looking happy and better than—"

"I spoke with Mr. MacDougall. He said we would change to the Douglas farm," Spencer interrupted harshly.

"Let us be civil, Mr. Thomas. Need not be defensive."

"I did as ye asked. What else doth ye want of me?"

"Doth Mr. MacDougall ask anything in return?" the man asked, ignoring Spencer's question.

"He asked yer name."

"Fair enough," the man said, a cold smile curving his face. "Tell Mr. MacDougall my name be Mr. James Tomlin. Tell him we have done business before. As to your previous question. Should I need more from you, we shall always know where to find thee."

90

SIX

---◆---

THE GREAT MICHAEL

Chip felt as though his life was shattering all around him.
He could find no joy in anything. Without his family, he sank lower
and lower into depression. He began limiting his visits to see his
wife and children to once a week. As much as he wanted to be with
them, the pain of leaving them to return to his small room was
nothing less than torture.

The bakery had become nothing more than a passing
thought. Weeks had passed since he had darkened its threshold or
breathed in the wonderful smell of bread baking in the oven. The
passion and hope the place once rekindled within him had almost
entirely faded away.

Now, he found himself in a small dusty tavern called
O'Bryan's, staring at the pint before him with loathing and disgust.
Several times, the bartender asked him if he was going to drink it,
but a harsh glare was the only answer he gave. He had no desire to
drink, but knew it wasn't proper to enter an establishment without
at least ordering something.

For him, the place was no different than any other. The

same voices that tormented him everywhere else, followed him there as well. *Of course they did!* he mused darkly. *Be they not all in me head? How shall one ever outrun the voices lest ye cut them off at the neck? What be the use of living a life such as this?*

"Ye look like a man that be down on his luck."

Chip whirled around to see a weather-beaten sailor standing in front of him in a blue waistcoat and grey breeches, bearing the grit that only comes from being aloft at sea.

"Leave me be," he said, spinning back to face his pint.

"What be it that ye be doing?" the man asked, taking a stool beside him at the bar. "Bartender, I be having what he be drinking."

"Long as ye drinks faster than he." The bartender jerked a thumb in Chip's direction.

He considered tossing the pint at the bartender, but did not wish to be tossed from the tavern.

"I asked ye a question, lad."

"Doth that mean I must answer? I asked ye to leave me be."

"Aye, ye did mate. But where would I be supposing I let it be? I shall tell thee. I would be a captain without a crew."

"So ye be a captain," Chip retorted dryly. "Ye doth not dress like a captain."

"Oh, I left me finer petticoat aboard me ship. Ye hath to dress for the occasion when ye be about looking for fine new hands."

"Ye be in the business of recruiting mad men to ye crew?" Chip sneered, glancing at the man.

"Most that join me crew be mad … or close to it," the Captain chuckled. "Ye be mad then?"

"That be what me thinks."

"Why so? Doth ye see specters in the night? Doth ye talk with yer self?"

"Nay. All that be wrong with me be that I hear voices by day and suffer tormenting dreams by night." He had no idea why he was telling this man anything, but it felt good to talk.

"What be it that ye do?" the Captain asked, pressing the conversation forward.

"Not much of anything anymore."

"Sounds to me like ye be in need of work. Good honest work shall keep yer voices at bay."

Chip turned to stare at the man. "Work? Work aboard yer ship?"

"Aye, mate. She not be any ship either. She be the *Ottoman*, the finest vessel in the King's Navy."

"Ye want me to be a sea-crab in the King's Navy?" Chip scoffed at the notion, his eyebrows rising to his hairline. "Ye must be desperate. Sorry, Captain, but I hath had me fill of the Crown."

"Lad, we all hath had to bear the weight of this Union," the Captain sighed. "I doth not consider it enlisting. I consider it serving me people. We keep vessels safe from pirates, buccaneers, and any other form of privateer that threatens the shores of this land. We keep vessels safe that be filled with fellow Scots."

"How be it that ye be captain, and be a Scot? How be it that ye be entrusted by the Crown?"

"Simple, lad," the bartender interjected, while pouring a pint for the Captain. "He be the best captain there be. He be Captain Joseph O'Toole that ye be talking to."

Chip tipped his cap. "It be an honor to meet thee. Me name be Christopher MacDougall, but many call me Chip. I hath heard tales of yer many great escapes and brilliant victories."

"Wish they all be true, Chip me lad. I be confident that many ye hear be truth and sea tales intertwined."

"Supposing only half be true, then they still be impressive to me."

The Captain squinted at him, leaning closer, "Tell me, where be ye from?"

"Today, I be from a tiny room above this tavern." Chip tapped his glass with his fingers. "Not too long ago, I be living amongst the nobles of Edinburgh. Before that, I be a humble wharf rat. Go back many a year and ye would find me a baker from a modest township along the shores of Loch Tay. Take yer pick."

"That explains me confusion. I see fine clothes wrapped about what looks and sounds to be a hardworking Scot. That be a rare sight indeed. Now, aboard me ship ye shall dress as all the others—for we be family."

"What makes ye think that I be joining yer crew?"

"Because ye need to," Captain O'Toole replied solemnly. "Ye need us more than we need thee." He slapped Chip on the back. "Think it over. Me offer stands until the morn. Me ship be at the end of the wharf. First one ye come to in the Naval Yard."

Without waiting for an answer, Captain O'Toole downed his pint in one, paid the bartender, and left out of the tavern.

"Did not stay long."

"Did not need to," the bartender said smirking. "He came looking for a new mate, and he believes he found one."

Chip paid the bartender, then left the tavern to take a walk. When he finally looked up to see where he was, he found his feet had carried him back to Prim Street. His eyes immediately became fixed upon the door of the manor house he once called home. He found it hard to imagine that only a short while ago, he and his family were moving in, the future so bright.

Still trying to decide why his feet had carried him there, he walked up to the door and knocked.

"I was not expecting ye today," Mary said, greeting him with a timid smile.

"Might I come in?" he asked, that sickening feeling in the pit of his stomach returning. It happened every time he visited.

"Of course."

Mary stepped to the side, allowing him to enter. As she closed the door, he suppressed a shiver. His life there felt so foreign, like a wonderful dream rather than something that had really happened.

"Marcus went to school today," Mary said conversationally, trying to sound positive.

"Doth ye think he shall be okay?"

Her timid smile faded. "Aye. He was nervous, but the teacher, Mr. Anderson, assured me he would be well with him."

His mind drifted to a vision of his son sitting in a wheelchair, watching while his friends played and ran about him. Rage filled him once more at what his boy was going through.

"Why be ye here?" she asked, folding her arms across her chest. "Hath something happen?"

Chip breathed deeply. "I was approached today by Captain O'Toole of the King's Navy."

"What doth he want?"

Cleared his throat he sighed, "He wants me to join his crew."

"Be ye going to join up?"

Chip's gaze fell to the polished floor. "I-I doth not know."

"Ye be considering it then," she huffed, her eyes narrowing.

"Would be better than being drafted by the Edinburgh Town Guard," he scoffed, his anger boiling up again for reasons he did not understand. "They flash the knob, that bunch."

"At least then ye would be on dry land!" she shouted, her arms trembling.

"Ye asked me to leave, remember?"

"I asked ye to seek help!"

"Maybe this shall help me!" he shouted, stomping his foot. "Nothing else has!"

"This be why ye came here today? To ask for permission to join the King's Navy?"

"I did not come here to ask yer permission!" Chip growled. "I came here to—I know not why I came here!"

"Maybe ye should leave, Christopher. Go then, join the Navy. I be here to take care of the children. At least be kind as much to tell Spencer what ye plan to do. Or doth ye plan to abandon the bakery as well?"

"Supposing I was going to abandon the bakery, I would hath done so months ago!"

Anger poured through him like boiling water. Truth be told, he had come there to be asked to stay, to come back home. Now, he was furious. He stormed past her, wrenching the door open. He stopped when he felt her hand upon his arm.

"Swear to me, should ye join, ye shall not leave port without letting us know," Mary said, her voice choked. "For the children."

"Aye, for the children," he said, unwilling to look at her.

Mary released his arm, allowing him to leave, before slamming the door behind him. Chip could not grasp how she could treat him this way. He had always done everything he could to give her all she needed. *Now, when I need her most she turns me away!*

Once again, Chip walked without thinking until he passed his bakery. The repetitive cry of *"Food!"* drew him from his thoughts. Realizing where he was, he hesitated before turning around and going inside.

"Mr. MacDougall!" Donovan nearly dropped his broom to shake his hand.

"Where be Spencer?"

"He be in the back. Doth ye wish for me to fetch him?"

"Nay, lad. I shall fetch him me self. Spencer saith ye be doing a right fine job."

"Thank ye, sir."

Chip patted the young man on the shoulder before walking past, into the back room.

"Mr. MacDougall!" Spencer shouted, his mouth falling open. "I thought ye was Donovan!"

"Hello, Spencer," Chip smirked, shaking his loyal employee's hand. "There be something I need to tell ye."

He explained how he was considering joining Captain O'Toole's crew and instructed Spencer to report all earnings to Mary should he do so.

"Before I go. How doth the new farm be doing? Be they keeping up with ye orders of grain?"

"Aye, sir. The Douglas farm be doing well."

"Good, good," Chip said, forcing a smile. "Well, I must be on me way. Should I not see ye for a while, hold to the tagger until I return."

"Aye, sir. We shall make ye proud," Spencer said, biting his lower lip. "Sir, ye asked me the name of the gent that solicited us for the Douglas farm?"

"Aye, that I did. What be his name?"

"His name be James Tomlin. He saith that ye hath done business before."

Chip stood there quietly for several minutes, unable to

speak.

"Sir? Hath I ate me nails?"

This would be the perfect way to repay Mr. Tomlin for me mistake, Chip thought, making up his mind. "Nay. Ye hath done nothing wrong. Use the Douglas farm as long as they provide good grain."

Spencer nodded. "I shall."

Chip bid the two young men good night before heading back towards Leith and his small room. He had a haversack to pack.

------◆------

The next morning, Chip put on the clothes he used to wear as a docker and tossed his haversack over his shoulder. A surreal feeling sweeping over him. He then headed down to the wharf to see about whether he could find his way back to whom he used to be.

He reached the end of the wharf, only to be greeted by a stern looking English soldier carrying a riffle.

"State your business," the soldier snapped, eyeing Chip suspiciously.

"I be here to see Captain O'Toole," he said, standing as tall as possible.

"Follow me."

The soldier snapped his boots together as he turned on the spot, kicking a large wooden crate on accident. A hundred cries of

"Danger!" echoed in the morning air. Chip involuntarily cringed, earning a cross glare from the soldier. He followed the man roughly ten meters before reaching the plank of a modest looking naval ship.

"Someone fetch Captain O'Toole!" the soldier shouted as he walked up the gang plank and onto the ship's crowded deck, Chip following close behind. "He hath a new sandy for his crew."

An enormous and surly looking seaman sneered at Chip and the soldier, then walked towards the captain's quarters. Moments later, Captain O'Toole emerged onto the deck.

"Ah, me new maltoot hath arrived!"

The English soldier nodded to the Captain then turned and left the ship.

"Welcome, Mr. MacDougall, to the *Persica*," Captain O'Toole said, gesturing to the ship. "I see ye decided to dress in yer common attire. Excellent choice, though I hope ye brought yer money belt with ye. Ye shall be expected to spot the bull's eye for a while."

Several of the crew members around the Captain laughed.

"Forgive me, Captain, but I thought ye said yer ship was the *Ottoman*?" Chip asked, clutching his haversack strap a little tighter.

"It be. Good memory, lad. This ship merely be passage. We sail for the *Ottoman* at first light tomorrow."

"Sail?"

"Aye, the *Ottoman* be docked in Iceland. We sail to fetch her for the King's Navy."

"How long shall we be gone?"

"Barely a month. Just enough time for ye to get yer sea legs."

Chip's breath became shallow. "I must write to me family. Let them know that we be leaving port."

"Of course, lad." The Captain slapped him on the shoulder. "Right after ye sign up. The papers be in me quarters. Drop yer haversack here. Mr. Kellogg shall stow it below."

Chip gave the Captain a wary look.

"Let me be clear," the Captain said loudly. "Conveyancers not be tolerated aboard me ship. Ye need not worry of yer belongings."

A burly man stopped his swabbing and cursed under his breath.

"Ye hath something to be said, Mr. Boyd?" Captain O'Toole asked, folding his arms.

"Nay, Captain," the man replied, leaning on the handle of his mop.

"He be sulking over how Mr. Stives stole away the attentions of a local lass," a well-groomed looking man said, laughing as he approached.

"Nothing doing of that!" Captain O'Toole roared with laughter. "Mr. MacDougall, this be me first mate, Mr. Kellogg."

Mr. Kellogg shook Chip's hand. "Welcome aboard, Mr. MacDougall. Keep an eye open for Mr. Stubbs. He be the sassenach with the bowler hat. Not to be trusted."

Chip nodded. "Aye, I shall."

He followed the Captain to his quarters, where he officially signed up for the Royal Navy. Once it was official, Captain O'Toole handed him some parchment and quill. He wrote a quick letter to Mary and apologized for not having the chance to say goodbye to Marcus and Anna.

"Now ye be officially a sea-crab," Captain O'Toole laughed, slapping him again on the shoulder.

"Sir, when ye found me in the pub, ye said ye be in search of more hands. Yet ye crew be a hangman's gathering."

"Ye be observant, Mr. MacDougall. Me crew be too grand for the Persica, indeed, but barely enough to sail the Ottoman. Ye shall see."

Chip nodded to his new captain, then exited the quarters. That night, he slept topside to avoid the bodiless yowls that echoed in the hull below. His dreams were filled with a wrathful Mr. Prose demanding his life in exchange for the rat.

The next morning before the ship set sail, a young boy stopped to collect letters. Chip paid the boy a schilling to deliver his directly. The boy nodded enthusiastically before hurrying along his way.

He watched from the stern of the ship as the shoreline drifted farther and farther away. Captain O'Toole assured him that, as a new hand, he would be too busy to miss Edinburgh and Leith, and that they would be back before he knew it. He quickly understood what the Captain meant. If he did anything besides work, eat, and sleep for the first week, he could not recall.

As Chip slept topside one night, the sound of thunder startled him. He awoke to see storm clouds forming in the distance. The wind was picking up, blowing through his hair and causing the main sail above him to ripple violently, the ropes cracking like whips. He looked about for Captain O'Toole and Mr. Kellogg, but they weren't topside. Nobody was.

"Mr. MacDougall!" shouted a voice that made his hair stand on end.

Chip turned to see Mr. Prose standing at the wheel of the ship, the wind blowing the tails of his petticoat. His voice cut like a knife through the sounds of the waves crashing against the hull. "Think you shall escape me at sea?"

"I hath not ye rat! It be dead! Leave me be!" Chip shouted, anger pouring through him.

Through the shadows and the light, he saw Mr. Prose smile. Next moment, there was a flash of lightning and Mr. Prose disappeared from the stern. The lightning flashed again and now, Mr. Prose stood directly in front of him. Chip took a step back, fear driving his anger away.

"Captain O'Toole and his crew have abandoned you," Mr. Prose said, in a voice that could freeze a man's heart. "You're the last rat aboard." He grabbed Chip by the throat, lifting him off his feet, nearly choking the life from him. "Time to join your crew, Chip!"

A wave that could have reached up to the heavens crashed

against the ship, sweeping Chip overboard. He felt himself being dragged beneath the waves as he struggled to comprehend which way was the surface, the water swirling about him.

Chip rolled to his feet, his breath ragged. He stood transfixed, shocked to see he was still aboard the *Persica*. Morning was almost upon them, only a few bright stars still visible.

"Morning, Mr. MacDougall."

He turned to see the Captain standing at the wheel of the ship, smiling in his direction. Normally at this time of morning, Mr. Kellogg was found at the wheel, the Captain still asleep in his quarters.

"Come up and join me, lad."

Chip walked up slowly, still shaking off the dream. The night crew shuffled about wearily, ready for some rest.

"Still doth not understand how ye rest topside. We need to help ye with yer demons."

Chip yawned. "Not certain it be possible, sir."

"I not be so easily swayed. That not be what I called ye up here for, though. Behold, the *Ottoman!*"

Chip's eyes followed the Captain's outstretched hand to the approaching harbor, resting upon the most magnificent vessel he had ever seen. Double the size of the *Persica*, with at least fifty cannon ports and four magnificent masts reaching up towards the heavens. Its flawless lines were accentuated by the light coming from the harbor town beyond, casting a long shadow upon the water.

"Land ho!" a seaman cried, from high above in the crow's nest.

"Best late than never at all, Mr. MacDuth!" the Captain shouted, rolling his eyes.

"Aye, Captain."

Arrival in port was a frantic cascade of movement, the crew hurrying to make ready the *Ottoman* for sail. Chip was charged with moving Captain O'Toole's personal belongings over to his new quarters. The crew would be split in two, with Mr. Kellogg captaining the *Persica* back to Leith alongside the *Ottoman*.

"Put yer backs into it, lads!" the Captain shouted. They'll be plenty of time to enjoy the taverns when yer chores be done!"

Chip lugged the last of the Captain's fifteen chests aboard the *Ottoman* and into the captain's new quarters. Winded, he took a seat upon the chest, wiping his brow and looked about the massive cabin for the first time. It was a luxurious sight, with finely crafted wood, tapestries, and linens. Between the two long windows at the stern of the ship, hung an oil painting of an angel wearing armor and carrying a sword. The angel stood victorious over a monstrous creature, his foot upon the back of the its head. He found himself transfixed by the image. Most depictions of angels he had seen before, were either praising their maker or watching over people.

"I see ye hath discovered the secret of the *Ottoman*," Captain O'Toole said, standing behind him. Chip stumbled as he jumped up, whirling around to face him. "Easy now, Mr. MacDougall. Ye be not in any trouble."

"Sir," Chip said breathlessly. "I be—"

"Admiring a marvelous painting," the Captain interjected. "Need not worry."

"Sir … what did ye mean by 'the secret of the *Ottoman*'?"

"This here, be a painting of the angel, Saint Michael, or known to others as Michael the Archangel. It portrays his victory over Satan."

"Be it valuable?"

"To some. The reason it hangs in me quarters, be that this ship was once called the *Great Michael*. It was the finest ship in the King's Navy, until Britain ordered her be sold."

"Why sell such a grand ship?" Chip asked, thinking of how intimidating it would be in battle.

"This ship represented the pride of the King's Navy and of Scotland. Britain felt that with the uprisings over the then impending Union between England and Scotland, it best to remove such depictions of military strength from view."

"Now they bring her back under a new name?" he asked, not surprised by such deception.

"Nay. Britain would never allow this ship to return if they thought it be the *Great Michael*. We bring her back under a new name." The Captain picked up a long blanket. "For now, we shall cover the painting with this until we find a better way to hide it."

"Would it not be easier to take the painting down?"

"This painting hath hung in this cabin since the first day this ship hath sailed. It be the namesake and hath been through every battle. When we return to port in Leith, we shall find a way to hide this masterpiece from prying eyes."

"I know of a carpenter who might be able to help," Chip said, thinking of Jonah.

"It would be right for a carpenter to help," the Captain sighed, his eyes fixed upon the painting.

Chip knew there was something he was missing, but he dared not ask for sounding foolish.

"Mr. MacDougall, I shall trust ye to keep the *Ottoman's* secret. Not all aboard know of this."

"Aye, Captain. I shall."

———◦———

One week earlier …

A young boy walked up Prim Street, glancing at each house as he went. He came to the middle of the way, pausing and staring up at a pristine looking manor home. It had two floors and looked to be quite large. Making up his mind that this must be his destination, he pushed open the gate and walked up the path that led to the stoop of the house. He was about to knock when someone hailed him from behind.

"What be ye business here, lad?"

The young boy turned to see a stately gentleman, wearing a black petticoat and white breeches, standing behind him.

"Hath a letter for the people of the house, sir," the boy

replied. "The master of the house sends it."

"Ye hath a letter from Mr. MacDougall?"

"Aye, sir. Mr. MacDougall paid me one whole schilling to see it delivered."

"Mr. MacDougall be a fine and generous man," the man said warmly. "Give me the letter, for I hath business here today. I shall see it delivered to the family within. Here be another schilling for ye swift service."

The man handed the young boy a schilling.

"Thank ye!" the boy exclaimed, handing the letter over to him.

"Now, run along, lad."

The boy tipped his cap before sprinting down the path and up the street. The man opened the letter and glanced over it before placing the it into his pocket. He then knocked swiftly on the door.

"Aye, what might I for thee?" Mary asked, opening the door ever so slightly.

The man tipped his cap. "Be Mrs. MacDougall at home this morning?"

Mary eyed him suspiciously. "Aye. Who be ye?"

"Forgive me, madam. Me name be Jefferson Wallace. I be with the bank. I have some important information to discuss with Mrs. MacDougall."

She bit her lower lip. "Mr. MacDougall be in Leith. He be either in a room above the tavern O'Bryan's or in the Navy shipyard."

"Aye, Mrs. MacDougall, I presume?" Mary nodded. "Ye husband be not in Leith. His ship sailed this morning." Her face flushed, and her breathing became shallow. "Mr. MacDougall left word with the bank that should he be away, ye could stand in his stead."

"Be that done?"

"It be highly irregular. However, Lord Campbell, the residing governor of the bank, approved the request, providing I be the overseeing adviser."

"Oh," Mary said, lost for words.

"Might I come in?"

"Aye." She stepped aside to let him in. "Forgive me manners. This be much to take in."

"It be me fault, Mrs. MacDougall," Mr. Wallace retorted, entering the house and allowing her to close the door behind him. "It be much for any to take. It not be often that the lady of the house be given such authority while the husband be yet living. I swear, me business shall not take long."

"Sorry, but I did not know me husband's ship hath sailed. Doth ye know when it shall be returning?"

Mr. Wallace inclined his head once more. "Me forgiveness again. I was not aware that ye did not know. The port master said that the *Persica* would be returning in a month's time."

Mary turned away from him so he could not see her tears. Mr. Wallace smiled, lightly patting the pocket concealing the letter.

SEVEN

———◆———

HAND OF FATE

The first night aboard the *Ottoman*, something amazing happened. Chip slept the entire night without a single tormenting dream. The next day he felt refreshed and envigored, as though he had not slept a full night in years.

"Sleep agrees with you, Mr. MacDougall," Mr. Barrett suggested, shoving a large bag of grain onto one of the shelves in the hull.

"I still not be buying the rounds," Chip retorted cheekily. "Matters not how nice ye be."

"There be my proof. Yesterday, such a comment would have only earned me a surly growl."

The large seaman laughed, slapping Chip on the shoulder and nearly knocking him into the shelves. He that knew Mr. Barrett was right, but it wasn't the only reason he was in such a good mood. He'd been in the hull of the *Ottoman* all day and had yet to hear a single bodiless voice. He longed for peace and it was almost too good to be true. *Be it the ship or be it Iceland why I not hear their yowls?* he pondered silently. *Alas, time shall tell.*

Mr. Barrett yawned, "Come along, Mr. MacDougall. We've been aboard the *Persica* a fortnight and another two days loading this vessel. Time we scoured the harbor, whether you be buying the round or not. Captain said the crew could go ashore as soon as the hull was full and this barrel," he slammed a massive hand atop the barrel next to him, "marks the last."

"I follow thee, Mr. Barrett," Chip nodded, his heart pounding. *Time hath come to know.*

He followed his large companion out of the hull and across the gang plank. The moment his boot met the pier, the bodiless voices returned. *Alas, it be waiting for me. To attack and torment me.* The voices yowled in his ears and in his heart until he returned to the *Ottoman* with the crew. The moment his boots were back aboard the mighty vessel, the voices faded. He sighed, grasping the deck railing for support.

Mr. MacDuth laughed. "Ye only killed two pints, Mr. MacDougall! Surely ye not be in a stooper!"

"Nay. I be only tired."

"Ye all hath labored well," Captain O'Toole interjected. The crew nodded and cheered. "Get some rest lads. There be more work to be done in the morrow before she be ready to sail."

Captain O'Toole watched him carefully as the crew dispersed for the hull below. The following night, as the crew prepared to head ashore, Chip volunteered to stand guard.

"Mr. MacDougall, ye be up to something?" the Captain questioned sternly, his arms folded. "In all me years, never hath a maltoot under me command ever wished to stay aboard when the harbor called."

Chip shook his head. "Nay."

"First, ye be sleeping through the night and now ye doth not wish to leave the ship," the Captain assessed. "Ye hath taken the secret of the *Ottoman* to heart."

"Sir, I admit I be more relaxed aboard this ship. The source of me comfort, I not be sure."

"Should ye wish to remain aboard, I shall not stop ye," the Captain sighed. "Just remember, lad, we hath a long journey back. We shall accompany the *Persica* to Inverness before finishing the trek back to Leith. I be going to assign ye to the *Persica*, but I think it best ye stay aboard the *Ottoman*."

"Thank ye, Captain. I be grateful."

The Captain's tone took a serious turn. "Show yer gratitude by keeping an ear low and reporting anything that might be considered mutinous."

"Mutinous, sir?" Chip repeated in a hushed tone.

"Aye, Mr. MacDougall. These be troubled days still, and many Scots believe fighting be still in the stars. Winds of war still fill the sails of those that sympathize with Prince Charlie and his Jacobite rebellion."

"Why doth ye trust me?" Chip asked, his brow furrowed. "I hath as much contempt for the English as any other Scot aboard yer ship."

The Captain patted him on the shoulder. "I trust ye, Mr.

MacDougall, for ye be wise. Ye know what folly would befall yer home should the Jacobites seize control. For this reason, we must fight our yearnings and defend our country."

———•———

The *Ottoman* stayed in port three more days before setting sail again, escorting the *Persica* to the Port of Inverness. The crew had come to accept Chip, and Mr. Barrett decided it was time to teach him how to fight. He wasn't sure he really needed to learn until Mr. Barrett mopped the deck with him, literally.

"Hath you ever been in a scrape?" Mr. Barrett asked, picking him up from the deck by the coat.

Chip wiped the dirt from his face. "Aye. Just not with the likes of ye."

"Not many hath ever been in a scrape with the likes of Mr. Barrett, Mr. MacDougall!" the Captain laughed, emerging from his cabin. "He be one of the finest tappers England hath ever seen."

"Ye were a boxer?" Chip asked, staring up at Mr. Barrett while attempting to catch his breath.

"Aye. A champion fisticuffs for a time."

"Might I ask what happened?"

"Wanted to see more of the world and less of other men's blood."

"His abilities be why I recruited him," the Captain added. "The riffle and the sword not always be allotted ye in a fight. There be times yer fists be all ye hath. He shall teach ye the ways of the riffle and the sword as well. Friendly word. Never be owing Mr. Barrett a copper."

Chip's face twitched at the thought of what dire consequences the Captain inferred. The more he got to know the crew, he realized that nearly the entire lot had been hand-selected by the Captain. There were only a few aboard the *Persica* and the *Ottoman* that were assigned to his ranks. Those few included the notorious Mr. Stubbs.

Mr. Stubbs was a shady Englishman from the south of London who was given two options in life: join the Royal Navy or serve out an unknown number of years in prison for a lifetime of theft. His thieving ways caught up to him in London Harbor when he attempted to lift a chest from a Spanish payload. The chest was rumored to be worth a King's ransom.

Without the dreams and the bodiless voices, Chip started feeling more and more like his old self. The Captain quickly accepted Chip into his inner circle of crew, citing that the "True Mr. MacDougall" was of real value.

This return to himself also brought about a greater longing to return home. He tortured himself in the quiet times with mental images of his family. *Shall I be able to return home once me tour be over, or shall the voices and dreams return the moment I depart this ship?* These questions bothered him, always right before he drifted off to sleep.

On the fifth day of the voyage, Chip awoke to the sound of cannon fire in the distance.

"Calafort Inverness bheith faoi seige!" Mr. MacDuth shouted from the crow's nest.

"Speak English you paddy-whack!" Mr. Stubbs growled.

"He said the Port of Inverness be under attack!" Chip shouted, reaching for his cap and glaring at the gent in the bowler hat.

"Prepare to man the cannons, men!" Captain O'Toole shouted, taking the helm of the ship. "Mr. Barrett, signal for Mr. Kellogg to steer the *Persica* to the north! We shall take them from the south and cut off the ships from traveling the shoreline! We shall force them out to sea!"

"Aye, Captain!" Mr. Barrett shouted.

Chip stayed topside to help man the upper cannons. The Captain planned to down the enemy ships and cut off any land forces. *Barely two weeks in the Royal Navy, and I be about to see war. Surely this must be the Jacobites.* Regardless of his feelings, he knew the Captain was right. He was part of the Navy, sworn to defend the shores of Scotland and England from all foes.

The sound of wood colliding with something hard and splintering caught Chip's attention. He looked up in time to see the tip of the stern mast shatter from cannon fire. Instinctively, he lunged forward and shoved Mr. Barrett to safety. Mr. Stubbs could be heard cursing at the top of his lungs.

"Who is close enough to fire upon us?" Mr. Barrett shouted, rolling back to his feet.

"It be the *Persica*!" Mr. MacDuth shouted, this time in

English.

"It not be!" Chip shouted. "Mr. Kellogg be in charge of the *Persica*!"

"Not anymore!" Captain O'Toole roared, peering through a spyglass. "There be a mutiny aboard! Men, prepare to return fire!"

Chip felt the pit of his stomach leave him. He could see his feelings reflected in Mr. Barrett's eyes. The sound of another cannonball whistling past snapped him to his senses. *Blaggards! How dare they turn on us!* he thought savagely as rage filled him.

Moments later, the *Ottoman* was being brought about. Starboard cannons boomed, as they attempted to do the once unthinkable: sink the *Persica*. All thoughts of saving Inverness were lost as they battled the once kindred ship.

The ship he had been aboard only a week ago was no match for the mighty *Ottoman*. Chip loaded another round into his cannon as he watched another cannonball slice through the forward mast of the *Persica*. Soon she would be too battered to continue the fight. They were close enough now to see aboard without a spyglass. Mr. Tombs stood at the wheel, shouting out commands. He remembered how unsociable Mr. Tombs had been during their journey to Iceland and how he was one of the first to volunteer to sail back aboard the ship.

Chip could tell that Mr. Tombs was looking for a way to flee, but there was no reasonable way to do so, the *Persica* too battered to sail.

"Continue the engagement!" the Captain shouted. "Sink the

Persica!"

"Captain!" Mr. Stubbs shouted in protest.

"We shan't allow the blaggards to reach shore!" the Captain growled.

"Suppose there be captives aboard, Captain?" Mr. Boyd pleaded. "Shall we send our shipmates to a watery grave, knowing not whether they be traitors indeed?"

Captain O'Toole hesitated before shouting, "We not risk boarding the *Persica!* We know not which be mates and which be traitors! Should they take the *Ottoman*, we risk too much!"

Chip could tell that the Captain aggrieved this decision. He could not imagine Mr. Kellogg surrendering to Mr. Tombs. *Mr. Kellogg must be dead.* As the booming of cannons commenced once more, he saw a tear streak Captain O'Toole's cheek.

Less than a half hour later, an explosion signaled the hull had been breached, where the gunpowder was kept.

"Cease fire!" Captain O'Toole shouted.

Chip bitterly watched as the stern of the *Persica* began to sink. No signs of life on the deck of the sinking ship could be seen. All were either dead or had taken their chances in the frigid waters of the North Sea. He could see no dinghy boats leave-taking the wreckage.

The sound of cannons booming in the distance penetrated his thoughts.

"Prepare yer selves, lads!" the Captain shouted. "The enemy not be defeated yet. We must drive the blaggards out of Inverness!"

By the time the *Ottoman* was close enough to engage the Jacobite Army, it was too late. A cannonball crashed into the waters just meters from the port bow.

"Who hath fired upon us?" Captain O'Toole demanded.

"It be the Fort, Captain!" Mr. MacDuth shouted from the crow's nest. "She be under seige!"

"Prepare to come about! We must retreat to open waters!"

"What of Inverness, Captain? We leave her in the hand of these rebels then?"

"It be too late for them. The *Persica* did her deed well. She detained us long enough for the blaggards to seize the Fort. As mighty as the *Ottoman* be, she not take the Fort alone."

Mr. Barrett nodded solemnly. No ships pursued the *Ottoman*, having witnessed the onslaught the *Persica* withstood before sinking into the icy waters. Chip helped assist crew members which were injured. Fortunately, they had sustained no casualties from the battle. The trouble was, now they were alone. No matter how great the *Ottoman* was, the chances of withstanding an attack from a fleet with a skeleton crew and limited resources were slim.

"We shall sail for Leith," the Captain ordered after much deliberation. "We hath not knowledge whether the rest of Britain knows yet of this attack. We must deliver word."

There was a distinct murmuring amongst some of the crew.

"Let me make me self clear," the Captain continued, a growl to his voice. "Regardless of yer feelings over the current state of Britain, ye vowed to defend the Union from all invaders when ye enlisted in the Royal Navy. Any that harbor mutiny aboard this vessel shall be placed in shackles and shall be charged of treason when we reach Leith."

"There shall not be any mutiny aboard this ship, Captain," Mr. Boyd said, turning to face the rest of the crew. "I be Irish, and I be Scot. I hath seen more than me fair of lesser acts by the English, but these blaggards offer only bloodshed. There be not a better day ahead should they be allowed to continue their quest. Should ye wish not to fight for Britain, then fight for Scotland."

The crew looked amongst each other before nodding and shouting their approval.

"Hoist the main sail! We sail for Leith! Mr. MacDuth, take to the crow's nest and watch for ships. Should ye see any, call out immediately. We know not who yet be with us."

"Aye, Captain!" Mr. MacDuth shouted, before climbing up what was left of the rope ladder.

"Mr. Barrett, join me at the wheel. Mr. MacDougall, go below and inventory our supplies. We need to ration as much as possible, lest we be delayed."

Aye, Captain!" Chip and Mr. Barrett shouted in unison.

Chip knew the Captain was preparing for a long voyage. He gathered up a count of everything from food rations to gunpowder, checking it twice before submitting his findings to the Captain.

"These numbers be yer post until we reach Leith, Mr. MacDougall," the Captain said, looking over the parchment and handing it back to him. "I shall be depending upon thee to see that we not run out. None shall be allowed rations without permission. Fetch ye a riffle and keep it close. Should any attempt to overthrow ye, doth not hesitate."

"Aye, Captain."

He despised the thought of having to shoot a fellow crew member, but he knew what desperate times and hunger could do to a man. He fetched a riffle from Mr. Boyd, who guarded the armory room next to the supply room, and assumed his post.

———•———

They encountered another ship not even a day's journey from the Port of Inverness. The *Ottoman* became locked in a fierce battle. When it was over, the foreign ship was left to sink into the North Sea. More crew members had been injured, including Mr. Boyd, but to their great fortune none had lost their lives.

The following day they encountered yet another hostile ship. The crew of the *Ottoman* once more found themselves in a fight for survival. In the end, the *Ottoman* continued on victorious while the enemy sunk beneath the waves. Despite no loss of life aboard the vessel, the mood amongst the crew started to sour.

The fifth night of the voyage to Leith, the Captain conveyed his concerns to Chip, Mr. Barrett, and Mr. Boyd in private. "Sailing with a skeleton crew be task enough, but to continually engage in battle shall press the men to the break. I trust ye three to be me eyes and ears."

"There be murmurings indeed, Captain," Mr. Boyd interjected, leaning against the armory room wall while favoring his right arm.

"None hath attempted to breach the supplies, however several tend to linger," Chip added.

"Should we encounter another hostile ship before reaching Leith …"

"There not be any choice, men. Should we encounter another ship, we shall sail out to avoid confrontation. While we still be loaded with artillery, I fear a weary crew would leave us vulnerable. Keep yer eyes wide."

"Aye, Captain," the three replied in unison.

The sixth day proved to be the same. A foreign hostile vessel sat just off the shores of Aberdeen, the invading forces of the Jacobites attempting to take hold there as well. The vessel fired upon the *Ottoman*, missing just south of the bow. The Captain ordered the crew to hold their fire and to sail farther out to sea.

"Should they follow us, Captain?" Mr. Stubbs shouted.

"They shall not leave their forces unprotected!"

Indeed, the vessel stayed put as the *Ottoman* sailed farther out to sea. They sailed the open waters for days, much longer than it should have taken had they been able to hug the shoreline. On the twelfth day, Mr. Stubbs mused, "We must be halfway to Denmark!"

"If ye be wishing to visit, Mr. Stubbs, we can toss ye over and let ye swim the rest of the way," Mr. Boyd suggested.

"You need not be so cross, Mr. Boyd. Surely Mr. MacDougall lets you a scrape from the rations every now and then."

"Continue yer accusations, Mr. Stubbs, and I shall help ye over the side," Chip growled. "Back to yer hammock or back topside."

"As you say, Mr. MacDougall." Mr. Stubbs tipped his bowler cap before heading back topside.

Food supplies were starting to run thin. They had planned on storing up more in Inverness, but that had been thwarted by the mutiny of the *Persica*. Chip found himself to be less liked with each passing day as the rationing of food took its toll on the crew. Only the Captain, Mr. Boyd, and Mr. Barrett remained steadfast.

Twenty days after leaving Inverness waters, the ports of Leith came into sight. Smoke from cannon fire filled the air as the *Ottoman* bared down on an intense battle just outside the North Port. Two foreign vessels were locked in an intense exchange with two Naval ships protecting the harbor. It was clear the Navy ships were beginning to lose.

"Prepare yer selves, lads!" the Captain shouted. "Man the portside cannons and pack them tight! Shore up the sails! We hath the advantage! When we come about, fire on my command!"

The Captain spun the wheel, bringing the *Ottoman* about at a swift clip. Chip gripped the ship's railing for stability as the mighty vessel turned into position. He remembered how Mr. Stives had admired the topside cannons when they first boarded the ship, pointing out how they would give the *Ottoman* an advantage over most vessels due to their long range. A cannonball whistled through the air in the *Ottoman*'s direction, splashing down well short of its intended target.

"Ready, men! Fire!"

The *Ottoman* rocked as every topside portside cannon fired at once. Chip swabbed his cannon, Mr. Boyd packed the charge, and together they loaded the cannonball before pulling the cannon back into place by guide ropes. Immediately, Chip grasped the side of the ship, as Mr. Boyd adjusted the cannon's trajectory.

"Fire!" the Captain shouted.

Mr. Boyd lit the fuse. They both turned away to shield their faces as the cannon boomed again, sending the round projectile hurdling through the air. Chip looked up in time to see their cannonball find its mark, along with twelve others, pounding the side and deck of their target. Over and again, he and Mr. Boyd repeated the same process. It wasn't a strange feeling for him, the repetition reminding him of his days as a docker, repeating similar movements over and over, while unloading a ship or stacking crates.

Return fire from the enemy ship became less and less until finally the Captain ordered the *Ottoman* to cease fire, the vessel showing signs that it was beginning to take on water. As for the second enemy ship, it had turned and was attempting to flee to the north.

"Hoist the sails full!" the Captain shouted. "We shall run

the blaggards down before they make open waters!"

Another Navy vessel from the harbor was pursuing the enemy ship as well, but Chip knew they had no real chance of catching it. Only the *Ottoman* could prevent the ship from reaching open waters. Once it was in range, the Captain pulled parallel, then ordered the portside lower cannons to open fire.

Chip watched as the vessel's main mast shattered, the reign of cannonballs blistering the already battered hull. He could see its crew scrambling for empty dinghies or diving into the water, knowing they would never survive the coming onslaught. The *Ottoman* mercilessly pounded the enemy vessel, until the soon-to-be wreckage sank beneath the waves.

The Naval ship, the *Victoria*, flagged down the *Ottoman*, requesting permission for their captain to come aboard. Once aboard, the two captains went to the captain's quarters to speak in private. They emerged a half hour later and Captain O'Toole gathered the crew about him as the *Victoria's* captain departed back to his ship.

"Men, Leith hath been overrun by the rebellion," Captain O'Toole grimly advised. "We must sail to London for supplies then we shall return here to reclaim control of the Port."

"Captain, hath Edinburgh fallen as well?" Mr. Stives asked.

Chip feared for his family as he awaited the Captain's answer.

"Captain Sinclair saith Union soldiers resist the blaggards at all sides. They be aware of the state of Inverness. Even now, the

Duke of Argyll leads Union soldiers to Inverness to combat the rebellion there."

Chip felt the bittersweet angst building in his chest. He felt relieved to hear that Edinburgh was resisting and at the same time frightened his family might still be in danger.

"Hoist the anchor and man the main sails!" the Captain shouted. "Quickly men! We must make haste!"

"Aye, Captain!" the crew shouted in unison.

"Mr. MacDougall."

"Aye, Captain?" Chip replied, as he helped raise the anchor.

"Go down below and take yer post guarding the rations," the Captain ordered. "And send Mr. Stubbs to me. I be sure ye shall find him close to the supply room."

Chip frowned at the thought. "Aye, Captain."

He sighed as he entered the hull. He knew if he found Mr. Stubbs where the Captain suspected, there would be resistance. Sure enough, he found Mr. Stubbs helping himself to some food.

"Mr. Stubbs." Chip growled, startling the bowler hat clear off the man's head as he jumped. "Captain O'Toole wishes to see ye topside. Yer to leave the rations behind."

"Mr. MacDougall," Mr. Stubbs said, regaining his composure, "you gave me a fright for sure. Do you know why the Captain wishes to see me?"

"He not say. Only ye to report to him."

Mr. Stubbs made to leave the hull, but Chip extended his arm, blocking the man's way. The strong aroma of whiskey filled his nostrils as it floated up from the Englishman.

"The Captain told me to man the rations," Chip said sternly. "Empty yer hand, then go see the Captain."

"Mr. MacDougall … have a heart," Mr. Stubbs said, trying to sound friendly. "I was only hungry."

"Ye eat with the rest of us. We eat even portions, including the Captain, until we reach port."

"Our dear Captain," Mr. Stubbs mused. "A leader by ways."

"Aye. That be why he commands respect."

"Not even a month at sea and you be his faithful seaman. From where do your loyalties come?" Mr. Stubbs quipped.

"I be loyal to Captain O'Toole and me country."

"When you say country, you mean Scotland. What of the rebellion? They be for Scotland as well."

Chip knew what Mr. Stubbs was inferring. He was trying to get Chip to say something, so that he might have leverage.

"I doth not sympathize with the Jacobites," Chip said, losing his patience. "Doth not pretend ye understand me or me countrymen, Mr. Stubbs. Like Mr. Boyd, I too hath suffered at the hand of the Union. We doth what be best for Scotland and should it be best for England as well, so be it."

"It be the hand of fate, Mr. MacDougall, not the hand of the Union that sets our path," Mr. Stubbs spat. "One day these ships shall be full of English soldiers and you Scottie dogs shall be back in your pens."

Chip grabbed Mr. Stubbs and shoved him forcefully into

the side of the hull. The fear in Mr. Stubbs' eyes prevented Chip from beating the man for the things he had said.

"What is the problem, Mr. MacDougall?" Mr. Barrett asked, walking up behind Chip.

A sick grin covered the face of Mr. Stubbs.

"The Captain ordered Mr. Stubbs topside to see him. Mr. Stubbs thinks himself better. Thinks he be privy to our rations as he pleases."

Mr. Stubbs' grin faded quickly as Mr. Barrett pushed past Chip, knocked the rations from his hands and grabbing him by the back of the neck.

"You not be any better than the rest of us, Mr. Stubbs," Mr. Barrett. growled "Leave not the Captain waiting long, lest we be forced to tell him why you did not come quickly."

Mr. Barrett released Mr. Stubbs who stumbled, as he ran for the steps that lead topside, his eyes wide with fear.

"That's why Mr. Kellogg told you to keep an eye on him," Mr. Barrett grunted. Chip thought about Mr. Kellogg and bit his lip, trying to hold back the anger that rose from the loss of their mate. "I should have let you flog him for what he called thee."

"I be called worse before. I believe he thought ye were going to help him."

Mr. Barrett frowned. "Aye, because I be English. He not be understanding me grand-mum be Scottish. He speaks of fate, yet he sets his own."

"In a way, we all hath set our own fate," Chip said, thinking of how he had ended up there.

"Be it fate, Mr. MacDougall, that has placed us all together here?"

"What doth ye believe?" he asked, curious as to what the large man would say.

"I believe that we are all here for a reason. That there is a purpose for us, whether we yet know what it is. I used to believe I cheated death every time I walked away at the end of a bought. Now, I realize the reason I walked away was because my fight was not yet over."

"Ye be wise, Mr. Barrett," Chip said, pondering his words.

Mr. Barrett chuckled. "That, or I suffered too many strikes to me head. I shall let you be the judge."

———◆———

Mary was busy preparing the evening meal when a knock at the front door caught her attention. She hastened to the door, opening it to see Mr. Wallace from the bank standing there with his hat in his hand.

"Mr. Wallace. Please come in at once. It not be safe."

"Thank ye, Mrs. MacDougall," Mr. Wallace said nervously. "Me apologies for stopping by unannounced."

"What be the matter?"

Mr. Wallace peered around the room. "Where be ye children? I doth not wish for them to hear this from me."

"The children be upstairs," Mary replied, her chest tightening. "What be wrong?"

"Mrs. MacDougall, ye may want to sit down," Mr. Wallace replied calmly, fetching a chair from the corner for her to sit in. "Mrs. MacDougall, I be truly sorry to be the one that delivers the news to thee." He took a deep breath. "The ship ye husband was aboard, the *Persica*, went down in the North Sea. None survived."

Mary didn't wail or scream. She sat there transfixed on the cuff of Mr. Wallace's sleeve. She remembered seeing Christopher wearing a shirt like that for the first time. He looked so handsome in it that she never wanted him to stop wearing it. She remembered how uncomfortable he was whenever he dressed up. How nervous he was the day he asked her to be his wife. How nervous he was the day Marcus was born. He was so scared he might drop him that he shook the whole time.

"Mrs MacDougall?" came Mr. Wallace's voice, cutting through her mind. She was completely unaware that tears were pouring down her cheeks. "Mrs MacDougall, be there something I might for thee?"

Mary shook her head. There was nothing that anyone could do for her. She had lost her husband twice. The first time to his own mind, and now to the North Sea.

"Be there someone I might fetch for thee? I doth not wish to leave ye alone after delivering such news."

"Nay, Mr. Wallace," Mary replied, feeling dazed. "Me family be too far away. I shall go and visit me church to pray."

Mr. Wallace handed her a handkerchief to wipe her face. "Doth ye need help with yer children?"

"Nay, Mr. Wallace. Thank ye for yer kindness, but I shall manage."

"I shall send someone around from the bank in a few days' time to check on thee," Mr. Wallace said, nodding and turning to leave.

"Mr. Wallace, why be ye so kind to me and me family?" Mary asked, looking up.

Mr. Wallace stopped and turned back to face her. "Ye husband inspired people. I was captivated by him. I often wondered over the past year what he might do next and where his inspiration came from. It be a pity that I now understand the source of his strength on this day."

Mary nodded, though she did not agree. Christopher had always been her strength and her motivation to keep her family going in his absence. She could never imagine a world without him. She had envisioned that one day he would come home.

The door closed behind Mr. Wallace and Mary fled to the study, locking herself away before succumbing to the grief welling up inside her.

EIGHT

———————— ◆ ————————

THE SEVEN

On the fifth day at sea, London Harbor came into view.
Captain O'Toole and Captain Sinclair decided to take the longer
voyage out away from the shoreline. They agreed that any further
entanglements before they could refresh their low supplies could be
disastrous. Any attempts to stop in other Lowland ports for
supplies risked being boarded by either rebels or sympathizers.

Chip had just dozed off when he heard Mr. MacDuth cry,
"Land ho!"

Stretching and yawning, he joined the rest of the crew
topside, as they entered London Harbor. Most of the crew were
excited to be able to stand on dry land, if only for a few hours. Chip
wasn't excited at all. He did yearn to exit the ship, but the fear that
his demons might be waiting for him on the wharf beyond was
overwhelming.

"Mr. MacDougall, please come with me," Captain O'Toole
replied when Chip volunteered to stay aboard.

Chip followed the Captain to his quarters, unsure of what
he had done wrong. *Surely the Captain would not punish him for*

volunteering to watch the ship.

"Mr. MacDougall, doth yer resolve to stay aboard this ship come from the fact that ye hath been at peace since ye boarded this vessel?"

"Aye, Captain, it doth." Chip was relieved to hear the Captain understood.

"That be why I shan't let ye stay aboard."

"But Captain, sir—" he spluttered, his heart pounding.

"Ye must face yer demons, Mr. MacDougall. But we doth not hath to face our demons alone."

The Captain opened up a desk drawer and removed what looked to be a wooden cross, attached to a looped piece of yarn.

"See this cross, Mr. MacDougall?" The Captain held up the necklace so that Chip could see it clearly. "It be made from this ship. Every time a plank be replaced, wooden crosses are carved from it. It be tradition that whenever a seaman reaches the end of his voyage aboard the *Great Michael*, they be given a wooden cross. It be a way for them to remember their time aboard and carry a bit of the blessing of St. Michael with them." He placed the necklace over Chip's head. "I believe ye need this now."

Chip held the wooden cross up in the palm of his hand, so he could get a better look at it. "Thank ye, Captain."

"Go. Join ye crew. Tomorrow, Mr. MacDougall, we set sail again. I expect ye to make sure our hull be full of supplies."

"Aye, Captain."

Chip joined the crew as they headed ashore for one

delicious meal before returning to prepare the *Ottoman* for a potentially long voyage. He held his breath as he set foot on the wharf, clutching the wooden cross about his neck with his hand. To his surprise and elation, he heard no voices other than that of his fellow seamen.

Chip's heart leapt for joy as he joined his mates at a nearby tavern, but refrained from the ale that flowed. He was enjoying his freedom too much to impair it. Though the tavern was dingy and smelt of fish, everything seemed brighter to him.

Several hours later, Chip and the crew returned to the *Ottoman* to prepare for the voyage ahead and the battle beyond. An additional hundred and thirty men joined the crew, many experienced gunners, assigned to the ship by Royal Navy. Together they began loading supplies, including a war's cargo of cannonballs and black powder.

———•———

Chip awoke the next morning to discover that more ships had joined them in the night. *The Margaret*, the *Harmony*, the *Sentinel*, the *Mary* and the *Henry* had come in to load up as well. They would join with the *Victoria* and the *Ottoman* on their voyage. The captains of the seven vessels went ashore to meet with Union generals before setting sail. Upon his return, Captain O'Toole gathered the crew topside.

"Men, today we sail for Inverness. We shall be joined by the

Victoria and the Margaret. They shall aide in securing the harbor while Union forces drive the blaggards out."

"What of the other ships, Captain?" Mr. Barrett asked.

"The Harmony, Sentinel, Mary and Henry shall sail to secure the Ports of Leith and Aberdeen. We shall sail ahead and around. We must reach Inverness Harbor before they reach Leith."

Chip saw the fire in his Captain's eyes and heard the grit in his voice.

"The blaggards hath drawn the line and sides hath been chosen," the Captain continued, drawing his sword and holding it high. "It matters not what hath happened in the past. We shall win the day and this rebellion shall come to an end. For yer country and for yer families we sail!"

The crew roared their approval as they scattered like flies, heading to their posts. Chip silently wished that he was aboard the four headed for Leith, but knew his fate lied with the *Ottoman*. To return home, there was no other choice. They must be victorious.

The voyage back to Inverness was anything but quiet or peaceful. Strong storms, seasonally uncommon for that time of year, had moved into the North Sea, slowing their progress and filling the voyage with unexpected danger. Great waves pounded the hull of the *Ottoman*, threatening to sink the mighty vessel. The storms became so intense that at one point the Captain had to order the main sails be lowered lest the masts be shattered by the gusts of wind.

When the storms finally subsided, allowing for the *Ottoman*,

Victoria and *Margaret* to press on, they had lost nearly two days' progress. Chip knew this meant the other ships would reach the Port of Leith first, and the Union army would reach the northern Highlands before they reached the Port of Inverness. If this happened, the chances of the three ships being thrust into an immediate battle was almost certain.

"Chip!"

Chip looked up to the crow's nest as he prepared to head down below deck.

"Go fetch the Captain from his quarters!" Mr. MacDuth shouted. "Tell him we be passing Peddler's Peak!"

Chip nodded then headed to the Captain's cabin. He knocked swiftly on the cabin door and waited for a response.

"Enter," called the Captain's voice.

"Sir, Mr. MacDuth asked me to fetch ye. He saith we hath passed Peddler's Peak."

Captain O'Toole sat at his desk, his head bowed low over several maps and charts. His eyes were closed, and he did not seem to breath until he looked up at Chip, who still stood in the doorway.

"Inverness draws near," the Captain sighed grimly. "I daresay that I not hath to tell ye what this means."

"Nay, sir, ye doth not."

"Ye wonder why I seem so concerned by what lies before us. I see it in yer eyes. Ye wonder why a captain such as me self, with all the battles I hath seen, would be troubled."

"Aye, sir, I do."

"Mr. MacDougall, every battle troubles me. Never, in all me voyages, hath a battle ended without loss of life. This truth ye must understand and accept, should ye wish to live through as many as me. The burden of loss of life, it weighs on me."

"Surely ye must be accustomed to death by now, sir."

"Mr. MacDougall, come and join me." Captain O'Toole gestured to the chair in front of his desk. "Peddler's Peak means we be another two hours from Inverness, even with a good headwind."

Chip took a seat in front of the Captain's desk and waited silently.

"Ye be an intelligent lad, Mr. MacDougall," Captain O'Toole continued, settling back into his chair. "This be why I shall share this with thee. Me secret to being the captain I be today be simple. I thank me first captain for being ruthless with a heart of coal. I vowed while in his service never to be like him." He took a sip from his glass of whiskey before continuing. "Here be me secret to survival: never fail to mourn loss of life. The day ye stop mourning loss, yer soul be snabbled."

"Sir, forgive me ignorance. How doth it help ye survive?"

"I value life over victory. I hath ended several battles with barely a scuffle, because the captains of other ships respected and feared me. They knew to resist was to invite the devil among the tailors, but to surrender meant life."

"How doth ye know when to spare yer foe and when ye must off them?"

"Ye must know yer foe." The Captain stood and turned to face the cabin wall. "Some foes might be bargained with, others shall not surrender. When I be five years of age, me grandfather fought against the first Jacobite Rising. He lost his life while preventing the loss of others. Ye must be willing to what ye must to prevent more loss of life." He pulled back the curtain hiding the painting of St. Michael. "When I be torn, I turn to me faith to be me guide."

Chip sat quietly, thinking of Mary and her faith. He once possessed such faith, but pain and torment slowly replaced his belief in someone that he could not see. He looked down at the wooden cross which hung around his neck, clinching it in his fist.

"Ye and I doth not share the same faith," the Captain said quietly.

Chip looked up quickly to see that the Captain was still facing the panting of St Michael.

"Ye doth not hath to answer me, lad. Ye cling to that tiny wooden cross, as though it be yer lifeline. I wear me cross only as a tribute to me faith."

Chip looked hard for signs of a wooden cross hidden amongst the Captain's shirt ruffles.

"I doth not see yer cross, sir."

"Me cross not be worn on the outside."

Before the Captain could explain, there was a loud knock at the cabin door. Chip stood up and turned to face the door, waiting anxiously.

"Enter," the Captain called out.

Mr. Barrett hurriedly entered the cabin. "Sir, two ships have been sighted in the distance! They look to be blocking our path."

"Mr. Barrett, signal the *Victoria* and the *Margaret*," the Captain ordered, dawning his coat. "Inform them of the sighted vessels then pipe up the crew. We must prepare for conflict."

"Aye, sir," Mr. Barrett said, leaving the cabin with haste.

Chip made to follow, but the Captain grabbed his shoulder.

"Mr. MacDougall, ye shall join me at the wheel. Ye hath shown yer self to be capable of following simple commands. Let us see how ye fair with something more complex."

Chip wasn't for certain, if the idea sounded appealing to him. Not wanting to disobey an order, he simply nodded, then followed the Captain up to the top of the stern. Mr. Barrett roused the crew, which sprang up from below deck, like ants from the earth.

"Prepare the portside cannons, lads!" the Captain shouted, taking the wheel.

"Always position the bow of the ship towards open water during conflict," the Captain instructed Chip. "We only fire the forward cannon when we hath not a choice. Keep sight of the *Victoria* and the *Margaret*. Should they deviate from our course, notify me at once."

"Aye, sir!"

Chip did as the Captain requested, though he found it difficult not to turn around and see what was transpiring behind

138

him. The Captain shouted out commands to the crew, as the *Ottoman* turned sharply. The sound of cannonballs colliding with the water, shy of the bow, was incredibly hard to ignore. The *Ottoman* opened fire on the opposing vessels. Shouts from the crew and the Captain informed him their cannonballs had found their mark.

The *Victoria* and the *Margaret* followed course, but did not open fire on the opposing vessels until they sailed much closer. Chip assumed it was because the two ships did not have the range of the *Ottoman's* topside cannons. They sailed around the two enemy vessels, forcing them to break position and attempt to re-position themselves against the onslaught. This was a mistake.

Captain O'Toole immediately brought the *Ottoman* about at a swift pace, catching the opposing vessels off guard. The *Victoria* and the *Margaret* remained parallel with the enemy vessels, drawing their fire. The Captain's maneuver exposed the stern of the nearest enemy ship, allowing the *Ottoman* close range cannon fire.

A devastating barrage from the lower deck cannons crippled the rudders of the ship. Unable to flee, the *Victoria* and the *Margaret* pounded the enemy ship until it began to take on water at a swift rate. The lead ship raised its main sail and made to flee.

"Mr. Barrett! Signal the *Victoria* and the *Margaret*. We sail on for Inverness. Leave the devils to flee, lest they decide to engage again. They hath delayed our voyage long enough!"

"Aye, sir!" Chip heard Mr. Barrett shout somewhere behind him.

"Mr. MacDougall, doth ye understand thy purpose?"

"To keep watch and report should either ship change course," he recited, turning to face the Captain.

"Aye. Should they break course, we would be exposed, the same as those enemy ships were just now. I gave ye an important job, and ye followed me orders like a true maltoot." Chip recognized the compliment and immediately nodded his thanks. "Ye shall doth the same when we reach Inverness."

Tension amongst the crew elevated as they sailed on. They all knew the two ships that delayed their mission would be nothing more than a brief interlude compared to what laid ahead. Captain O'Toole sounded steady and calm, as he called out commands, as though they were merely sailing out to sea.

A cool breeze whipped across the stern of the ship as Inverness Fort came into view. Cannon fire ripped the would-be serene moment apart as cannonballs splashed down several yards shy of the bow.

"They be a challenging us, lads!" the Captain shouted. "Mr. MacDuth, be sure to be on the lookout for vessels!"

"Aye, Captain!"

The Captain swung the bow of the *Ottoman* out to sea, making to stay clear of the Fort's cannon fire. The *Victoria* mimicked the *Ottoman*'s path while the *Margaret* sailed on, directly into the path of the Fort's cannons.

"Sir! The *Margaret* has not changed course!"

"By design, Mr. MacDougall! She shall draw their fire while

we move in from the north!"

The horror of the moment grasped him. The *Margaret* and her crew were about to sacrifice their ship and possibly their lives to secure the victory. The *Victoria* and the *Ottoman* would overpower the Fort and sustain the least amount of damage, but the *Margaret* would surely be lost.

Chip could see the *Margaret* rocking in the water, as the close-range attack began, the combination of the ship's cannon fire and cannonballs smashing into its hull. The low-level Fort was unable to focus its attention on the *Victoria* or the *Ottoman* with the *Margaret* so close, every cannon blast potentially deadly.

"Two enemy ships be coming about from the north!" Mr. MacDuth shouted.

Chip turned to see what Mr. MacDuth was seeing, and instead saw one of the new crew members standing between him and Captain O'Toole. He was a burly man with a tuft beard, wearing a thick pullover shirt and a tartan kilt of clan Wallace. Before he could say or do anything, the crew member brandished a short knife and thrust it into the side of the Captain.

"Captain!" he shouted, lunging at the traitor.

Chip quickly knocked the knife from the man's hand before thrusting his fist into the man's throat. The traitor dropped to his knees, clutching his throat and gasping for breath. He slammed his knee into the man's face, breaking his nose and knocking him to the deck. Chip looked back at the Captain. Though he was holding his side, he remained at the helm, supporting himself with the wheel.

The traitor struggled to his feet and attempted to draw his sword. Chip kicked the sword from his hand, then hooked the man's arm with his own before sinking his fist into the traitor's gut repeatedly. He slammed the man's back into the ship's railing, causing him to arch his torso in pain. He then smashed his fist into the side of man's face repeatedly. The man growled something inaudible as Chip withdrew his sword.

"Enough!" Captain O'Toole shouted with a grimace. "Show the blaggard to the brig! His life not be worth the blood on yer hands."

Chip backed away from the man and placed his sword back in its sheath, as Mr. Stubbs grabbed the traitor and shoveled him down the steps and then below deck. He looked down at his hands to see his knuckles covered with the man's blood.

"Captain, you be injured!"

"Doth not leave yer post, Mr. Barrett!" the Captain ordered. "Forget not the task at hand! It be merely a flesh wound. The blaggard missed anything important."

Chip wiped his hands on some rags, as the booming echoed about him. He was lost in his own thoughts, trying to come to grips with what had been going through his mind only moments earlier. He was so enraged at the traitor's actions that he was prepared to end the man's life—not out of fear for his own, but out of anger.

"Mr. MacDougall!" the Captain shouted, ripping him from his thoughts. "I thank ye for yer aide, but back to yer post! Forget not what be going on about us!"

"Aye, Captain!"

The Captain shouted more commands, ordering the crew to prepare to come about. The great ship turned and Chip caught sight of the two new ships that were preparing to attempt to halt the *Ottoman* and the *Victoria*. Unsurprisingly, he recognized the enemy vessels to be Spanish battleships. Prince Charlie having allies within Spain was highly suspected for years. The newcomers were still too far out for the *Ottoman* to engage.

Suddenly, the air had gone silent about them. The crashing of the waves against the hull could be heard once more. The cannon fire between the *Margaret* and the Fort had ceased.

"Captain, the Union Army has seized the Fort!" Mr. Barrett shouted.

A smatter of cheers went up from the crew. Chip knew if the Union Army had control over the Fort, the town of Inverness might well be in their grasps as well. Despite this, he could tell the enemy vessels were still preparing for a fight. The loss of the Fort had not changed their objective, though they remained out of range. They had lowered their main sail to half-mast and were turning into position to make a stand.

"Captain, why be these ships not fleeing?" Mr. Boyd asked, joining the Captain, Mr. Barrett, and Chip at the stern.

"They wish to detain us," the Captain replied, standing taller now.

"Shall we engage?"

"Aye, Mr. Barrett. Our orders were to clear the harbor and that be what we shall do."

"Captain, the *Margaret* hath signaled she be sea worthy," Mr. Barrett said, reading the signal flags through a spy glass. "Captain Kilbourn wants to know whether they should engage the enemy vessels."

"Signal the *Margaret* to hold position, lest any ships come up from the south." The Captain stepped away from the wheel. "Mr. Boyd, take the wheel and bring the *Ottoman* about starboard full."

"Aye, Captain!"

Captain O'Toole stepped forward past the wheel to address the crew. "Prepare the upper and lower port cannons! Ye shall fire upon me command! Doth not cease fire until I order ye to!"

"Aye, Captain!" the crew shouted as they made haste to be ready.

"Mr. MacDougall, go to me cabin and fetch a clean bed sheet and a bottle of whiskey."

Chip hurried off immediately to the Captain's cabin, having an idea what both were for. The Captain had him tear the bed sheet in two and un-stopper the bottle. He then soaked a small portion of the bed sheet with the whiskey before wrapping it around his waist to cover the knife wound. Chip tightened the sheet and tied it off, while the Captain drained the rest of the whiskey in one.

The Captain smirked, "Whiskey be an amazing liquid. It hurts me side to yell. Mr. MacDougall, stand here and shout out me orders."

"Aye, Captain."

"Tell the crew to drop the main sail and prepare to fire."

Chip cleared his throat the shouted, "Drop the main sail and prepare to fire!"

The crew looked up, not recognizing his voice as one of command. Upon seeing him standing beside the Captain, they immediately complied. He continued to bark out the Captain's commands as the *Ottoman* opened fire upon the opposing vessels.

The *Victoria* joined the *Ottoman* in what he could only describe as a boxing match. The four ships took hit after hit, though the *Ottoman* packed a deadlier punch. The sound of splintering wood, as the hull was repeatedly pounded, made Chip feel uneasy. Captain O'Toole assured him these were merely hits, and that no cracks were being made.

"Ye shall know, Mr. MacDougall, when the hull breaks." The Captain patted him on the shoulder. "The *Great Michael's* hull be over three meters thick. He truly be the finest vessel that I hath ever sailed."

Chip did not care to find out what it felt like when the hull of a ship broke. He had witnessed what happened to the unfortunate ships thus far that had dared stand against the *Ottoman*. He bit his lip as he thought of all those that had potentially been sent to a watery grave.

Suddenly, a cannonball struck the upper deck, blasting two of the crew backwards clear across to the other side, where they moved no more. A massive crew member, known as Big Dubbins, made his way to the vacant cannon and single-handedly pushed it back into place. Then, to the surprise of many, he grasped the ropes and began operating the cannon on his own.

The battle went on for hours and when the final cannon sounded, the *Ottoman* and the *Victoria* stood victorious. Several *Ottoman* crew members lost their lives that day, and many more aboard the *Victoria* and the *Margaret*.

"Cease fire, Mr. MacDougall. Mr. Barrett, signal the Victoria to cease fire as well. There be enough lives lost this day."

"Cease fire!" Chip shouted.

An eerie silence followed his command, as the cannon fire died away. The two Spanish vessels still rocked in the waters from the onslaught, but they were no longer a threat. Their hulls, cannon ports and masts were smashed and broken. He could see the crews waving sheets of surrender. The Captain had chosen to spare their lives.

Later, Captain Sinclair and Captain Kilbourn joined Captain O'Toole aboard the *Ottoman*. They did not seem to agree with the decision to not sink the Spanish battleships, but conceded it would have been a waste of ammunition to continue the battery. The Duke of Argyll boarded the ship that evening to meet with the captains. Mr. Barrett and Chip made to leave the cabin, but Captain O'Toole ordered them to stay.

"I wish to speak with only the captains and those in charge," the Duke said harshly.

"They be second in command aboard the *Ottoman*, ye

Lordship. I trust these two with me life."

Captain Sinclair peered over at Chip and Mr. Barrett, eyeing them with mild interest.

"Very well, Captain O'Toole," the Duke grumbled. "Captain Kilbourn, I commend ye on yer bravery. That move with yer ship turned the day."

"Thank ye, Duke. It was Captain O'Toole's idea though, and a brilliant move it was."

"Well, yer bravery shall not go unnoticed. Captain Sinclair, ye shall sail out to the west in the morning. A ship carrying Prince Charlie sailed before ye arrived. We believe he be headed for Skye. Make sure of it."

"What be yer orders should we find he has not left the mainland?" Captain Sinclair asked.

"See to it that he makes it to Skye. It matters not how he arrives, as long as he be alive. The King hath determined it best he live in exile for what he hath done. Should he die, he shall become a martyr. In exile, he dies a failure. This shall break the will of the remaining Jacobite Rebellion."

Captain Sinclair nodded. "I shall not fail."

"Captain O'Toole, ye and Captain Kilbourn shall remain here until ye receive new orders," the Duke continued. "Ye shall make sure the harbor remains under Union control."

Chip grimaced inwardly. He wondered how long it would be before they returned home to Edinburgh and Leith. The captains and the Duke commenced to break out the whiskey and share old seafaring tales. He and Mr. Barrett were reduced to servants, serving whiskey and fetching food from the galley. Captain O'Toole received a snort of distaste from the Duke when he told Chip and Mr. Barrett to help themselves to a glass of whiskey. Chip did so reluctantly, never really acquiring the taste for knock-down liquor.

"Treated the Captain as though he had done nothing," Mr. Barrett spat, as he and Chip went to fetch more whiskey.

"The Captain knows his own worth. He need not hear praise from the Duke."

"Aye, but it be disrespectful to not even acknowledge it was his plan that led to victory," Mr. Barrett surmised.

"There be one thing I hath learned aboard this vessel. It be that Captain O'Toole be tough. Words of the Duke, even those left unspoken, not hurt a man such as he."

Mr. Barrett chuckled, "Says the future Captain Chip MacDougall."

Chip rebuked him. "Nay. When this voyage be at an end, I be returning to me baking."

"You fight, you bake, you are second in command," Mr. Barrett mused. "Do you dance as well?"

Chip danced a jig and Mr. Barrett roared with laughter, as they headed back to the captain's quarters.

———•———

The following day, the Duke set off for London and Captain Sinclair set sail aboard the *Victoria* to see if Prince Charlie had left the mainland for Skye. Captain O'Toole began working with the new guard of Inverness to set scouting measures in order to better protect the outer barriers without spreading their forces too thin. The *Ottoman* and the *Margaret* took turns patrolling the outer waters of the harbor. While in port, half the crew would assist in the rebuilding of the Fort.

Days turned into weeks, and weeks turned into months. Chip longed to return to Edinburgh, but to leave without being dismissed would be treason. He wrote letters to Mary, explaining where he was and what had happened since he left. He told her how much he missed her and the children, and how he longed to see them.

Peace spread across Inverness. There were a few confrontations, but no serious battles ensued. The Jacobite supporters went into hiding, and Captain Sinclair sent word Prince Charlie had indeed fled for Skye.

"Men!" the Captain shouted one morning, gathering the crew. "The King hath decreed that we not be allowed to where the kilt any longer."

Murmuring spread through the crew like wild fire. Though others did, Chip hadn't worn his kilt since he joined the Navy. It remained tucked away safely inside his haversack.

"I know there be those amongst us that hath nothing else. Those that be in need of breeches, I shall provide the copper."

"But Captain, it be all I hath ever worn!" Mr. MacDuth exclaimed.

"The decree be for all of Britain, Mr. MacDuth. Ye hath not a choice. If ye need breeches, see me for the copper. That be all."

"Be this how the King repays loyalty?" Chip asked, once the crew had dispersed.

"He believes he be breaking the back of the rebellion," the Captain sighed. "Let us pray he doesn't start a fire instead."

"I be glad Mr. MacDuth didn't determine to part with his kilt topside." Mr. Barrett mused, a wry smile curving his face.

"Doth not give him the notion," the Captain warned before shaking his head.

———•———

Seven men sat about a round table in the center of a darkened room. Only a few oil lamps and a crackling fireplace gave light to the chamber. They sat silently, waiting for someone else to arrive, a lone empty chair sat vacant. Moments slowly passed, but none present showed signs of strain. Then, with no rhyme or reason, one of the seven raised and lowered a gavel against the table.

"This meeting shall now come to order," charged a commanding voice. He was clean shaven and wore a black jacket with gold buttons and red stitching. "We shall disclose in turn our reports."

"Should we not wait for him, Mr. Blake?" an older bearded man asked, wearing a black jacket with silver buttons and green stitching.

"We hath waited long enough," Mr. Blake scolded. "Being that ye be so talkative, Mr. Wall, why doth ye not start off tonight's meeting?"

"Very well," Mr. Wall groaned. "For the month—"

"What have we here?" a gentleman interrupted, taking a seat in the empty chair. "Starting without me? Bad form indeed."

"M-M-Mr. Prose," Mr. Wall stuttered. "W-W-We were just—"

"I be aware of what you were about to do, Mr. Wall. It seems you and Mr. Blake do not approve of my tardiness."

"We did not mean any disrespect, Mr. Prose." Mr. Blake inclined his head in Mr. Prose's direction. "We simply assumed yer schedule had prevented ye from attending."

"I am here," Mr. Prose said, indifferently. "Shall we dispose of the financial reports and proceed to the intent of tonight's meeting?"

The other men around the table shifted slightly in their seats.

"I wish for you to raise your leases by ten percent," Mr. Prose continued, not fazed by their reactions.

"Mr. Prose, sir," one of the men said, wearing a black

waistcoat with bronze buttons and gray stitching, "should we raise our leases we risk losing our tenants."

"I be aware, Mr. Terry. I be also aware that where one tenant leaves, another takes their place. One way or another, each one of you has become quite wealthy at my hand. All I wish be for thee to simply raise the price of your land deeds. I assure all of you that you shall continue to profit greatly."

"Of course, Mr. Prose," Mr. Blake said, bowing his head. "We shall comply with yer requests, as always."

A collective muttering of agreement echoed throughout the room.

"Now, Mr. Wallace," Mr. Prose said, looking directly across the table "do you foresee any changes, tenant-wise, to Toppum Street?"

"Nay, sir. The tenants of Toppum Street be most profitable."

"And what of Mr. MacDougall?"

"Sir, Mr. MacDougall remains a member of the Royal Navy. He continues to write to his wife, though I have intercepted all of his letters, as ye requested. Mrs. MacDougall believes he be lost, drowned aboard the *Persica*."

"Excellent," Mr. Prose said, smiling and folding his hands together in front of him. "The greatest pleasures are always the unexpected ones."

NINE

———◆———

HOME AGAIN

Chip stood at the helm of the *Ottoman* and looked out into Inverness Harbor, watching the waves roll in with the tide. A year had passed since he first sailed aboard the great vessel into the harbor, battling to victory alongside his fellow crew mates, under the leadership of Captain O'Toole. He remained under the leadership of the Captain, but now he stood at the helm as the first mate.

The *Ottoman* made weekly voyages into the North Sea, patrolling for signs of foreign vessels that did not belong. Though none were ever encountered, the Captain continued to demand they stay sharp and alert. Chip's job was to keep morale high amongst the crew and to report any concerns with any seaman. Overall, the crew respected him and took well to his post.

"Mr. MacDougall, sir."

Chip looked from the stern to see a stout seaman, wearing breeches that were a bit short in the legs hailing him from the deck below.

"Aye, Mr. Brown."

"Sir, the local dosser requests permission to come aboard."

"Permission granted," Chip growled bitterly.

"Today might be the day," Mr. Barrett offered hopefully.

"Nay, me friend. Me day passed a while back."

"Lose not your hope. There be many reasons why you have yet to hear from home."

"I hath wrote every week since we hath been in this cursed port," Chip growled. "Supposing me whither be going to write, she would hath done so. The dosser brings hope to all 'cept me."

"You know I have not a whither-me-go to send me affections," Mr. Barrett said lightheartedly. "Do not count me among the fortunate." He reached out, grasping Chip by the arm. "You shall return to them soon. The Captain swears that we be not much longer for this place."

"Aye, he did," Chip agreed, watching the waves of the North Sea spray up just beyond the break. "Me whither be cross with me the last we spoke. This be me only console that there be something to return to."

The word came on a Wednesday that the *Ottoman* would be reassigned back to Port Leith. Several members of the crew chose to stay behind in Inverness, having settled down and began families there. Captain O'Toole had no trouble replacing the wayward crew members and within two days' time, the *Ottoman* set sail for Port Leith and Edinburgh.

The voyage was one of mixed emotions for Chip. His mind

painted different pictures of what he might find upon arrival. One moment he imagined scenes of joyful reunion, the next he envisioned strife and turmoil. Sometimes he wondered if he might find some tragedy awaiting him. No matter what lie ahead, he knew one thing, he was going home.

———◦———

The voyage to Leith proved easier than the voyages around the northern land masses of Scotland that Chip had become accustomed to. The wind didn't bite him to the bone, and the waters didn't break against the bow with fierce vengeance. Though, in his longing for home, the voyage felt longer than it had the year before. When the ports of Leith came into view, several members of the crew, including Chip, cheered. The Captain summoned him to his quarters, as the crew prepared to bring the *Ottoman* to dock.

"Be there any way I might persuade ye to stay aboard?" the Captain asked, offering Chip a seat.

"Nay, sir. It hath been a pleasure to serve ye, Captain, but I must be about to see in on me family."

The Captain sighed, uncorked a bottle of whiskey, and poured himself a glass of the amber liquid. "When I met ye, ye were a man of troubles. Hath ye found solace aboard this ship?"

"Aye, sir," Chip replied, glancing up at the curtains that hid the portrait of St Michael from view. "I be grateful of the day ye asked me to join yer crew."

"Ye hath proven to be quite the seaman and a valuable first mate. I shall miss ye."

"I shall miss ye as well, Captain."

"Then join me in a round," the Captain said, pouring Chip a glass. "I know ye shy away from whiskey, but doth me this honor." He accepted the glass from the Captain. "As of tomorrow, ye shall not be one of me crew. From now on, call me Joseph."

"Ye shall always be Captain to me," Chip retorted, taking a sip from his glass.

Captain O'Toole inclined his head, downing his glass in one. He slammed it onto his desk and refilled it. Chip knew he would never forget his time aboard the *Ottoman* and his journeys with Captain O'Toole.

The next day, before bidding farewell, Chip set off to make good on an old oath. It did not take him long to hunt down Jonah McCullah inside his favorite haunt, O'Gill's. He was startled though by Jonah's ghostly reaction.

"It not be!" Jonah shouted.

He slapped Jonah on the shoulder. "I know I be gone a year, but ye act as though ye be speaking to a specter."

"But I be speakin' to a specter! Everyone believes ye a dustman! Offed the perch aboard the *Persica*!"

"Everyone?" Chip repeated, frowning hard.

"Aye." Jonah shook off his shock, as a smile crept across his face. "Ye might want to give the misses a fair warnin' before walkin' in!"

Indeed, he pondered. "Jonah, should this be true then I must be on me way. Before I go, there be someone I want ye to meet."

Jonah laughed. "Lead the way, specter Chip!"

Chip tossed an arm about his old friend's shoulders, as they made their way to the *Ottoman.* He introduced Jonah to Captain O'Toole and explained to the Captain that Jonah was the one to build the special cabinet in the Captain's quarters. Jonah vowed to keep his work a secret and would be honored to help hide the portrait of St. Michael from unworthy eyes.

He bid farewell to Jonah, the crew, and the Captain before setting off for home. Chip arrived on Prim Street to find it almost as he remembered. The street was busier than before. He realized the once vacant fields at the far of the street were being filled. The street was expanding, with more manor homes being built along its path.

Chip made it to the gate of his home, but froze when he looked up to see the frame of a man standing at his door. The man had his back to him, but he could tell the man wore the stately clothes of a businessman. He pushed open the gate, alerting the man to his presence.

"Mr. MacDougall!" the man exclaimed. Chip now recognized him to be Mr. Wallace from the bank. "Ye be alive!"

"Mr. Wallace," he greeted, extending a hand. "That I be."

"Mr. MacDougall, I had heard ye died aboard a ship."

"It be a misunderstanding. What be ye doing at me home this time of the evening?"

"Actually," Mr. Wallace replied hesitantly, "this be not yer home any longer. I just sold it to a family from Bristol."

"What be the meaning?" Chip retorted hotly. "Where be me wife and children?"

"Moved, Mr. MacDougall. Mary … I mean, Mrs. MacDougall purchased a home on another street. The upkeep be just too much for her and the children with ye gone …"

Chip's eyes narrowed at Mr. Wallace's use of Mary's name. He was not a jealous man, but if Mary thought him dead it could make her vulnerable to the affections of another.

"I thank ye for watching out for me family, Mr. Wallace," he said softly. "Pray tell, what street hath they moved to?"

"Long Street, Number Nine Long Street. Before ye go, there be something that ye should consider."

"What be that, Mr. Wallace?" Chip asked, a hint of danger in his voice.

"Ye have been gone for over a year. Doth not expect them to adjust quickly to yer sudden return."

"I shall take care of me family," he breathed. "Good day to ye."

Without another word, Chip spun on his heel and marched down the path and up the street. It took several minutes for him to reach Long Street, walking slowly until he reached Number 9. The house was only slightly smaller than their old house. Before he had a chance to consider a next best move, a scream announced that Mary had opened the front door. Her figure falling to the stoop, signaled she had fainted. He rushed up the path, to her side.

"Mary," he said softly, brushing the hair from her face.

Mary slowly stirred then stiffened at the sight of him, her face filled with emotions too complex to decipher. He smiled awkwardly, attempting to break the tension.

"Be ye really here?" she asked, touching his face with her hand.

"Aye, Mary, I be," he replied, touching her hand with his.

Chip gently helped her up to her feet and into the unfamiliar house. There was a small sitting room to the right, and he guided her there, so she could sit.

"I doth not understand," she said, staring at him. "How did ye survive? I heard yer ship sank in the North Sea!"

"I not be aboard the *Persica* when she sank. I—"

"Madam, I heard a scream from upstairs—" an older woman interrupted as she hurried into the sitting room. "Who be ye?" the woman demanded the moment her eyes fell upon him.

"I be Christopher MacDougall," he countered, a hint of aggression in his voice. "Who be ye?"

"I be Ms. Douglas," the woman replied indignantly. "Mrs. MacDougall hired me to help tend to the house and the children while she be away."

"Away?" he repeated, turning to look at Mary.

"Thank ye, Ms. Douglas, for checking on me, but I be fine now. I would like to speak with me freshly resurrected husband in private."

"Aye, Miss," Ms. Douglas said, nodding her head in Mary's direction. "I shall be in the kitchen should ye need me."

Ms. Douglas shot him a glare before leaving the room, that confirmed one thing: she did not care for him. *The feeling be mutual.*

"Aye, Christopher. Away," Mary said, regaining his attention. "Since ye hath been gone, someone hath needed to tend to the needs of this family."

He could hear the bitterness in the statement. He knew she was strong and would not simply hire others to do chores for her, but at the same time he had truly considered what stress would be set upon her by his departure.

"Where be Marcus and Anna?" he asked, glancing up the stairs.

"They not be here right now. They be off playing with friends."

"How be Marcus?" he asked, trying not to let his hopes get too high.

"He be confined to the chair," she sighed. "He hath come to understand it be forever, and he be learning to live this way."

"How doth he get up the stairs?" His heart ached as he imagined someone having to carry Marcus up and down the steps.

"He hath a room here on the main floor. Anna and I sleep atop. We could not find a house with enough rooms on one. Mr. Wallace looked a great while, but twas not meant to be."

Chip felt the anger boil in his stomach again at the mention of Mr. Wallace. A dark thought crept through his mind once more and he knew that he had made a grave error by going away.

"Mary," he said softly, "I know now that I should not hath gone away. Forgive me. Give this foolish man another chance to be the man that I need to be."

"It not be so simple." She raised a hand and touched the tiny wooden cross that hung about his neck. "While ye were off finding yer faith, life here hath continued. The children and I hath found our way past our loss of ye ... together. Supposing ye reappear from the dead and things not go well, it shall be like losing ye all over again."

"What would ye ask of me? Would ye wish I stay away from me family and play a dustman?"

"Of course not. They shall be happy to hear ye be alive and well—though that be the question. Be ye well again?"

"I hath found me solace. Shall ye let me come home?"

"Nay, Christopher," she replied sadly. "Many things hath changed since ye hath been gone."

"Doth any of these changes include Mr. Wallace?"

Mary took a step back from him. "Ye were gone for over a year. We were told ye had died."

"I wrote ye every week!"

"We received none." She bit her lower lip, her eyes raking the floor. "Be ye sure ye—"

"I not be touched in the head!"

His voice echoed in the room as Mary looked away, covering her mouth with her hand. He could tell he had frightened her.

Ms. Douglas rushed into the room. "Everything alright, Mrs MacDougall?"

"Everything be fine, Ms. Douglas," Mary replied, looking back at him. "Mr. MacDougall was about to leave."

"Mary, please—" Chip reached for her hand, but she withdrew it from his reach.

Mary turned away. "Just go. Please, Christopher."

Something was wrong. Chip could sense it. He could not place his finger on what it was, though he had his suspicions it had something to do with Mr. Wallace. "I shall be around tomorrow to see me children."

Mary refused to look at him. "That shall be fine."

Chip nodded curtly to Ms. Douglas before turning and walking briskly to the door, doing his best not to slam it behind him as he left. When he reached the gate, he turned back and looked at the house that was foreign to him. As he did so, he worried if the family that lived within—his family—would be foreign to him as well.

———•———

Lost in his own thoughts, Chip found that his feet had carried him back to the dusty tavern where he had first met Captain O'Toole. He asked the bartender if the small room he had once rented was available. To his surprise, as though waiting for him, the room was still vacant. He paid the month's rent to the bartender, then made his way upstairs, back to his prison.

The next day, Chip found himself for the first time in over a year without something to do. It felt uncomfortable, as though any moment Captain O'Toole would come in and demand to know why he was just sitting around. Unable to take it anymore, he headed into town to see what had changed. Once again, he found his steps following a well-known path. This time they lead him to Toppum Street and to the door of his bakery, but was it still his?

Chip slowly entered through the front door. Before he could say a word, he was greeted with a warm roll being tossed at his chest. When the roll did not pass through him, Spencer leapt across the counter to greet him.

"I heard that ye resided in an eternity box!" Spencer exclaimed, shaking Chip's hand and slapping him on the shoulder.

"Me demise hath been greatly exaggerated."

"What be the commotion out—" Donovan started, exiting the storage room. "As I live and breathe!"

Donovan didn't run to greet Chip as Spencer had. Instead, he walked over to greet him—supporting his weight with a walking cane. He shook Chip's hand, smiling brightly as he held himself upright, his right leg remaining stiff.

"Donovan, what happened to ye, lad?"

"Some of the rebellion soldiers thought that bread should be free for them," Donovan said smirking. "Did not take too well to being told they had to pay."

Chip bit the inside of his lip, a mixture of anger and guilt filled his chest. Memories of English soldiers murdering his friend and burning his father's shop to the ground flooded through his mind.

"The beaton saith me knee be twisted badly in the scuffle, and that it may get better in time."

"I should hath been here, lad," Chip sighed, placing a hand upon his shoulder.

"Ye were off fighting the blaggards," Donovan retorted. "Ye be a hero."

Chip didn't feel like a hero. He had run off in order to leave his demons behind. Instead, he had left his family and friends to suffer.

"How did ye escape the *Persica*? We be told she went down."

Chip told them the stories of his adventures. Both Spencer and Donovan listened in awe, as neither had ever seen more than the shores of Edinburgh and Leith. Several customers that entered the shop that day suffered the same shock to see their favorite baker standing there alive and well. He knew it would not take long for all of Toppum Street to know of his return.

———◆———

Chip waited until evening before departing the bakery and heading for Number 9, Long Street. He dreaded returning to his family's new home, but desperately wanted to see his children. The reunion with his children was exactly what he had envisioned.

"Papa!" Anna shouted as she sprinted to meet him at the gate, tears streaking her cheeks.

Marcus sat in his wheelchair, waiting for him to enter the house. The moment Chip did, he wrapped his arms around his father's waist. "I hath missed ye, Papa!"

Chip patted Marcus on the side of his head. "Me brave boy. I hath missed ye too."

Mary entered the room, wearing a forced smile. "Children, show yer father to the sitting room. He not know this house."

Anna took him by the hand, her smile brighter than the sun. "It be this way, Papa."

"I not care for this house, Papa," Marcus grumbled.

Chip glanced at Mary, who wore a solemn expression. He sat and visited with his children, telling them stories of his journey. He listened to all the new things they had been doing while he was away. He disliked the stories of how Mr. Wallace had been around while he was away.

Marcus had come to accept the fact he would probably never walk again without assistance. He silently admired his son's courage. He attempted to speak with Mary in private before leaving, but she would have nothing of it. Chip promised his children he would visit with them again soon.

He was lost in his own thoughts, as he returned to the wharf that evening. He did not notice the man in the familiar bowler hat leaning up against the outer wall of the fish shop until the man hailed him. Chip turned to see Mr. Stubbs from the *Ottoman* and two other gents standing in the shadows. It was dark now, and the oil lamps that lined the streets were casting shadows in every direction.

"There he be!" a drunken Mr. Stubbs sang. "Captain O'Toole's favorite first mate, Mr. MacDougall!"

Mr. Stubbs staggered towards him, smiling and laughing. Chip eyed the two larger gents as they followed Mr. Stubbs.

"Celebrating yer return?"

"Celebrating?" Mr. Stubbs repeated. "Thanks to you, I was cast off the *Ottoman* the moment we made port!"

"How be that me fault? I did nothing to ye."

"Oh, did ye now," Mr. Stubbs slurred, mocking Chip's Scottish accent. "It seems to me you reported me to the Captain for helping myself to some extra rations, memory serves me."

"That be over a year ago," Chip retorted. "How hath that any merit with ye being cast out now?"

"O'Toole said it be one of the many reasons he had for not keeping me. The ways I sees it, you be owing me another year's wages."

Chip eyed the two large men again. "I see ye hath enough schillings to drink away yer senses. I owe ye nothing."

"We shall see about that!" Mr. Stubbs spat.

Immediately, the two burly men grabbed at Chip. He struck one in the leg, causing him to curse in pain. Stubbs hit Chip hard in the stomach with a rock, sending him to his knees. The three men shoved him into a nearby alley, beating him and taking his money belt. Stubbs spit in his face, laughing. Chip tried to get to him feet, but the sole of a big boot was all he saw before all went black.

———————

Mr. Wallace stepped out of the coach and ordered his driver to wait. The steed that was harnessed to the carriage pranced nervously, and Mr. Wallace couldn't help but share the beast's reservations, as he took in the isolated grounds that surrounded the house he was visiting. If he had his way, he would climb back into his coach and leave. That, however, was not an option afforded to him.

The grounds, with their stately stone walls and kept greenery, accented the prestige that stood before him. It was apparent to Mr. Wallace that the owner, Lord Campbell, was as particular with his grounds as he was austere in his business. He did not look forward to his meeting with Lord Campbell, but he knew he had no choice in the matter.

Mr. Wallace knocked curtly on the door and waited. An older man, no doubt the butler, answered the door, staring at him with an eyebrow raised slightly.

"I be here to see Lord Campbell," Mr. Wallace said firmly. "The Lordship be expecting me."

"Please come in." The butler motioned for Mr. Wallace to

enter. "Whom may I say be calling upon the Lordship?"

"Mr. Jefferson Wallace," he replied in a stately fashion.

"Aye, the Lordship be expecting ye. I shall inform the Lordship ye hath arrived. Please wait in the sitting room."

As the butler made his way up the grand staircase that sat in the middle of the foyer, Mr. Wallace nodded, then proceeded to the sitting room. There he observed that the tables and bookshelves were spotless and that a maid could be seen cleaning in the study across the hall. It was apparent the young Lord ran his home and his life with a military flare. The sound of hard sole shoes alerted him of his host's arrival.

"Mr. Wallace, forgive me delay," Lord Campbell greeted, shaking his hand firmly. "I just finished quilling a letter to our correspondence in France, regarding our need for more inclusiveness in matters of trade that enters the ports of Leith."

"Forgive me, Lord Campbell," Mr. Wallace said as respectfully as possible, "but doth ye think it wise to request inclusiveness from France when we still not be for certain whether they aided in the rebellion?"

"From whence whom would ye look to for insight, supposing not from our trade allies?" Lord Campbell placed his hand to his chin in thought as he observed Mr. Wallace.

"I only breathe words of caution, me Lord," Mr. Wallace replied, understanding the need to tread carefully. "Me understanding be that Britain still be considering whom was aiding the rebellion. Until that be determined, it would be wise to look to our contacts within the ports of Leith for reliable information. However, I be sure that ye being the newly appointed Governor of the Royal Bank of Scotland hath privilege to information I doth not. If they indeed be our allies, then none other be needed."

Lord Campbell nodded, smiling for the first time. "Well said, Mr. Wallace. My cousin, the Duke of Argyll, hath always spoke highly of ye. I indeed hath information that ye doth not. The Spanish funded the rebellion against the Union in hopes they could gain a foothold in the north. The French were approached by the rebellion leader, Prince Charlie, but were denied funding."

"Supposing the French knew of the rebellion plans. Why did they not warn Britain?"

"Such loyalty, Mr. Wallace. Unfortunately, I doubt yer loyalties are wholly with the bank and with Britain."

"Lord Campbell, doth ye challenge me to be a sympathizer of the rebellion?" Mr. Wallace retorted indignantly.

Lord Campbell's brow furrowed slightly. "Nay, Mr. Wallace. However, I challenge yer loyalty to the bank and to me. Whom doth ye serve?"

"Me Lord, I serve Britain and the Royal Bank of Scotland. By extension of the bank, I now serve ye as well."

"Ye claim loyalties, Mr. Wallace, yet ye front me as though ye be afraid I might upset a balance of power."

"Ye read more into me concerns, me Lord. Me concerns only be for the well-being of the bank and of Britain."

"Then forgive me reluctance. The day in which we live, one

not be overly certain."

Seeming to accept Mr. Wallace's answers, he and Lord Campbell retired to the study, where they proceeded to discussing the purpose of his visit: becoming better acquainted with the new bank governor. Several hours later, he departed, destined to call upon Mary and see how the return of her dead husband was setting in. He closed his eyes to rest and reflect as the carriage moved along. The sound of the trotting steed soothed him.

"Because I asked them not to, Jefferson," came a voice from inside the carriage that made the hairs on his neck stand up.

"Mr. Prose!" Mr. Wallace quickly opened his eyes, nodding as he did. "I was unaware of yer presence, me Lord."

"Indeed," Mr. Prose said, smiling. "In answer to your question … the French did not inform Britain, because I asked them not to. I profit far more from war than from peace."

"Of course, me Lord," Mr. Wallace said, nodding once more.

"Your loyalty did not go unnoticed, Jefferson. I be quite pleased. Do not fret for our young governor. He shall serve our needs well."

"Aye, me Lord," Mr. Wallace agreed, before changing the subject. "Mr. MacDougall hath returned, as ye said he would. I shall be stopping in on Mrs. MacDougall to see how she be doing this evening."

"Excellent, Jefferson. When he comes around to see you at the bank, make sure you keep him abreast of your visits to see about his family. Do this subtly. Mr. MacDougall is twice the man he once was. I would not wish to have to replace you, Jefferson."

"Ye wish for me to provoke him?"

"Aye, Jefferson, but only lightly. In the case of Mr. MacDougall ... I believe the scale is ready to tip."

Mr. Wallace bowed his head. "Me Lord, what be it that Mr. MacDougall be ready to do?"

He looked up to find himself alone again. *With whom or what hath I gotten me self involved?* he wondered. He had pondered this many times before, but resigned himself to the fact that he must do Mr. Prose's bidding. He was too afraid of what might happen if he did otherwise.

TEN

———— ◆ ————

HUMPHREY

Chip came to slowly, wiping the blood from his face. His nose and ribs throbbed from the punches and kicks. He felt a mixture of anger and appreciation. He knew the blaggards could have easily killed him in the process.

"Quick! Move! He not be dead yet!" a voice from Chip's nightmares shouted.

His eyes, blurry from the sweat and blood, could make out the outline of something sitting on his chest. Chip struggled to his feet, as the object on his chest fell to the ground and disappeared.

"Nay! Nay!" Chip shouted, grasping at the wooden cross which hung about his neck. "Not again!"

He staggered like a drunk in the small alley, as he tried to regain his footing and, more importantly, his sanity.

"Look! The mongrel speaks with himself!" the unnatural voice jeered.

"How dare ye call me mongrel, ye demon!" Chip growled, wiping his face with his hands.

"He hears us?" another distinct voice asked, a mixture of

shock and concern laced within its tone.

"Impossible. There not be a mongrel that understandeth us," the first voice answered, sounding irritated.

"It be demons then. Just because ye doth not show yer self to me and speak in me native tongue, doth not mean I doth not know what ye be. Show yer self to me at last!"

Chip stood his ground, determined not to run no matter what he saw. He was done with living in fear. *It be only natural if there be a God and His angels, then there be demons as well*, he reasoned. *If God shall not help me, then I shall face the demons me self.*

A rustling to his right caught his attention. He looked down to see two wharf rats crawl out from under a wooden crate and stand there next to him. The insanity of the moment engulfed him. He felt as though they were looking up at him. He took a step back. The rodents cringed, but did not scurry away.

"What be this?" he questioned, just above a whisper.

"Doth ye understand us?" the first voice asked timidly.

"Ye appear to me as a rodent, demon?" Chip retorted in a husky voice, feeling something between fear and rage bubbling in his chest.

"N-nay, strange mongrel," the second voice stuttered, "We be rodents."

Chip backed further away from the two rodents. "Impossible! Ye be demons sent to torture me!"

"Quick! Flee before he kills us!" the first voice shouted, just as one of the wharf rats ran back under the crate.

Chip watched as the remaining rat climbed up the crate and onto the ledge of a window so that he and it were nearly eye level.

"How doth ye understand me?" the second voice asked.

To Chip's horror he could see the jaw of the rat move. "Go away, demon!"

"I be a rodent, not a demon," the rat retorted indignantly. "Ye called me out, now ye wish for me to leave?"

"I wish to never hear ye or any other demon again! Ye hath tortured me for too long!"

The rat stretched out its body towards him, its nose twitching frantically. "How long hath ye been able to understand me, I mean rodents? Doth ye speak to all rodents or only rats? Come back! I hath more questions!"

Chip fled the alley, stumbling as he did. He felt as though the final vestiges of his sanity were slipping away. He looked back towards the alley. To his horror he saw the tiny wharf rat running after him. He bit his lip against the pain and ran, pushing himself to get as far away from the demon as possible. *If it be a demon, shall I ever outrun it?*

He made it back to his small room, sinking down into a cushioned chair. He grimaced from his injuries as he looked about the room, but didn't see any sign of the rat. Relieved that the demon had chosen not to torture him more that night, he passed out. That night he had no dreams of demons, of rodents, or of Mr. Prose. That night, as he slumped in his chair inside his small room above the dusty tavern, he laid in peace.

———◆———

Chip awoke the next morning and grimaced as he felt the pain, remembering the beating he took at the hands of Mr. Stubbs and his gents. He wiped his eyes and blinked as the morning sun shone through the window over his small kitchen table.

"Oh good, ye be awake."

Chip jumped and nearly vomited, as he scanned the room for the source of the voice. Finally, he spotted the demon rat standing near the door to the room.

"Go away—demon!"

"Still on about I being a demon," the rat said, yawning.

Chip chucked a boot at the rat. "That be because ye be a demon!"

The tiny rat dodged the shoe, then scurried up onto the back of a chair. *A boot shall not drive away this demon.*

"I searched all night to find ye. At least answer me questions, then I shall leave ye be."

"I doth not trust ye, demon. Ye hath tortured me long enough!"

The rat was nearing exasperation. "I not be a demon, and until I found ye on the ground, I hath not set eyes on ye before."

Chip slammed his fist on the arm of the chair. "I shall not be tricked by yer deceiving ways!"

The tiny rat hopped down from the back of the chair and

made its way over to the table. "Ye be hurt. Be this from the three mongrels that left ye on the ground?"

An idea came to Chip. *If I might trick the demon, then maybe I might get it to tell me why it be sent here to torture me.* He tilted his head to one side. "Answer me this, rat. Why doth ye call me mongrel?"

The rat looked about cautiously, as though expecting another boot. "It be what all rodents call yer kind. What doth ye call one another?"

"We be humans ... or men."

"Be I the first rat ye hath spoken to?" the rat asked, his nose twitching wildly.

"Aye, ye be the first rat I hath spoken to." Chip rubbed the bridge of his nose, succumbing to the madness. "At least the first that hath spoken back. Doth rats hath names?"

"Names? We be rats."

"How tell ye one from another?" Chip asked, easing up to fetch a towel. The tiny rat edged back at his movement.

"By smell. How doth mongrels tell one from another?"

Chip wiped the dirt and blood from his face at the sink. "We hath names."

"Sounds hard," the rat replied, edging closer in Chip's direction. "What be ye name?"

Demons be tricky. Doth not be deceived, he reminded himself. "Me name be Chip." His side aching, he took a seat at the table. "What might I call ye?"

"Call me? I be a rat. Would ye like to call me by a name?"

176

"It would make it easier," Chip sighed, hoping he might finally trick the little demon.

The rat sat back on its hindquarters. "What would ye call me then?"

"Know ye not a name that ye would like me to call thee?"

"I know not any names."

Chip squinted at the rat. "So ye still hold ye be not a demon?"

The pest spun in circles, as though frustrated with him. "I be not a demon! I be a rat. I be born a rat. I shall die a rat."

"Were ye the one on my chest?" he asked, trying to settle down the tiny creature.

"Aye. Ye were warm, and I were cold."

Chip stood up quickly, causing the tiny scoundrel to run for cover. "Nay! Nay! This not be natural! Should ye not be a demon then I be cursed to hear yer kind!"

He fetched a fresh coat and cap, tucked his shirt back into his breeches, then made his way towards the door.

"Where be ye going?" the rat asked timidly, peering out from behind a chair.

"To the *Ottoman*, so that I might be rid of ye forever!" he snarled, slamming the door behind him.

Chip reached the port, only to be greeted with horrific news. The *Ottoman* sailed that morning for London and would not be back anytime soon. He sighed in frustration, as he headed back to the wharf, ignoring the calls of "Danger!"

For the first time, he recognized where the cries came from. Movements caught his eye, as rodents scurried deeper into hiding from the humans that walked the streets. He had always seen the creatures moving about the wharf, scavenging for food. Somehow, he had been cursed by something or someone.

Lost in his own thoughts, he accidentally bumped into someone walking in the opposing direction. "Pardon me."

"Mr. MacDougall?"

Chip looked up, shocked to see Captain Sinclair, of the *Victoria*, standing there in front of him. "Captain Sinclair, sir."

Captain Sinclair smiled. "I thought it be ye, Mr. MacDougall. Captain O'Toole told me how he not be able to persuade ye to stay aboard the *Ottoman*. He took yer loss as a personal failure." Chip bit his lip, uncertain of how to respond. "That be a compliment."

"Thank ye, sir. I be just down to the dock to see about the *Ottoman*, but I be told it hath sailed for London."

"I wouldn't know. I hath officially resigned from the Royal Navy, me self."

Chip was speechless. "I know not what to say."

"It be of me own doing, Mr. MacDougall. I be a privateer captain now. Me new ship be the *Elpida*—one of the growing fleet of vessels that shall make trade with the Colonies much easier."

"Ye be sailing to the Americas?"

"That be correct. Ye be welcome to join me crew. There be more money to be made than with the Royal Navy, and it be the chance to see the Colonies firsthand!"

"That be tempting, sir, but I hath things to tend to here," Chip said, thinking of the rat he left in his room, his family, and his sanity.

Captain Sinclair slapped him on the shoulder. "I shall leave the offer open, Mr. MacDougall. Should ye change yer mind, the *Elpida* be docked at the far north dock."

"Thank ye, sir," Chip said, shaking Captain Sinclair's hand. "I shall keep it in mind, should something change."

Be this just chance meeting or be there something more to it, he wondered. He dismissed the meeting, for it mattered not. Something or someone had cursed him and he needed help. He needed Mary.

———•———

The streets were packed with people that time of day and it took Chip nearly an hour to reach Number 9, Long Street. Through the open window, he could see Ms. Douglas bustling about upstairs. Ms. Douglas' comment swirled around in his mind of how she watched over the house and the children while Mary was away. Gathering his courage, he knocked upon the front door. Several minutes later, Ms. Douglas answered.

"Ah, Mr. MacDougall. Mrs. MacDougall not be in."

"Doth ye know when she might return?" he asked, as friendly as he could.

"Mrs. MacDougall did not say. I shall tell her ye stopped by."

He tipped his cap. "Thank ye Ms. Douglas."

Ms. Douglas nodded before slamming the door in his face. His insides shook with anger as he stood there on the stoop, staring at the door that wasn't his, though his money had purchased it.

If only hath I told the Bishop when I the chance. Maybe he could hath helped me see this curse for what it be! Chip agonized silently. He closed the gate behind him and proceeded back up Long Street. "The Bishop!" he exclaimed, causing several people on the street to stop and look at him.

Chip tipped his cap to the onlookers, then quickly made his way towards the church. He opened the door to the church and poked his head inside. The small church looked to be empty. He stepped inside and noted that immediately the whispered voices of the rodents that plagued the town died away.

"Maybe this be where I should stay," he mused aloud.

"Church be a place for comfort and assurance, not a place to hide," a man said, standing near the pipe organ. "Lest ye have the calling."

Chip removed his cap. "Forgive me. I not see ye there. I be looking for Bishop Seamus."

"There be not a need for apologies, sir," the man replied, walking up to him. "Bishop Seamus be out visiting today. Be there something I might for ye?"

He shook the man's hand, looking him over as he did. The

man was about his height, had sandy brown hair, blue eyes, and was dressed similar to the Bishop. "I came here to seek advice from Bishop Seamus."

The man smiled. "Please, call me Brother Hesperus. Be there something that I might for ye?"

"Brother Hes—Hes—"

"Hesperus. It be an old name."

Chip sighed, "Bro. Hesperus, I doth not know whether ye could help. I not be meaning disrespect. I doubt Bishop Seamus could hath helped, had he been here."

"Should ye wish to speak, I shall listen to thee. Here, let us sit."

Nodding, Chip joined Bro. Hesperus in a nearby pew. Something about the man's voice was oddly soothing, and he was desperate to talk to someone. He took a deep breath. "Bro. Hesperus ... I believe that I be—that I be cursed."

"What makes ye believe this?" Bro. Hesperus asked calmly.

"This shall sound as though I hath gone mad."

"Please, tell me what troubles ye. I shall not judge thee."

Chip felt comfortable with the man, so he decided to be honest. "I-I hear rats."

"Please help me understand, Mr. ..."

"Forgive me. I be Christopher MacDougall. Me wife attends yer church."

"Pleasure to meet ye, Mr. MacDougall. Now, help me to understand. We all hear rats. They be all around us. The town be overrun with them."

Chip cleared his throat, his gaze dropping to the floor. "Forgive me. When I hear rats, I understand what they say."

"Ye mean ye think ye understand what they be saying?"

Chip shook his head. "Nay. I not hear their squeaks. They speak in Gaelic to me."

"How long hath this been going on for ye?"

"I did not recognize it to be rats I be hearing until last night. Before, I just thought it be bodiless voices tormenting me, calling to me from beneath the stones and hedges."

"The voices that called to ye from beneath the stones and hedges—what doth they say?"

"Mostly they just shout 'danger'. Though once I heard them from the kitchen, speaking of me daughter. I hurried in just in time to catch her as she fell from climbing a shelf."

"Did these voices warn ye she was about to fall?"

"Aye."

"When did ye come to believe the voices were those of rats?" Bro. Hesperus asked, his eyebrows arched as he stared intently at him.

Chip told him what had happened the night before and of the little rat that was possibly still waiting in his room for him to return. Bro Hesperus sat quietly for a moment before speaking.

Surely this minister thinks I hath taken leave of me senses, he mused silently.

"Ye saith the voices warned ye yer daughter be in danger?"

"Warned me?" Chip repeated. "I would not say they warned me, but I heard them speaking of her."

"Suppose ye hath not heard these voices. Doth ye believe yer daughter would hath been hurt?"

"Aye, I do."

"Lad, ye claim this to be a curse, yet what it be in the end be up to thee. Sometimes things that be intended for evil can be used for good instead." Bro. Hesperus pointed up with a finger. "He hath been known to do such more than a few times."

"Ye saying this be a good thing?"

"I be saying it be what ye make of it," Bro. Hesperus replied calmly. "Tell me, why doth ye believe understanding a rodent be evil?"

Chip pondered his question for a moment, biting his lower lip. He was trying to remember his Christian teachings from his childhood. "A rodent be an unclean animal, and speaking with any animal be not natural."

"In the story of Creation, did God create all the creatures in the Garden of Eden?"

"Aye."

"Yet there be but one creation spoke of in the Bible," Bro. Hesperus continued. "All animals, clean and unclean, were created by God. At the time of Creation, all animals were clean. Only after sin entered the world did things become unclean."

"Surely, ye not be saying that understanding any animal be natural?" Chip interjected in disbelief.

Bro. Hesperus smiled. "I be simply saying even the direst of circumstances might be turned into something positive. Take the example of Paul and Silas. They were set in prison for doing not one wrong thing, yet they made something good out of it."

"I know me teachings," Chip said in a clipped tone, trying to grasp the sheer fact this minister was making this curse into something positive.

"Then turn to them when ye need them. Guidance often be readily available to those who be willing to receive it."

Chip stood and shook the pastor's hand, ready to leave. "Thank ye for ye time."

"We be always here for ye whenever ye need us."

Chip reached the door when the minister hailed to him again.

"Remember yer teachings as but a young lad. The dreams be gone, and the voices shall be too when ye not need them anymore, Chip."

"What did ye say to me?" Chip retorted, spinning around.

Bishop Seamus stood near the door to his office. "I saith nothing to ye, sir. Mr. MacDougall? Be that ye?"

"Where did the young pastor go?" He scanned the small church, but saw no sign of him.

"Mr. MacDougall, I be the only one here, and I hath just returned. Ye be okay? Ye doth not look well."

Unable to speak, Chip fled the small church. Bishop Seamus called out to him to return, but he didn't stop running until he reached his small room above O'Bryans. He collapsed to his knees, holding his side, as pain raced through his chest.

"Be ye okay?"

Chip rolled over to see the tiny rat standing near the chair he hid behind earlier. His first thought was to shoo the creature away, but then he thought of what the strange man had said. He groaned, massaging his chest. "I be okay. I just be in pain from last night and from running."

"Running? Were the mongrels after ye again?"

"Nay. I be just in a hurry." Chip pushed himself up to a sitting position on the floor, his knees bent up to his chest to reduce the pain. He pondered the words of the strange Bro. Hesperus. *He saith that me dreams be gone, but what doth I need from rats to make this end as well?*

"Did ye find this *Ottoman?*" the rat asked, his nose twitching.

"Nay. It hath gone, but I found something else."

The rat cringed and he realized it was waiting for him to try and harm it.

"I shall not harm ye, rat," Chip continued. "Tell me though, why doth ye kind call out danger whenever I be near?"

"We call out danger when all mongrels be near."

Chip pondered what he was hearing. *I nearly did me self in simply because I did not understand! If it not been for Captain O'Toole, I would hath!*

"Be ye well, mongrel?"

Aye," Chip replied. "I be simply trying to understand. Supposing ye be afraid of us mongrels, rat, then why risk following me?"

"Ye be the first that understandeth what I say. I wanted to know how."

"I wish I could tell ye, but I me self doth not know. I doth know this though. Ye be a brave rodent." He felt as though he was giving into the madness.

"I be not brave. I be foolish."

"How so?" Chip asked, smirking at the tiny creature.

"I followed ye, believing ye could answer me questions. I believed this would make me special."

"I believe ye be special and brave."

"Ye think me special?" the rat repeated, spinning in a circle.

"I think ye be special because ye doth want to be different. Ye be brave because I could hath killed ye."

The tiny rat's nose twitched rapidly. "Ye think me brave as well?"

Chip sighed, "Aye ... and bravery, as Captain O'Toole would say, deserves a name."

"A name?"

"Aye. Should ye be staying with me then ye shall be needing a proper name. I shan't go about calling ye 'rat'."

The rat spun in circles once more. "I be staying with ye?"

"I shall not be placing ye in a cage. It shall be up to ye." Chip and the rat stared at each other for a long moment. "Shall ye stay?"

"I shall stay," the rat replied. "I wish to be special."

Chip rubbed his hands together. "Then ye shall need a name. I believe I shall call ye Humphrey. It twas me great uncle's name."

"When ye say 'Humphrey', then I shall answer."

"That be how having a name works," Chip huffed, marveling at the madness before him. "Now, there be some rules ye must follow."

"What be rules?"

"They be things ye doth not do while in me room," Chip explained. "First rule. Ye eat nothing in this room unless I give it to ye."

Humphrey cringed and he knew what that meant, having seen the same reaction from his own children.

"Supposing ye hath broken any of the rules I be about to give ye, it be okay," he continued, noting this made Humphrey relax. "Second rule. Ye shall doth yer needs outdoors."

"I doth not understand."

Chip then went into detail. First, about where the rat was to relieve himself, then about the difference between indoors and outdoors. "Understand now?"

"Aye. Be there any other rules?"

"Aye, little one. I shall only speak with ye in the privacy of this room. Should other mongrels see me speaking with ye, they shall believe I hath lost me senses."

"Could ye not tell the other mongrels that ye can speak with me?"

"Nay. I barely believe it me self. Why should I believe another might doth better?"

"Why would they not believe ye?"

Chip sighed, "Ye must trust me, little one." He could tell that most conversations with Humphrey would be largely one-sided, and he would have to treat the rat like a small child. "Mongrels not be open to new beliefs."

"As ye wish."

Chip laid down that night, watching the tiny creature scurry out the window for an evening of hunting food. Humphrey told him he would be back before morning. He believed he was cursed, yet his mind still interpreted it as madness. Whatever it was, he felt it had fully taken hold and that his life would never be the same again.

That night he dreamed of his life as a little boy, growing up in the bakery with his father. His father was teaching him how to make dough, when a strange man entered the bakery. He remembered not liking the man for interrupting his time with his dad, but did not argue when he was sent outside. Something about the man made him feel uncomfortable. Whatever the man was up to, he had confidence that his father could handle it.

ELEVEN

---◆---

THE LOST GIRL

Chip awoke the next morning to find Humphrey sitting at the end of his bed, watching him sleep. He rolled his feet off the bed and rubbed his eyes, but the tiny rat did not move. He realized he had dreamed while he slept, but couldn't remember what it was about. Strangely, he found this comforting.

"Morning, Humphrey."

"Aye, it be morning," Humphrey replied.

Chip cleared his throat, "That be the way that we mongrels greet one another."

"Rats greet one another by licking one another about the face and biting off long hairs."

"New rule. Doth not ever lick me face or bite me hair," Chip said in a commanding voice.

"Aye, Master."

"What did ye call me?" he asked, peering at the small rodent.

Humphrey sat up on his hind legs. "I called ye Master."

"Why doth ye call me master?" Chip asked, scratching his

chin as he stood up.

"I wish to learn from ye, so I call ye Master. I only mean respect."

"Very well, Humphrey," Chip said, as he prepared to shave.

He watched out of the corner of his eye as the small rodent made its way from the side of his bed to the table where his lather sat. He fetched the hot water from the top of the pot belly stove, the razor from his drawer and began to spread the lather across his face and neck. Humphrey sat there, liken until a small child, and watched as he shaved. When he was finished, the small rat followed him into the water closet, where he poured the contents of the bowl down the open drain.

"Why remove the hair from yer face?" Humphrey asked, watching the last of the water go down the drain.

"Some mongrels do. Some mongrels doth not." Chip wiped his face with a towel. "It be a preference, and I choose a clean face."

"Rats see hair upon face as a sign of dominance. The more hair, the more dominant. When I be but a youngling, all the hair was bitten from me face to show me place."

Chip could tell that remembering the act bothered the small rodent. "We mongrels tend to determine one's position by what we wear," He held up his coat for the rat to see, "and the money we hath in our pockets. Thanks to Mr. Stubbs and his gents, I be now in need of money."

"Hath ye ways to get more?"

"Aye. There be more inside a mongrel dwelling that be mine. I be off to fetch more from there now."

"What be this money good for?" the tiny rat asked, his nose twitching.

Chip pulled on his coat and placing his cap upon his head. "I swear I shall explain when I return. Remember me rules."

"I remember." Humphrey's nose twitching again as he watched him leave.

Chip smirked as he headed down from his room above the tavern and headed off to the bank. He thought about stopping by the Edinburgh Town Guard to alert them to the actions of Mr. Stubbs and his associates, but felt it would be of little use. *The word of one Scotsman claiming three Englishmen robbed him would not go far,* he reasoned.

The shouts of "Danger!" echoed about him, but they no longer bothered him now that he knew their source. In a strange and maddening way, the knowledge of where the voices came from gave him a sense of power.

Chip entered the bank, looking about the mighty structure and remembering the first time he'd come. Today, he walked directly up to the teller and made his request, presenting his seal.

"Mr. MacDougall!" the teller exclaimed, clearly startled. "Ye be deceased!"

He laughed at the teller's words, receiving a cross look from the young man. "Those that perceived me dead, where greatly mistaken."

"Unfortunately, Mr. MacDougall, this be not a laughing matter," the young teller said, clearing his throat. "Please follow me."

Chip failed to conceal the dark look that crossed his face, as he contemplated seeing Mr. Wallace again. He followed the young man down the long hall that led to Mr. Wallace's office. The young teller opened the door to the office then motioned for him to enter.

"Mr. Wallace be in a meeting. Please hath a seat while I fetch him."

Chip nodded then took a seat in the same chair that he had sat in the last time he was in Mr. Wallace's office. He had been incredibly nervous the first time he was ushered in. This time, he felt nothing but a mixture of annoyance and anger. *Why hath not Mr. Wallace, knowing I be alive, corrected this issue? Be it an oversight or be it done with purpose?*

"Mr. MacDougall," Mr. Wallace said, entering his office and taking a seat at his desk, smiling in a way that made Chip feel uneasy. "I did not expect ye to visit so soon."

"Neither had I. Unfortunately, several men robbed me of me money belt last night."

Mr. Wallace frowned. "That be most unfortunate, Mr. MacDougall. Were ye injured?"

"I shall heal."

"Well, Mr. MacDougall," Mr. Wallace rubbed his hands together, "it be bank policy that the account owner must grant access to funds. Since ye were declared deceased, Mrs. MacDougall now be the account owner. However, this being unusual circumstances, I believe I shall be able to make an exception and grant ye some funds now until Mrs. MacDougall be able to sign the appropriate documents."

Chip felt his anger boiling close to the surface, but he managed to remain in control. He felt as though Mr. Wallace was enjoying this in some way. "Thank ye for understanding. I presume ye shall hath this matter settled as soon as possible."

"Aye, Mr. MacDougall. I shall take the appropriate documents to Mrs. MacDougall this evening."

"Thank ye," Chip said, biting the inside of his lip.

The thought that Mr. Wallace would be visiting Mary this evening sent ripples of fury through him. The only thing that kept Chip in check was the fact that Mary would take it as an insult if she heard tale of his jealousy.

Mr. Wallace withdrew a small piece of parchment and quickly quilled a note onto it. "Take this note to the tellers, Mr. MacDougall, and they shall supply ye with a new money belt and the proper funding."

Chip accepted the note, nodded his thanks, then stood and turned to leave.

"One day, Mr. MacDougall," Mr. Wallace said, causing him to stop and look back, "ye must tell me of ye voyages aboard the *Ottoman*. She be a fine vessel."

Chip frowned. "How be it ye were not aware I still be alive, yet ye knew of me voyages aboard the *Ottoman*?"

Mr. Wallace swallowed hard. "Well … yer son, Marcus, be proud of his father."

"And I also be proud of me son," Chip retorted, his breath becoming shallow. "His courage in the cold face of fate be inspiring."

"Indeed."

"I thank ye for watching after me family while I be away. Though tell me, how often hath ye and doth ye still visit me family, Mr. Wallace?"

Mr. Wallace cleared his throat. "Mr. MacDougall, ye family have been through much this past year—"

"Ye doth not need to lecture me, Mr. Wallace, on how much me family hath suffered in me absence!" Chip growled, his face becoming expressionless and cold.

"Mr. MacDougall, forgive me lest I sounded disrespectful. I be only trying to explain why I hath visited yer family while ye were away."

"Now, I be back," Chip said coldly. "Supposing ye be a gentleman, ye shall respect that it matters not what me family may be going through—they be me family and Mary be me wife."

Mr. Wallace inclined his head. "I hope that one-day ye shall understand that all I have done be with yer family's best interest at heart. On that day, I hope ye might even consider me friend."

"On that day, ye must tell me how ye knew that I was aboard the *Ottoman*—for I hath yet to tell me son the name of the vessel I be aboard beyond the *Persica*," Chip snapped. "Good day to

194

ye."

Before Mr. Wallace could say another word, Chip exited the office, his mind racing and his anger breaking. If he had not been moving with such haste, he might have noticed the look of fear that crossed Mr. Wallace's face as he left his office. He concluded his business with the bank, then headed on his way, distancing himself from the establishment as fast as possible.

———•———

Chip returned to his small room above the tavern to find Humphrey waiting for him, accompanied by a slightly larger rat. He raised one eyebrow, as he stared at his tiny friend and larger companion. Silence drifted through the room for several minutes before Chip remembered that rats did not understand human expressions.

"Who be this, Humphrey?" Chip asked, taking a seat at the kitchen table.

"He hath not a mongrel name, Master."

"Where doth he come from?"

"He comes from me pack."

"Ye speak to this mongrel as though he understands ye?" the other rat quipped, staring at Humphrey.

"I understand what ye be saying, rat," Chip said, laughing as the large rat jumped and cringed.

"This be me master now," Humphrey proclaimed, turning

his face in the direction of the large rat.

"I be not anyone's master, Humphrey," Chip interjected, not caring for the title.

"Ye be mine," the tiny rat retorted, his nose twitching.

"What makes me yer master?"

"Ye be me master, because ye be the greater and I be the lesser. Me life be limited to the life of a rat. Should I return to me pack—I shall be nothing more than I be now. Should I stay with ye—I hath the chance to be special."

"Special," the larger rat scoffed. "How doth being the pet of a mongrel make ye special?"

Humphrey rounded on the larger rat until they were standing nose-to-nose. "What other mongrel doth ye know that understandeth what we say?"

The larger rat did not answer the question, but Humphrey turned back to face Chip as though he had received his answer. *Be they able to speak without words,* he wondered. *I must remember to inquire of Humphrey later.*

"Supposing I be greater, why doth ye call me mongrel?" Chip asked, choosing to ignore the exchange between the rats.

"It be what we rats hath always called yer kind."

Chip realized that the small rodent didn't see the term "mongrel" to be offensive and meant no offense by it. He slapped his knees with his hands. "Well, I be hungry. I think I shall prepare some porridge."

Chip walked over to the cupboard and pulled out a bag of

oats, a small jar of honey and a small pot. He placed the oats and honey on the table before filling the small pot with water from the tap. Out of the corner of his eye he could see the two rats watching him.

"Master, did ye get more of the money that ye needed?"

Up until that moment, Chip had put aside his anger about what had happened at the bank, the two rodents serving as a good distraction. "Aye, Humphrey," he replied gruffly.

"Stop speaking to this mongrel!" the larger rat exclaimed. "Doth ye not see it not be natural! Now, the mongrel be upset!"

"I not be upset with Humphrey, large rat," Chip said in an even tone, pushing aside his anger.

"I be not a large rat, mongrel. There be many rats that be larger than me."

Chip didn't doubt this statement, as he sat the small pot of water on the stove to heat. "Did yer master send ye to fetch Humphrey?"

"I hath watched over the rat that ye call Humphrey, mongrel, since he be a pup. Our master knows not of this."

Chip could tell that the larger rat did not care for him and was certain that their pack's master would not be a friendly rodent.

"A pup?" he repeated, adding some oats to the boiling water.

"A rat young-ling," Humphrey explained, sniffing the air hopefully. "The same as a mongrel pup."

"We mongrels call our younglings 'children'."

Humphrey climbed up onto a nearby shelf. "Not all mongrels then. The bad mongrels call their younglings 'nuggets'."

"What bad mongrels doth ye speak of?" Chip asked, curious as to what Humphrey might define as a bad mongrel and where he had heard that derogatory term.

"Not insult his kind! Yer new master may decide ye not be worth a pet!"

Chip dipped some oats into a bowl, stirring in honey. "Ye rats doth like to shout. Doth ye like porridge as well?"

"What be porridge?" Humphrey asked, his nose sniffing the air again.

Chip, spooned some from his bowl and placed it on the table. "This be porridge."

Humphrey sniffed then tasted the spoonful of porridge before spinning in circles. "I hath tasted this before behind a mongrel dwelling. It be pleasing."

The larger rat scurried up onto the table to sample the porridge for himself. Unlike Humphrey, who only took a small bite, the large rat ate all of it. Then, he instinctively made a move towards the bowl of porridge before remembering Chip was present and backed away slowly.

Chip smiled. "It be okay. Ye and Humphrey may hath this bowl. I shall fetch another."

Humphrey hesitated while his fellow pack member did not. The large rat was up on the side of the bowl before Chip had fully turned around. Humphrey did eventually join his fellow rat, but at a safely measured distance from his larger counterpart.

As Chip sat down at the table he shook his head at the madness he had accepted as reality. His life was spinning again. He thought that returning home would bring peace and joy to his life once more. He knew that returning home after a year away would require some adjustments, but he never considered he would end up back in a small room above some tavern entertaining rodents. *Sitting, eating, and talking with rats at the table. Speaking with people that don't exist. Surely these be signs that I be losing me sanity.*

"What troubles ye, master?" Humphrey asked, crawling down from the side of the bowl.

"Please, call me, Chip, and it be nothing." He didn't wish to discuss his feelings with the tiny rat. "Tell me, where hath ye heard mongrels call their children 'nuggets'?"

He remembered being called it as a child by Englishmen when his father wasn't around. Many viewed Scottish children as useless.

"Many places, Master. The most being in a mongrel dwelling near the water. There be many mongrel pups there. We often go there for food that hath been placed outside. The mongrels that live there be bad. Not nice like ye."

Be he referring to one of the orphanages near the wharf? Chip wondered. "Humphrey, what doth they do that be so bad?"

At his question, the large rat scurried out of the porridge bowl and bumped Humphrey so hard he nearly knocked him off the table.

"There be no violence here, rat," Chip said firmly.

"There be things we must not speak of, mongrel Chip."

"We may speak freely," Humphrey retorted. "Me master shall not harm us."

"It not be yer new master that trouble me," the large rat growled. "Darkness surrounds that mongrel dwelling. Death of mongrels fills the air within."

"Be it that they not feed the children there? Doth they not hath enough food?"

"Food?" the large rat repeated. "There be plenty of food. That not be the trouble."

"What be the trouble then?" Chip pressed, his interest rising.

"It not be known what it be that happens to the mongrel pups within, Master. All we know be that the mongrel pups dwell within and the smell of death lingers there."

Chip leaned slowly back in his chair. He didn't question how the rats knew such things. He was certain that the rodents, being scavengers by nature, had entered the dwelling looking for scraps of food. By the large rat's response, the children weren't dying of starvation. This piqued his curiosity even higher. "Tonight, Humphrey, ye shall show me where this mongrel dwelling be."

"Doth not dare!" the large rat squeaked, rounding to face Humphrey. "Should ye dare, ye shall be responsible for the death of the pack!"

Humphrey pushed past the large rat to face Chip. "Master,

the dwelling be unsafe. The mongrels that dwell within be bad."

Chip folded his arms and stared at the large rat. "How would me visiting this mongrel dwelling threaten the safety of yer pack?"

"The food that comes from that dwelling feeds me pack. It be the only dwelling we rats enter without the danger of death. The mongrels there doth not harm rats."

"Me pack be quite large," Humphrey interjected. "Food be hard to come by. Many rats would starve without the food from that dwelling."

"As ye care for the safety of yer pack, I also care for the safety of these mongrel pups ye speak of," Chip said firmly. "I shall make certain yer pack doth not starve."

"How would ye fulfill such?"

"Should something happen, I shall provide food for ye pack," Chip replied, chewing on his lower lip at the thought of buying food for a multitude of rodents.

He could tell his answer startled the large rat almost as much as it had startled him. Humphrey, on the other hand, spun in a circle in excitement.

"Ye would undertake this?" asked the large rat.

"Aye, rat, I would."

"Then we shall show ye where the mongrel dwelling be tonight."

Through the darkness, Chip followed the two rodents down back alleyways and up vacant streets. Twice he had to remind them he couldn't squeeze through small cracks in fences like they could. *I be glad I be wearing me breeches and not me kilt,* he mused, climbing another wall.

He could have easily found the orphanage on his own. It was gaining the trust of the larger rat and Humphrey that had him scaling walls and sliding along dark alleys. The only true difficulty would have been deciding which orphanage it was, as there were three that stood close to the waterfront, a stark reminder of what their fight with England and disease had cost them.

"It be just ahead," Humphrey said, running ahead of him.

Suddenly, Humphrey and the larger rat slid to a halt before scurrying under a nearby wooden box that sat just outside a small shop. "Danger! Hide!"

Instinctively, Chip dodged into a nearby alley and pressed himself against the stone wall. He listened carefully and could hear boots on the cobbled street coming closer. *Be this just the rat's natural reaction to humans or be there something dangerous about the person approaching,* he pondered as he stood there.

The boots stopped just outside the alleyway. Chip squinted to see if he could make out the figure casting a long shadow on the street, the oil lamp shining down from above them.

"I know you are in there," a man's rasping voice cooed. "I

can hear your breathing. It shall be okay. Come with me and you shall not be in any trouble."

"Where shall we be going?" Chip asked, stepping out into the light, ready for a fight.

"A thousand pardons, sir!" the man gasped, taking a step backwards.

Chip surveyed the tall weedy man that stood before him. His eyes reminded him of Mr. Stubbs', which placed him more on edge. His thoughts must have shown, as the man's expression turned to one of concern.

"I did not mean to disturb you, sir. I was looking for a young girl. She has run away from our orphanage and is lost."

"I hath not seen any young lasses tonight. How old be this girl?"

"She about nine, sir," the man replied, not looking Chip in the eyes.

"I shall be vigilant then. Suppose I cross paths with the poor girl, where shall I bring her?"

"St. Thaddeus orphanage. I thank you, kind sir."

Chip extended his hand, and the man quickly thrust his hand forward to accept the offer, his over-sized sleeve slipping up his arm. As he shook his hand, his eyes fell upon a scar on the man's wrist in the shape of a star. The man noticed where he was staring and quickly let go, shoving his sleeve back down.

"Good evening," the man said, quickly turning to leave.

Once the man was gone the two rats emerged from under

the wooden box. Chip squatted down and beckoned the rodents come closer. "Be that man from the mongrel dwelling?"

"Aye, Master. That mongrel be always there."

"Then I wish not any longer to see this dwelling. There be a mongrel pup that hath run away from the dwelling. We must find her. Any questions I hath, she shall be able to answer."

"Find her?" the large rat repeated.

"Aye. We must find her before that mongrel does."

Chip stood up as his eyes scanned the street. He knew they had to find this girl before that man did. Something about seeing that scar distressed him, though at that moment he could not remember where he had seen it before.

"Ye saith ye shall feed me pack," the larger rat said, snapping him from his thoughts.

"Be this what ye shall require for ye to assist me?" Chip grunted, not wishing to barter with the rat at that moment.

"Aye."

"Very well then, rat. Should ye and yer pack do as I saith, I shall feed them."

"We shall find ye when we find the pup," the larger rat said before bolting off like a streak of lightning.

Chip looked down at the tiny rat, searching for an explanation. "Where hath yer friend gone to?"

"He hath gone for the pack," the tiny rat replied, sounding amazed.

"Shall ye stay and search with me?"

"Aye, Master."

———•———

Several hours passed as Chip and Humphrey searched for the 'lost' girl. It was apparent to him that the young girl was in hiding and did not want to be found. This only steeled his resolve to find her and to find out what was going on at this orphanage.

"Mongrel!" a voice shouted behind him.

Chip turned to see the larger rat racing down the street towards him, darting in and out of the shadows. He stooped down to greet the approaching blur of fur.

"We hath found yer pup! She be in an abandoned mongrel dwelling not far from here!"

"Well done, rat. Take me to her."

"Then ye shall feed me pack?" the rat retorted, searching for reassurance.

"Aye. Ye hath me word."

"Follow me!" The rat turned and raced back up the street.

Chip and Humphrey hurried after the larger rat, Chip struggling to keep up. They crossed several streets before arriving at a burnt-out stone building that looked unstable. Chip entered the building carefully through a window, the door being blocked by rubble. He could hear several voices conversing ahead of him as he slowly followed the rats under and through fallen wooden beams that laid at odd angles.

As he drew closer, he realized the voices were those of several rats having a frantic conversation.

"This mongrel pup shan't feed the pack," a voice said. "Look, it barely survives."

"He saith that finding the pup shall bring the pack food," another voice retorted.

"Doth he wish for the pack to eat this mongrel pup?" a third voice interjected, sarcasm dripping from its tone.

The moment they sensed his presence, the shouts of "Danger!" filled the air. He could see the rats scattering for safety.

"Humphrey. Let the other rats know I not mean them any harm."

"Aye, Master."

Humphrey scurried away to speak with the other rats while he approached what looked to be the sleeping form of a young child. Not wanting her to alert all of Edinburgh and Leith, he placed his hand over her mouth as he woke her. She squirmed violently, and he was forced to grab her to keep her from running away.

"Calm, girl!" he hissed into her ear. "I mean ye not any harm. I be not from St. Thaddeus. I hath come to help ye."

The girl stopped squirming in his arms, opening her eyes for the first time, as she tried to look at him. When the light through the windows and holes in the walls hit her face, he froze. She looked as though someone had struck her several times in the face with their fist.

"I be going to lower me hand from yer mouth. Lest ye want the man from the orphanage to come, doth not shout."

The girl nodded as Chip slowly lowered his hand. She stared at him in silence for several minutes.

"This be yer place?" the girl asked.

Chip smiled. "Nay."

"Ye wish to help me?"

"Aye. Me name be Christopher, but ye may call me Chip. Ye doth not need to fear me. Doth ye hath a name?" The young girl nodded, but said nothing. This caused his smile to broaden. "What be yer name, child?"

"Isabella."

"Doth ye hath a last name?"

Isabella shook her head. "I not know me last name."

"Okay then, Isabella, let us go somewhere safe." He looked up over the rubble. "Humphrey." The tiny rat scurried up onto a beam. "We need somewhere near and free of mongrels that be safe to go to. Doth ye know of a place?"

"Aye, Master."

"Then we shall follow thee."

The young girl stared up at him in awe as he swept her up into his arms. She slowly relaxed as he carried her gently out of the wreck of the structure. With a pang in his chest, holding her reminded him of his Anna.

TWELVE

---◆---

ISABELLA

Humphrey led Chip to a small building in the middle of a nearby graveyard that had once been a groundkeeper's shack. It was furnished with several chairs, a table and a small iron stove. The place had not been inhabited for ages, judging by the amount of dust that blanketed the floor and furnishings.

Chip placed Isabella down in one of the chairs. A scurrying sound caught his attention and he was surprised to see several more rats making their way into the shack, squeezing under the door frame.

Humphrey climbed up onto the table. "Master, this mongrel dwelling be cold. Ye make heat like ye doth at yer dwelling?"

"Aye, supposing the things I need be present."

"Sir, doth ye speak with rats?" Isabella asked softly, staring up at him.

"Aye, I do," he answered truthfully. She was only the second person that he had told this to. "They speak to me as well. This tiny rat on the table be Humphrey."

"Hello Humphrey," she whispered, staring wide eyed at the

tiny rat.

Humphrey sat up on his hindquarters. "Hello mongrel pup."

"Sir, what doth he say?"

"Humphrey saith hello." Chip searched about for any leftover pieces of coal for the stove. "He thinks it be too cold and I agree."

"He really saith that?" she asked excitedly, staring at the tiny rat.

"Aye. Doth ye not believe me?"

"I believe ye, sir," she said, looking up at him. "Never heard of someone before that doth speak to rats."

"Neither hath I," he muttered, digging out some forgotten pieces of coal from beneath the stove, tossing them in and striking the flint.

"Sir, it makes ye special. I wish I be special."

Chip lit what was left of a candle that sat on the table and bit the inside of his lip hard to keep from flinching at the sight of the young girl's face. A sudden desire rose inside him to find the weedy man that had been searching for her and beat him until he looked like her. No child deserved to be harmed in this manner.

"Ye hath good manners," he said, taking a seat next to her. "Please child, call me Chip."

"Not good." Her face fell to the floor. "Never been good. I best call ye sir, lest I forget and upset ... someone else."

Chip pondered her unspoken meaning. "How long hath ye

been at St. Thaddeus Orphanage, child?"

She scrunched her nose. "Long as I remember, sir. Me parents died when I be but a baby."

"Who hath done this to yer face?"

Isabella looked down again and refused to look at him.

"Master?"

"Aye, Humphrey. What be it?"

"There be a mongrel bed here. The mongrel pup might need sleep and food."

Chip smiled at the rat. "Aye, ye be correct me little friend. Isabella, be ye hungry?"

She nodded, but refused to look up at him. Chip knew that she was scared and didn't want to talk about the orphanage just yet. He would have to gain her trust before she would be ready to open up. He also knew that if he went to the Edinburgh Guard or the English Soldiers, they would send her back to the orphanage and tell him to mind to his own business.

"There be a bed here," he said softly. "Lie and rest. I shall fetch ye some food and bring it back."

"Sir ... thank ye."

"Ye be most welcome." Chip rose to his feet. "The rats shall not harm ye."

The large rat scurried into the light. "Mongrel Chip, shall ye be bringing food for me pack?"

He studied the rat for a moment. "Very well, rat. Bring yer pack here and I shall bring food for them as well. Humphrey, watch over the girl. Keep her safe."

"Aye, Master. The pack shall not harm the mongrel pup."

Chip looked down at the young girl. "Isabella, Humphrey shall watch over ye."

The young girl smiled as Humphrey edged closer to her. Chip watched as she carefully reached out to touch Humphrey, reminding him again of his Anna. He longed to be with his daughter and his family, yet he knew that for now it was for the better. He wasn't certain what he would do if anyone ever hurt Anna the way this poor girl had been hurt. All he did know was that it wouldn't be good.

Careful that no one saw where he came from, Chip sneaked out of the graveyard and headed for the one place he knew he would find food. Thirty minutes later, he arrived at the bakery. The aroma of fresh baked bread greeted him as he entered.

"Mr. MacDougall! What brings ye by this morning? Returning to the bakery?" Spencer asked hopefully.

"Not yet. I hath a task to complete first, but I shall return soon." Chip spied a cane propped up against the counter. "Where be Donovan?"

"Running deliveries this morn. He be doing much better. His walking stick be here more than he!"

"Ye make me sound to be a lay about."

Chip turned round to see Donovan standing tall in the doorway, the picture of health.

"Mr. MacDougall, sir! I not know it be ye!"

"Morning, Donovan," Chip greeted his young employee. "It be good to see ye."

"It be good to see ye sir, as well. Hath ye returned to the bakery?"

"I hath come to purchase some loafs of bread for some starving souls."

"Buy bread?" Donovan repeated. "But, sir! This be yer bakery!"

Chip smiled at his loyal employee. "I be needing quite a bit and I not be stealing from me own establishment. This bakery provides for me family as well."

"How many loafs doth ye be needing, sir?" Spencer asked.

Chip wondered exactly how many rats were in Humphrey's pack. "A dozen loafs should do."

"It be a black eye how many people be starving these days," Donovan muttered, making his way behind the counter.

Donovan and Spencer quickly fetched the loaves of bread. He had taught Spencer to bake plenty of extra pones, so it didn't take long for them to fill his order. He placed the money on the counter, but Spencer just shook his head.

"I shall not be cheating me own bakery," Chip argued.

"Sir, I know ye and Mrs. MacDougall be estranged, but this be yer bakery as well."

Another few minutes of arguing and Spencer conceded, placing the schillings in the drawer. Chip waved goodbye, knowing his bakery was in good hands.

He felt rather odd sneaking through the graveyard with a basket full of bread, but knew that it would not be good for someone to see him there. Reaching the small shack, he opened the door, but had to cover his mouth to keep from shouting at the sight that met his eyes. The entire floor was covered by moving fur. Nearly a hundred rats filled the small shack, climbing over top one another to make way for him. Shouts of "Danger!" and "Food!" went up as he entered.

"Humphrey!"

The tiny rat scurried up onto the table, followed by several other rats.

"This be yer pack?" Chip asked in disbelief, speaking over the shouts that surrounded him.

"Aye, Master. Be that food for the pack?"

"For the pack and for the lass," he replied, sitting the basket on the table. The pack's constant repeating of the words that had nearly drove him mad, quickly became too much. "Rats! Be ye silent!"

Most the pack fell silent. Some instinctively hid inside the cupboard or under anything they could find. One voice from within the mass of fur uttered a scoff, "The mongrel speaks as though we hear and obey."

"Ye shall hear and obey, rat, should ye wish for me to bring ye food."

The small shack fell silent at these words. Isabella, who had awoken during the scuffling of the pack, looked at him in awe once

213

more. "Not a squeak. They hath not been silent since they arrived. Ye truly doth speak to rats."

Chip was still not use to the idea of speaking to rodents. Hearing it confirmed by the young girl only continued to solidify his new reality. "Aye."

She sat up on the rickety cot. "That be how ye found me. The rats led ye to me. They truly be me only friends."

Chip moved through the pack to the cupboard. He opened it and found a dull knife to slice the bread with. Several of the rats moved away from him nervously as he carried the knife over to the table, only Humphrey remaining atop. He sat down at the table and began to slice the bread. Slowly, the other rats dared come close to him, the aroma of the fresh baked bread too tempting to resist. He tossed the slices of bread into the midst of the pack and laughed as they climbed over top each other to grab at the slices.

"There be plenty for all," Chip said assuredly.

Isabella made her way to the table to join him, the rats having vacated chairs for the bread that was being distributed. Not one of the rats dared to approach the basket of bread for fear of the unknown mongrel that sat among them.

"Hath the rats always spoken to ye?"

"Nay," Chip replied, thinking about just how long it had been since he first heard their whispered cry.

"One day they might speak to me too," she said, smiling for the first time as she took a bite of bread.

Chip smiled and secretly hoped that such a thing never

happened to this young girl. He was certain though, that understanding the whispers of rodents would probably be less of a burden than what the innocent child in front of him had already suffered.

"Be ye thirsty? There be a pump outside."

Isabella nodded and he rose to fetch them some water. After finding a pale that wasn't rusted through, he stepped out into the chilly morning air to investigate the pump. It required a bit more force than normal to get working again, but soon he returned with the water and rummaged through the cupboards until he found some cups.

"Ye saith that the rats be yer only friends. Hath ye not any other friends at St. Thaddeus besides rodents?"

"I did. His name were Samuel. He cared for me. Protected me."

Chip noted the past tense in which she spoke of this Samuel. "Be this Samuel an orphan as well?"

"Aye," she replied, shifting in her seat. "He be there with me far back as I remember. He called me his lil' sis. He taught me all I know. How to tie a knot. How to read. How to write me name. He played with me. Helped me when I be hurt. Held me when I be sick ..."

Isabella choked up and fell silent. This Samuel had been like a brother to her and Chip knew what it meant to lose someone.

"Did ye hath any other friends?"

She shook her head in response.

215

"What happened to Samuel?"

Isabella swallowed hard. "They saith he died in his sleep."

"What doth ye think happened to him?"

"Ye shall think me mad should I tell thee," she retorted, folding her arms about herself.

Chip smiled. "I speak with rats. It be madder than this?"

She sat back in her chair, relaxing her arms as she looked back up at him. He could tell that she was making up her mind about something.

"Children leave St. Thaddeus often and never return. They tell us that they hath died, but Samuel said they be sent to a new land."

"A new land? Ye sure that he not hath been speaking of Heaven?"

"I be sure," she replied, nodding. "Samuel not been speaking of death. He said the older orphans be sent to a new land aboard a great vessel."

There be only one place referred to as a new land, Chip pondered. *And only one reason why they would send Scottish orphans to the Americas … slavery.* This thought made him wroth with anger. Isabella drew back from him into her chair.

"It be okay child," he said, forcing a smile. "I not be upset with thee."

Chip patted her shoulder with his hand and she relaxed again. "When did Samuel disappear?"

Isabella's eyes became as large as saucers. "Ye believe me?"

"Aye," he replied, smiling reassuringly. "Tell me Isabella, when did he disappear?"

Isabella scrunched her nose again. "Two or three weeks ago ... I think. I been in the box for many days. I not be sure."

"Box?" he repeated, frowning.

"Should ye be bad, they lock ye in a small wooden box. Should ye be really bad, they keep ye there for several days at a time."

Chip tried to remain calm as he envisioned the little girl in front of him screaming as they locked her away. "What hath ye done that they lock ye in this box?"

"I saith bad things ..."

Chip could see the little girl before him being upset over the loss of her friend Samuel. He imagined her being shoved into a small wooden box and forced to remain there for days. *If there indeed be a Hell ... how much worse could it be than the hell she's been living in?*

"Be this why ye ran away?"

"Whilst I be in the box, I heard them talking. They thought I be sleeping. They saith it be me time. That I be too much trouble."

"Ye hath yet to call those that work at St. Thaddeus by name. Doth ye know their names?"

"We only call them 'sir'. They call one another by name, but we dare not."

"Where be the Nuns, child? St. Thaddeus be a Catholic orphanage."

"The Sisters left the orphanage long ago. Only Sister Carmella and Sister Francis stayed."

"Doth ye know how old ye be?"

"I be nine ... I think," Isabella replied, scrunching her nose again. "I not be sure."

"Doth ye know what day ye were born?"

Isabella simply shook her head.

"Hath this St. Thaddeus always been this way?"

"Aye sir," replied Isabella. "The Sisters were always busy. They hath not time to fuss with things like birthdays. We be grateful for food and shelter. They saith that it be more than we deserved. Being learned not be a need."

Chip contemplated what he was hearing and what he could possibly do about it. One thing was for certain, Isabella wasn't going back to St. Thaddeus Orphanage under any circumstances.

"Ye be going to stay here," he said, handing her the last slice of bread. "Supposing it be safe to move ye, I shall take ye to me place. Ye shall not be going back to St. Thaddeus."

Isabella jumped up from her seat and threw her arms around his neck, several of the rats scurrying over top one another to get out of her way.

"Thank ye," she whispered as he patted her lightly on the back.

"It shall be okay child. They shall not harm ye again."

She released his neck and sat back down in her chair, her smile marred only by the bruises on her face. Chip bit his lip as he considered what he could do. If she was correct, those that did survive their time there faced a fate worse than death. *How might I bring to light what be happening there without risking her safety?*

"Humphrey!"

Humphrey climbed back onto the table. "Aye, Master."

Chip rose to his feet. "I need ye to watch over the mongrel pup. I must see about some matters. Keep her safe until I return."

"Aye, Master."

"What of us, mongrel?" a large rat asked, climbing up onto the table, his coat so dark that it was almost black. "What would ye hath us do? We be indebted to ye."

Chip bit his lip again as he considered the rat's offer. Humphrey shrank away from the rodent and he presumed that this be the pack's master.

"Master rat, I presume?"

"I be the master of me pack," the rat replied.

"Could ye pack find which ships hath child—I mean, mongrel pups aboard?"

"What be a ship?"

"It be what mongrels use to cross water."

"I shall send a portion of me pack to find the ships that ye seek."

Chip nodded to the rodent. "Thank ye, Master rat."

"I never met a mongrel that understandeth rodents."

Chip sighed, "Neither hath I."

He figured the best place to find out any information about

an orphanage near the docks would be from someone who had spent most of his life working there.

"I shall return," Chip said reassuringly to Isabella, who nodded.

With that, he left the small shack and sneaked out of the graveyard in search of answers. Once again, he had a purpose—to help Isabella and possibly many more children in the process. *Be this what Bro. Hesperus meant by making something good out of it?* he wondered. Either way, it was a distraction from the other problems in his life and he welcomed it.

———◆———

Mary sat deep in thought as the hackney rolled along down the streets of Edinburgh. Her life had taken so many turns in the last two years, she could barely remember who she was before. Somehow, a hard yet simple life had transformed dramatically into an easy yet difficult existence.

Mary no longer had to worry about whether her children would starve or freeze to death in the middle of the night. No longer did she have to sit up at night while the house slept and worry about what new tax might be brought against her family. Now, she sat up at night and worried what her estranged husband was going through and whether he was well.

A cough startled her from her thoughts. Lost in her own musings, she hadn't even noticed that the carriage had come to a halt. The driver stood, holding the carriage door open for her. She quickly gathered her things and prepared to exit the hackney when a gloved hand appeared, palm up and open, waiting for hers.

"Thank ye, Mr. Wallace," she said, accepting his hand as she stepped out of the carriage.

"Morning Mary. Please, call me Jefferson. We be friends, after all."

Mary returned his smile. "Thank ye, Jefferson. I was not expecting ye to greet me."

"What manner of gentleman be I to let ye enter alone."

Mary payed the driver then explored the street with her eyes, before focusing her attention on the building that stood before her. She was still skeptical whether she was doing the right thing.

"Mary, ye not be hurting him," Mr. Wallace said, sensing her thoughts. "Ye simply be protecting yer children and yer self."

"Christopher would never harm me or the children," she retorted, walking alongside Mr. Wallace as they headed up the steps and into the Royal Bank of Scotland.

"Nay, not intentionally. Ye saith yer self that Mr. MacDougall hath changed. I saw it me self when he visited the bank. He be quite troubled. In such a state, one not say what he might do."

"Ye saith this Jefferson, yet Christopher knows what it would cause his family."

"Ye saith ye know not what he be doing. While ye be

separated, ye must protect yer children."

Mary sighed, "Very well, Jefferson. I shall do as ye suggest."

"I swear that ye not be hurting ye husband," he said reassuringly.

Mr. Wallace led her into his office, helped her with her coat, then excused himself to fetch the papers required for the transaction. *I must trust Mr. Wallace,* she told herself. *He saith this shall not harm Christopher.*

Moments later, Mr. Wallace returned with the papers and another older gentleman. "Mrs. MacDougall, this be Mr. Wall. He be the bank notary. He shall witness the signing and notarize the document."

"Mr. Wall."

Mr. Wall bowed. "Mrs. MacDougall."

The three of them sat down around Mr. Wallace's desk to go over the document. Mr. Wallace read aloud the document to Mary, though she truthfully only understood a small portion of what was said. When he finished, he explained to her what the document meant.

"This document simply states that Mr. MacDougall not stake claim to yer house or yer land. It states that ye purchased said house and said land in his absence. Should anything happen, ye could sell the land and be financially set."

"I shall sign this," she sighed, "with the full understanding that it not be more than the house and the land."

"Absolutely, Mrs. MacDougall," Mr. Wallace confirmed.

Mary glanced at Mr. Wall, who smiled and nodded reassuringly. She picked up the quill, dipped it into the ink and wrote her name at the bottom of the parchment before placing the seal below it with the wax and stamp. Mr. Wall took the parchment, examined it, then placed his notary seal on the lower right corner.

"That all that be needed." Mr. Wallace turned his eyes to the older gentleman. "Thank ye, Mr. Wall, for being witness."

Mr. Wall stood, then bowed to Mary once more. "It was a pleasure, Mrs. MacDougall."

He then nodded to Mr. Wallace before excusing himself from the office. Mary felt odd being left alone with Mr. Wallace. He called himself friend, but she knew deep inside that he desired more. Such would remain impossible for her now. When she thought Christopher to be dead, she had considered what her life would hold and whether the handsome Mr. Wallace would become a part of it. Since the day she met Christopher, he had been her future. Now that he'd returned, her future rested in the hands of her husband once again.

"Mary," Mr. Wallace said, stirring her from her thoughts.

She forced a smile. "Forgive me."

"Apology not needed. I know such things be difficult."

Mr. Wallace fetched her coat then helped her put it on, resting his hands on her shoulders for a moment before putting his own coat back on.

"Mr. Wallace, ye doth not need to see me out. I shall hail a hackney."

"Not needed. We shall take me coach. There be a wonderful pastry shop along the way to yer house. I be wanting some for the morning."

"It be too much trouble, Jefferson," Mary said, trying not to offend him.

Mr. Wallace bowed. "Trouble? Nay. It be me pleasure."

Mary sighed as she consented, allowing him to lead the way. He was a charming man and only a few weeks ago she was flattered by his attentions. Now, she found them most distressing.

———◆———

Chip reached the wharf, surprised to find that Mr. Malone had given up his post at the docks to become the owner of a small Inn in southern Edinburgh.

"Ye gave him his opportunity," Jonah explained. "When ye gave him the money, he decided it be time for him to change the moniker. Ol' Malone had more coppers stashed away. He be just waitin' till he had enough, be me guess."

"Where be this Inn?"

"It be the Malone Inn on High Street. Not be hard to remember. Now, why be ye in search of Ol' Malone? Owes ye somethin'?"

Chip shook his head. "Course not. Ol' Malone knows things and now I be in search of answers."

Jonah chuckled, "I would go with ye, but the docks be

needin' me. Ye let me know should ye need somethin' of me."

Jonah placed a hand on Chip's shoulder, causing him to smile. He knew that Jonah meant every word.

"I shall, me friend."

Chip set out from the docks, headed for High Street in search of Malone Inn. Instead of hailing a hackney, he chose to walk. It helped him keep his mind clear. Regardless of what he had once thought, the streets were his friend.

Twenty minutes later, he turned up High Street to see a small wooden sign hanging off the side of one of the buildings that read, "Malone Inn." He pushed open the heavy door to find a small but inviting room with a greeting desk. Stairs led up and away to the left while a hallway led down and to the right.

"May I help ye?" a kindly looking old woman asked, entering from the hallway.

Chip removed his hat. "Ma'am, I be looking for Mr. Gregor Malone."

"He be in the back. Whom shall I say be calling?"

"I be Christopher MacDougall."

The woman hurried away without saying another word. Chip glanced around at the many decorations that filled the small lobby while he waited.

"Chip!" Gregor Malone exclaimed, walking out from the hallway and grasping him by the shoulders. "I thought ye be snabbled!"

He patted Gregor on the arms and smiled. "Many hath

thought the same."

"Come! Join me in the back. Let us give a bottle or two a black eye. We hath much to talk about!"

Chip nodded then followed his former boss down the hallway and into a small living quarters. Gregor fetched a bottle of whiskey and two glasses from the cupboard then motioned for Chip to join him in a small sitting room.

"What doth ye think of yer investment?" Gregor asked, referring to the Inn.

"I gave ye the benders as a gift. Not one thought that ye would become a Keeper."

Gregor chuckled. "Course not! Never told a soul, besides me mother."

"That be yer mother?" Chip asked, motioning towards the hallway.

"Aye, that be the reaper that raised me."

"Did me best with this one," came a woman's voice behind Chip.

"Mrs. Malone," he said, standing up to greet her.

"Someone raised ye right, Mr. MacDougall."

"Thank ye." Chip said, sitting back down.

"I be upstairs should ye need me, son."

Gregor nodded. "Aye, mother."

They waited for her to leave before speaking.

"She be a good woman," Gregor sighed. "Never thought me plate-fleet would come in an' allow me to repay her. Thanks to ye I hath."

"Ye doth well?"

"Business be good, but ye hath not come to check on Ol'
Malone. Should there be something I might do for thee … name
it."

"Ye know more of the docks than any I know," Chip said,
getting right down to business. "What doth ye know of St.
Thaddeus Orphanage?"

Gregor's face fell solemn as he stared at Chip. "Why doth
ye ask?"

"I be concerned about the children within," Chip replied,
staring into the eyes of the old docker.

"Why be ye concerned? What hath ye seen?"

Chip measured his words. "Someone was searching for a
runaway orphan. He seemed bothered by the child's disappearance,
though I felt that there be more to it."

"Ye would be best to forget the blaggard and the child,"
Gregor sighed. "Supposing he be from the orphanage, it would
only be trouble for ye."

Chip chewed his lower lip as he contemplated how to
proceed.

"What hath ye done?" Gregor asked, squinting at him.

The look on Gregor Malone's face was a mixture of
concern and what looked like a hint of fear. He trusted his old boss,
but his reaction made Chip a little apprehensive.

"I shan't say."

"Why not?" Gregor snapped. "Tell me that ye hath not intervened."

Chip rubbed his hands together in front of his face, pressing his nose against his thumbs.

"Ye need not say a thing, nor doth I wish ye to," Gregor growled, looking frustrated. "Be ye a mopus?"

"What be going on at this St. Thaddeus, Gregor, that hath ye ready to comb me head?"

"The place be owned by 'Them'," Gregor hissed, turning pale.

Chip frowned. "Them?"

"Come now, Chip! Ye know of whom I speak!"

Chip frowned harder. "Nay, I doth not know, Gregor. Why doth ye speak in riddles?"

"Chip, ye hath lived in Edinburgh for many years now and hath worked in Leith," Gregor retorted, his frustrations growing. "Ye even be a topping man and strapper now."

Chip raised his eyebrows in surprise.

"Not act so surprised. Surely ye doth not think such a thing would remain privy. I visited yer bakery once, only to find ye hath joined the King's Navy."

"I know not whom this 'them' be that ye speak of," Chip said, reverting the conversation back on course. "Tell me, who they be that ye fear them so?"

Gregor sighed as he poured himself another glass of whiskey before draining it in one, as though searching for courage.

"Surely ye hath heard tale of ..." he dropped his voice to just above a whisper, "the Shadow Clan."

THIRTEEN

---◆---

HARD DECISIONS

"The Shadow Clan?" Chip repeated incredulously, staring at his old boss with a mixture of confusion and amusement. "Come now, Gregor. That be tales for children."

"They not be childish tales!" Gregor snapped, absentmindedly stroking his thick beard. "They be a mixed lot. Strappers, nobles, blaggards, reds and lotmen alike. The docks belong to them. I would soon rather lay me head in the maiden and wait for the blade to drop, than to challenge their hand."

"What makes ye believe such?"

Gregor poured himself another glass of whiskey. "Years before ye started at the docks, a young docker went missing one morn. We searched the docks until we found him, his head bashed in with a stone. The foreman told us the young docker had slipped off the wharf and bashed his head against a stone. We knew this to be false, but were told not to argue should we wish to continue to work."

Chip felt an uneasy chill. "Ye think that this docker be offed by this 'Shadow Clan'?"

"I know it be them that offed him. It be after his death that I knew old gooseberry be active amongst the docks. Lowly things were being done in the dead of night. Never allowed there too early in the morn or too late in the evening."

"Why did ye stay?"

"Hath ye been without worry too long already?" Gregor retorted hotly. "Doth ye not remember how ye came to work there?"

"Forgive me, Gregor. I meant not any disrespect," Chip said, stressing his sincerity. "Why doth ye think that they offed the lad?"

"He always arrived at the docks earlier than the rest. I believe that he saw something he should not hath. Thus, they silenced him."

Chip sat for a moment, considering what Gregor was telling him. "Ye believe that these same people, the Shadow Clan, be involved at this orphanage?"

"Remember how the Sisters would pass by as we worked?"

"Aye, I do."

He remembered seeing the small flock of nuns pass by daily while they were loading and unloading ships. He never really gave them much thought as he was too busy with the chores of the day.

"A year ago, before I left the docks, the Sisters stopped being passersby. They were always pleasant, like small moments of inspiration."

Chip nodded, though he had not felt the same connection.

He had nothing against the Sisters of St. Thaddeus, but being of a different faith he did not see them in the same light as Gregor must have.

"One day, I hailed a Sister as she passed," Gregor continued. "She told me of the orphanage being sold and that only three of the Sisters would be staying. All affairs would be tended to by the new strappers. She be deeply disturbed by this."

"What doth ye think they need from this orphanage?"

"That I not know. Whatever it be, it not be good."

Chip pondered again what Isabella had told him about the disappearing children.

"Why doth ye care so?" Gregor asked, breaking the silence.

"I think … they be trading the children to the Americas … as slaves," Chip replied, measuring his words.

Gregor frowned. "What makes ye think this?"

"I hath heard tale of unnatural deaths within the orphanage," Chip explained cautiously. "I believe the children not be dead, but sold for trade."

"Say this be. Why doth ye care?"

"These children be Scottish, Gregor," he retorted hotly, anger boiling up at his former boss' lack of concern. "Shall we watch as they be sold like sheep?"

"Chip, ye hath two children of yer own. It be noble that ye wish to help yer fellow kinsmen, but ye need to consider yer own first."

"Me wife cares for me children," Chip said, frowning.

232

"Since me return from the dead, she hath not wanted me. We ... we be estranged."

"I be truly sorry. I know not how ye feel. Should there be a chance, doth not give up. I only wish I but one more day with me Charlotte."

Chip furrowed his brow. "I did not know that ye were once married."

"Aye. I lost me whither to illness many years gone by. I miss her presence. It be like the sun rose when she entered the room."

"I know the feeling."

"Hold to yer faith, lad. She could bare ye once, thus there be hope," Gregor chuckled.

"Aye, though I shan't pretend that I heard not what be happening."

Gregor growled, "Ye wish to fill an empty box with ye own body?"

"What did ye say?" Chip asked, his mind racing as he stared at his old boss.

"Ye heard they be trading the children off and claiming they be dead. Should they be claiming death, there must be empty eternity boxes."

"Aye," Chip agreed, his tone hushed.

He knew that Gregor was correct. It would seem rather odd for multiple orphaned children to have passed and there not be any graves for their bodies. *They could be claiming disease, which would permit them to burn the bodies,* he reasoned. *Yet too many cases of disease would point to a potential outbreak and thus force the orphanage to close.*

"Heed me warning," Gregor said, looking tense as he stirred Chip from his thoughts. "Doth not tease old gooseberry. These blaggards be too powerful."

"Thank ye for yer advice. I shall consider what ye saith."

"Ye stubborn Scot," Gregor hissed. "Ye shall consider me warning as much as I shall consider leaving this bottle of whiskey be. Ye shall what ye hath resigned to do before ye came. I hath only aided in yer madness."

"It not be madness to help yer kinsmen. It be ye who taught me this. Besides, ye be as stubborn as I."

Gregor leaned forward in his chair. "Doth me one. Swear to me that ye shall not end as the young docker I once knew."

"I shall doth me best. I must leave now, but I shall come see ye again."

As Chip rose to leave, Gregor stood as well, embracing him as though it might be the last time they saw one another.

"Supposing there indeed be a God, may He be with ye."

Chip cleared his throat, trying not to become emotional. "Aye, and may He be with ye."

Gregor stepped back from him, placing his hands on Chip's shoulders, something between a smile and a smirk upon his face. Something in the moment made Chip hesitant. *What would become of Marcus and Anna without their father?* he pondered. *Would they ever forgive me should something happen?*

"Should ye find yer self in need of a helping hand," Gregor turned to walk with Chip, "send word and this old salt shall fetch me staff. I not be the heavy hand I once be, but I still be good in a scrape."

"Aye, that I shall," Chip said, smirking as they walked together down the hallway, making their way towards the entrance of the Inn.

Chip found solace in the words of his old boss. He knew Gregor Malone's word was good as gold. If anyone was to ever ask him to name two good things that came from his days as a docker, meeting Jonah McCullah and Gregor Malone would always be his answer.

———•———

Chip walked down the streets of Edinburgh, lost in his own thoughts. He looked up from the rhythmic hum that the heels of his boots made against the cobbled stones to see a street sign marked Long Street. He sighed as he resigned to the fact that his feet would always carry him to Mary and the children, for they were his true home.

Chip stood there, staring at the street sign. Just as he decided to swallow his stubborn pride and go see Mary, the trotting of hooves upon the cobbled street caught his attention. He stood there and waited. As the coach passed, he glanced through the open window and his heart nearly stopped. When he felt his heart beat again, he wasn't sure, for its beats were drowned out by the sound of the blood thundering inside his head.

She not even notice me standing there. How could she, when she be too deep in conversation with Mr. Wallace from the bank to notice her husband, Chip thought savagely. His arms shook and his jaw clenched tight. Neither had anything to do with the bitter wind that bellowed about him. The rage that burnt inside him made it feel like a summer's day. His father had tried to teach him that violence was always the last response and patience was always the best choice. He could hear his father's words echoing in his head. *The Devil shivers with delight when a patient man reacts.* This, however, tested his resolve to its fullest.

Chip resolved to stand at the corner and watch as Mr. Wallace flashed the gentleman, assisting Mary from the carriage. He continued to watch as Mr. Wallace followed her into the house. *No gentleman would escort an estranged woman into her home! Even as uncultured as I be, me father taught me certain things!*

Chip lost track of time as he stood there, waiting for Mr. Wallace to leave. He didn't recognize the wind that blew continually harder or the stares from passersby. The coach that stood in front of his family's home held his focus until Mr. Wallace reemerged from the residence. He had to fight the urge to deal with the man. What Mary would think of him if he gave in, was the only thought that kept him steady.

He waited several minutes after the carriage left before starting the longest walk of his life. He reached the front door and stood there for another moment or two before knocking. Mary's laughter reached him first as she approached the door.

"Christopher," she said breathlessly, opening the front door.

If Chip had been thinking clearer, he would have realized that Mary looked pleased to see him. Unfortunately, anger and jealousy raged inside him beneath the cold exterior that he was portraying.

"Mary," he said coolly. "Be the children home?"

"Aye," she replied, looking slightly crestfallen. "They be in the front room. Marcus be reading to Anna."

His eyes became focused on the far wall behind her. "May I see them?"

"Aye," she replied quietly, stepping back to allow him in. "Please, come in."

Chip nodded as he made his way inside the house. Mary escorted him to the front room without uttering a single word.

"Papa!" Anna shouted, running to hug him about the waist.

Marcus rolled his wheelchair round in front of the sofa so that he could slide into it.

"Stay where ye be, son."

Chip snatched Anna up into his arms then walked over and sat down beside his son, discarding his coat into an empty arm chair. Marcus hugged him tightly while Anna sat in his lap.

"Doth not let me interrupt. Read to us, me boy. Show me what ye hath learned at school."

237

"Okay, Papa!"

He sat there and listened as his young man read from a small poetry book. Anna rested her head on Chip's shoulder as she listened. Mary leaned against the doorway's facing and watched, her hair laying on her shoulders just the way he remembered. He could feel his resentment melting as he sat there amid his family, marveling as he listened to his boy reading. He had not learned himself to read until he was nearly grown.

"Be that Mr. Wallace at the door, Miss?" Ms. Douglas asked as she bustled into the room. "Shall he be staying for supper? Shall I be needing to ..."

Ms. Douglas' words trailed off at the sight of Chip sitting amongst his children. Marcus gave Ms. Douglas a look of exasperation that would have made his grandfather proud while Anna looked close to tears. Chip resolved to ignoring her comments and focusing on the things that were important.

"Marcus," Chip said, earning a nervous glance from his son "I believe that ye were on this page here."

Chip pointed to a page in the small poetry book, earning a smile from his son.

"Aye, Papa."

Ms. Douglas snorted in obvious disapproval before leaving the room, Mary following her out.

"I doth not like her, Papa," Anna whispered, resting her head on his chest.

Chip gently patted the side of her face as Marcus started to read again. He knew that he only had two choices. He would either find a way to work things out with Mary or remain estranged from his family. Removing the children from their mother was not an option. They needed her … he needed her.

Once Marcus was finished, they sat there for a while, catching up on all that had happened. They told him of school and of all the new things that they were learning. Chip told them that he had acquired another rat as a 'pet'.

"Why did ye not bring him with ye, Papa?" Anna asked, folding her arms and looking so much like her mother.

"I not be planning to visit ye today, Angel. I promise I shall bring him round the next time I come."

"Hath ye named him, Papa?"

"Aye. I call him, Humphrey."

"Ye named him after yer uncle Humphrey?" Mary quipped as she entered the room, her eyebrows rising.

"I might hath," Chip retorted, suppressing a smirk. "It be a good name."

"A befitting one as well. He hath enough whiskers the last we saw him."

Mary quickly left the room before he could retort. When it came time to leave, she escorted him to the door. Ms. Douglas entered the front room to sit with the children as she and Chip exchanged cold glances.

"The children be glad that ye came by," Mary said, offering him his coat.

He tugged it on. "I be their father. I miss being with them as much as they miss being with me."

"I heard ye tell Anna that ye plan to bring yer pet rat about the next time ye visit," she said, trying to maintain some form of conversation, though it was apparent that she was struggling.

"Aye. He be a small rat. Should I fear that Ms. Douglas might murder me pet?"

"Ms. Douglas would not harm any living creature."

"I not be so sure. She be a bit cold."

"She only be startled to see ye."

"Aye. Especially, when she be expecting Mr. Wallace."

"Mr. Wallace saw me home from the bank earlier," Mary countered quickly.

"Doth he normally stay for supper when he sees ye home?"

Mary's face filled with color. "It not be that way."

"What way be it?" Chip asked, trying to remain calm. "Who be here more? Me or Mr. Wallace?"

"Thank ye for stopping by, Christopher," she replied, biting her lip and ignoring his question. "Please come around again soon."

Mary opened the front door and held it, waiting for him to leave. Chip pulled his coat tightly around him and left without another word. He knew that he needed to get away before the raging animal inside his chest exploded. He was desperate to find a way to heal his family, yet at that moment he could see none.

It took Chip nearly an hour to make his way back to the shack in the graveyard. He pushed open the door to find Isabella lying on the cot in the corner, covered in what looked like a fur coat. As he drew closer he realized that the 'coat' was thirty or forty tiny coats. Humphrey sat nestled near her face. The air was crisp in the room, despite the coal burning stove. He marveled how some of Humphrey's pack and the young girl were keeping each other warm. The rest of his pack were curled up together on the floor.

Chip sat quietly at the table, not wanting to disturb them. He tried to stifle a cough, but was unsuccessful. Humphrey looked up to see that his master and slowly eased himself away from the young girl, making his way up onto the table.

"Master returns."

"Aye, I hath returned. How be the young lass?"

"The young mongrel be sleeping, Master. We hath kept her warm. She shall be hungry when she awakes."

"Aye," Chip agreed. "We all be hungry. We'll not move her until night, lest those that be searching find her."

"Shall Master take the young mongrel to ye dwelling?"

"Aye. Supposing it be possible and until I discover another way to keep her safe. I must first find a way that she might enter undetected."

Chip sat there for several minutes in silence, clearing his mind of his visit with his family and remembering his visit with

Gregor Malone. "Tell me Humphrey, hath ye or yer pack ever seen a deceased mongrel leave the dwelling where she comes from?"

"Leave?" Humphrey repeated, sounding confused. His tail becoming still.

"Aye. Carried out by other mongrels."

"Nay, Master. I hath not witnessed. I shall ask me pack."

"Wait until they awaken. I doth not wish to wake the lass."

"I be awake."

Chip looked over at the cot to see the eyes of the young girl staring back at him. "I not mean to wake ye child."

"I be only resting," Isabella replied. "It be too hard to sleep. The rats be warm, but they tickle."

Chip smiled at the thought of the girl being tickled by over a hundred tiny feet. Isabella returned his smile, though her bruised face still marred its innocence. He still found it hard to look at the evidence of her abuse, especially after just being with his Angel.

"Tell me child, hath ye ever seen the other children removed from the orphanage?"

"Nay, sir."

"Hath ye heard of where St. Thaddeus claims that they go?"

"Claims, sir?"

"When St. Thaddeus speaks of the missing children," Chip said, clarifying his question, "what doth they say hath happened to them?"

"They say that they bury the bodies."

"Be there a service for the deceased?" he asked, trying to

place the pieces together like a puzzle.

"There not be a service. They saith we not be deserving of such," she replied, her eyes falling for a moment.

Chip could tell that she was remembering things that had happened at the orphanage. *How much hath this poor child been through?* "Doth ye know where they saith they bury the bodies?"

"St. Anthony's."

Chip sat stunned by her response. "Be ye sure child?"

"Aye, sir," she nodded.

"What troubles ye, Master?"

"We be in St. Anthony's Cemetery," Chip breathed, feeling suddenly uneasy.

He knew at that moment, the people they were trying to avoid could be just outside their door. The look on the young girl's face told him that she realized this as well.

"Be that what mongrels call this dwelling, Master?"

"Nay. That be what they call the land we be upon. It be where mongrels bury their dead. The mongrels that search for this girl might come here."

Humphrey sniffed the air, then scurried down off the table towards a nearby huddle of rats. A moment later, the large black rat emerged from the pile of fur and followed Humphrey back to the top of the table.

"Ye think dangerous mongrels might be near the pack?"

"Aye, I do, Master rat."

"I shall send scouts," the rat said. "Should there be

mongrels about, they shall search them out."

"Thank ye, Master rat."

The large rat merely twitched its nose before scurrying off the table and back down to the huddle of rodents. Seconds later, five or six rats hurried off, squeezing under the closed door. Chip glanced over at Isabella, who was staring at him in awe again.

He tried to clear his mind and focus on the problem at hand while they waited for the rodent scouts to return, but his nerves were too tense. The idea that any moment one of the rats would return to report that a mongrel was in the cemetery or that someone would try to enter the shack while they waited was keeping him on edge.

"Tell me, Humphrey, why did ye sniff the air when I told ye of me concerns?"

"I be smelling for mongrels, Master, but there not be any besides ye and the young one near this dwelling."

"What did he say?" Isabella asked.

"He be sniffing for the smell of people."

"That be useful," she said thoughtfully.

"Why doth ye say that, child?"

"He can tell ye when people be near." Isabella sighed wishfully. "I wish I could hear him."

Chip was about to try and explain to the girl that it wasn't such a wonderful thing to understand rodents when there was a scurrying near the door. He looked over to see the rodent scouts returning from their mission.

"There not be a mongrel near this dwelling that not be inside," one of the rats reported to the Master rat. "Least not any that be breathing."

"That be good," the large black rat replied.

Chip did not wait for the Master rat to relay their findings, having heard clearly. He extended his arm towards Humphrey and without a word the tiny rat climbed up his coat sleeve and onto his shoulder. He dusted off his breeches as he rose to his feet. "We need to find another place."

"What of yer dwelling, Master?"

"It be too dangerous to return to me small room above the tavern. I know not any good way to sneak her in as the governor of the place be watching always, lest a tenant pay with the sails."

Humphrey drew himself up close to Chip's coat collar. "Where shall ye take her then?"

"This place be yer idea, Humphrey. Know ye any other place where we might stay?"

"I know one other that might be suitable for mongrels, Master. Be it safe? I know not, for I thought this be safe. I only know that mongrels not enter it."

"This be a good place Humphrey, lest not for the connection it carries to the orphanage. We hath not any choice but to search for new shelter. We shall wait till dusk then we shall make inquiry of this dwelling."

"Humphrey knows of another place where we might stay?"

"Aye."

Isabella smiled. "He be a smart rat."

"That he be. He also be a hungry little rodent. They all be, and I be betting that ye be hungry as well."

"Very much sir," she replied, perking up at the thought of food.

"Then I shall fetch some food for ye and for Humphrey's pack."

"I could show ye the dwelling while ye be out fetching food," Humphrey suggested, his nose twitching.

"The lass be right. Ye be indeed a smart rodent."

Humphrey spun in a circle on his shoulder before scurrying down the front of his coat and down his breeches onto the floor.

"I shall return shortly with food, child."

Isabella nodded.

"We shall be waiting, mongrel Chip."

Chip smirked at the large black rat, straightened his cap and opened the door. Humphrey immediately scurried through the doorway, Chip following close behind.

He expected to be led to an abandoned cottage or hut, but where the young rat took him was quite unexpected. It was a small abandoned spirits shop in the south of Leith. It had large open windows, but the cellar was secluded and would make an excellent place to hide until he could decide what to do. The smell of whiskey was strong, but it would still be an upgrade from the drafty groundkeeper's shack.

"Excellent work, me little friend. This shall do nicely."

Humphrey spun in a circle. "Thank ye, Master."

"Now, let us gather in some food from the local merchants."

He waited until nightfall to move Isabella. Surprising to Chip, the Master rat decided that the pack would follow them to the new shelter.

"Ye wish to come with us?"

"Aye," the large black rat replied. "Ye ability to understandeth me kind and the promise of food be enough to stomach the presence of mongrels. We shall scout ahead, lest there be unwanted mongrels about."

"We shall follow thee then."

When they arrived, Isabella welcomed the new place. It was further away from the orphanage and despite it being a cellar, it was much warmer than the shack. There was a small stove and cot down there as well, no doubt used to warm a worker or two that stayed the night there guarding the whiskey.

Chip brought down a table and chairs from the shop above while contemplating the many decisions he had made over the last few years. Many had been hard to accept. Yet helping this young girl was the easiest of all.

———•———

Mr. Wallace steadied his nerves as he knocked on the solid oak door of an antiquated, yet magnificent manor home. One might describe it as a palace, for it possessed all the characteristics of a place you might expect a monarch to live. The lush green estate was slightly browned by the effects of winter, but one could imagine how vibrant the grounds would be during the summer months.

He silently mulled over his actions of the past few days. *He hath summoned me here many times before*, Mr. Wallace mused, trying to reassure himself. He knew that his actions were under extra scrutiny those days. If he had missed even the slightest detail … He shuddered at the thought. As he stood there meditating, a small elderly housekeeper answered the door.

"Mr. Wallace, come in. The Master be awaiting ye in the smoking room."

"Thank ye madam," Mr. Wallace replied, fidgeting with the front of his coat as he stepped over the threshold.

"I shall hath ye coat."

Mr. Wallace removed his coat and handed it to the elderly lady, merely glancing in her direction. He straightened the cuffs of his sleeves and adjusted his collar, his eyes now focused on his destination. As he edged closer he could hear the scratching of a quill on parchment stop. Before his nerves got the best of him, he cleared his throat and knocked once on the open door.

"Do you intend to keep me waiting?"

"Nay, Lord Prose," Mr. Wallace stammered, entering and bowing his head slightly. "I doth not wish to intrude."

Mr. Prose sat behind a large ornate desk in a high back Victorian arm chair, going over a stack of parchment. Behind him, a grand fireplace with a roaring fire dancing high in its grate. The position of the desk and chair in front of the fireplace gave the illusion that Mr. Prose himself sat amongst the flames.

"Wish to intrude," Mr. Prose repeated, not looking up from his papers. "Jefferson, you are an intelligent man. Yet there are times that you not make any sense. I have summoned you here. How are you interrupting me?"

"Forgive me, me Lord. It be a foolish statement."

"Indeed, it be," Mr. Prose agreed, looking up from his work at last. "Jefferson, please be seated."

Mr. Wallace quickly took a seat in front of Mr. Prose's desk, removing his cap and placing it in his lap.

"Me Lord, it hath been done as ye wished."

Mr. Prose observed Jefferson for a moment, leaning back in his Victorian chair, his arms folded. "Jefferson, do you still believe that I require you to inform me of your actions?"

"Nay, me Lord."

"Then you must be seeking my approval," Mr. Prose said, staring at Jefferson, his eyes cold and unforgiving. "Tell me, what do you believe you have done to earn my disapproval?"

Jefferson felt as though his heart was about to beat out of his chest. "I doth not know, Lord Prose. I hath done all that ye hath asked of me."

"Indeed, you have." Mr. Prose flashed a cold smile and Jefferson could feel the hairs on the back of his neck begin to rise. "With such vigor, I might add. I not recall the last time you were so... detailed."

Jefferson stared at the cap in his lap. "I live to serve ye, me Lord."

"You desire something, Jefferson," Mr. Prose stated, his voice even and calm. "It's written in your eyes."

Jefferson felt a chill creep up his spine. For as long as he had known Mr. Prose, he had never been able to keep anything from him. "Aye, me Lord. There be something ..."

"Someone," Mr. Prose corrected, his eyes dancing with amusement. "You desire Mary MacDougall. This is why you have been so attentive to your task."

Jefferson sat there in silence as Mr. Prose's words lingered in the air like mist. He knew not what to say or even how to react. He more than just desired Mary MacDougall – he longed to be near her, to hold her hand for longer than just a mere moment as she stepped out of a coach.

"Has it turned yet, Jefferson?" Mr. Prose asked, Jefferson's eyes snapping back to Mr. Prose's face. "Have you begun to despise Mr. MacDougall? To hate him?"

Jefferson felt very his soul waging war over how to react. He wanted to shout out the answer, declare his hatred for Mr. MacDougall. He also wanted to flee Mr. Prose's presence.

"It matters not yet, Jefferson. Mary MacDougall still be important to the task at hand. You shall continue as you have been instructed. Not let your desires for this woman distract you from your task. You know what be the consequences of failure."

Jefferson bowed his head. "I shall not disappoint ye, me Lord."

Jefferson looked back at Mr. Prose and recognized his dismissal. He rose from his chair, bowed low, then turned to depart, all the while, Mr. Prose sat quietly watching him with his hands folded in front of him. The moment he had left the room, he could hear the scratching of a quill on parchment resume.

Jefferson departed the manor estate, understanding fully why he had been summoned there. The warning was clear. Stay to task or suffer the consequences. He cursed himself for being foolish enough to believe that Mr. Prose wouldn't know. Then and there he vowed to himself that he would not let his feelings get in the way—no matter what.

FOURTEEN

———◆———

THE GRAVEYARD AND THE SPIRITS

Several weeks passed and Chip found himself becoming quite attached to the young girl. Her face was almost completely healed, and she had gained several pounds. It made him happy to see that the girl was doing well, though he wasn't certain what to do next. Trust was a valuable commodity those days and he was in short supply. He wanted to trust Mary, to tell her about Isabella. Several times he had considered telling her during his visits, but decided against it, lest she slip while speaking with Ms. Douglas.

Gregor Malone's Inn posed another option for refuge, but Chip knew that if Malone was caught harboring a runaway orphan he would be in dire straits. The same was to be said for Jonah. He could lose everything, including his family. Chip knew the risks he was taking, and he wasn't about to bring that burden to anyone else.

Something else was silently nagging at him. He needed to know if Isabella's story of her fellow orphans being sold as slaves was the fantasies of an orphan making sense of things that she didn't understand or if it was the truth. While Gregor had been really shaken by the idea of challenging the owners of the orphanage, the rats had not been able to find any ships with children aboard. This left him with the burning question: *Could there truly be some illegal practices going on there?*

As Chip sat there thinking, another thought struck him. He looked around the cellar, searching for Humphrey amongst the sleeping rodents. It was morning and they had just returned from another night of scavenging.

With no signs of the little rat, Chip gave in to whispering, "Humphrey."

Immediately, Humphrey appeared near Isabella's sleeping form, his ears perked and his nose twitching.

"Come here, little friend."

Humphrey immediately dropped out of sight then scurried onto the top of the table only seconds later. "Master called?"

"Humphrey, doth ye smell things that be buried in the ground?"

"Some things. Supposing the smell be strong."

Chip sat back in his chair once more as he mulled over this sudden new idea. As insane as it sounded inside his head, if it worked it would wipe away any doubts he had about Isabella's story. "Humphrey, we need to go—"

"Ye be leaving?" Isabella interrupted, wiping the sleep from her eyes as she sat up on the side of the cot.

"We shall be back shortly child," Chip said, standing up. "There be something that I need to see about."

Isabella merely nodded. Chip extended his arm and

Humphrey immediately scurried up his sleeve and onto his shoulder.

"Where be we going?" Humphrey asked, his claws clutching to Chip's coat.

"There be something I need to be sure of."

Can me little friend possibly tell me whether there be orphaned children buried in St. Anthony's? Chip mulled over his new thought as he navigated the bustling streets of Leith. Even if the boxes were indeed empty, who would believe him? If he dug up the graves to check, he would be arrested for certain. Somehow, before he sought the assistance of the gentlemen in red, he needed to assure himself that what Isabella had told him was real.

———◆———

Chip arrived back at the graveyard, entering this time through the main gates. Humphrey remained nestled out of sight under his coat collar. He carefully looked all around, but there was no sign of any life inside the grounds, human or other.

He searched the grounds, looking for something that might guide him in the right direction. St. Anthony's wasn't a small cemetery, having grown over time to accommodate the ever-increasing number of deceased. Due to the patchwork of growth, St. Anthony's was more of a labyrinth than graveyard, with tree lines isolating one area from another.

Chip was sure that the orphanage would not make

headstones for the graves. *Would there be any markers at all or just small disturbances in the ground,* he wondered. Fortunately, the little snow that had fallen in the past week was all but gone, burnt away by the sun.

"Master, what be it that ye be looking for?" Humphrey asked, his nose twitching as he clutched to Chip's shoulder.

"I need assurance what the young lass believes be true."

"Doth ye not believe what the mongrel pup hath told ye?"

"Children sometimes make up stories to deal with death," Chip explained quietly. "I need to know what this be."

"Why not ask those that search for her?"

"I hath been given good reason not to trust them," he whispered, turning the corner of another tree line. "Be they not the mongrels ye deemed bad?"

"Aye. They be bad to mongrel pups. Doth ye believe that they be bad to grown mongrels as well?"

"Aye, I do," he sighed, remembering that he and his little friend didn't see the world the same.

"Be ye not afraid then that they might harm ye?"

Chip was deliberating how to answer when he saw what he had been looking for. There, at the end of this section of the cemetery was rows of small mounds, each with a rock to mark their placings. He bit his lower lip as he began to count the mounds. At least fifty such graves, all in tight groupings, lined the edge of the section of graveyard where he now stood.

"I believe we hath found what we be searching for."

Humphrey became quite still on his shoulder as they approached the mounds. He knew that his little friend was staying alert for the first sign of the 'bad mongrels'. Chip knelt and brushed his hand over a mound of dirt. It had been there for a while, though not completely settled. *This ground be stirred within the past year.*

"Master? Be ye well?"

"Aye, me little friend," Chip replied, stroking Humphrey's fur with a finger. "I hath spent too much time in me life in and about graveyards such as this."

"Why stay in these places, if ye not care for them?"

Chip rubbed his face, smirking at Humphrey's innocent question. "Many years ago, me father passed. I would go and visit his grave every week for years. Whenever I knew not what to do, I would go and sit by his headstone. Mary, me wife—err mate, would always know where to find me. She would drag me home and lecture me about letting go."

"Letting go?" Humphrey repeated. "Of what, Master?"

"It be what a mongrel saith when we think about the troubles of our past too much. I be really close to me father as a child and I wanted to be like just him. Did ye know ye father, Humphrey?"

"Me sire, Master?"

"Aye."

"Nay. He be dead before I be birthed."

Chip felt a bit of sadness for his little friend. He understood that the pack be his family, but he wondered if rats felt the same emotions as humans.

"Master, why doth ye wish to be like yer sire?"

"All mongrel pups wish to be like their sires, Humphrey. Even when we sire be bad."

"Was ye sire a good mongrel?"

"Aye. He would work without stop, so that there be food for every mongrel in me town. If ye had money to pay, he would take it. If ye hath not money, ye would hath food as well."

"Master, how did ye sire pass?"

Chip sighed as the memories swept over him. "One night, me father disappeared. It be days before the mongrels of me town found his body. He be face down in Cleary's Creek."

"Did a bad mongrel hurt him?"

"I believe someone did, though the other mongrels of me town believed otherwise. See, me father fell victim to drink. The mongrels of me town believed me father fell into the creek and couldn't pull himself out."

"Ye sire drowned while drinking from a creek?" Humphrey repeated. "I not believe it either, Master."

Chip laughed out loud, having to cover his mouth lest any heard his outburst. He wiped his eyes then looked at his tiny friend. "Aye. I not believe it either. Enough of me wallowing." Chip studied the ground before him. "Tell me, little friend, doth ye smell what be in the ground?"

Humphrey scurried down Chip's arm and hopped onto the brown grass that surrounded the graves. He watched as the rat

257

walked slowly around the mound.

"Nay, Master. I not smell beneath the grass."

Chip frowned as tried to think of a way that he could determine what was in the graves without digging up the ground. While he knelt there thinking, he absentmindedly watched the small rat run up and down the rows of graves, stopping at each mound.

"Master!" Humphrey shouted, running back to him. "I found fresh digging!"

"What hath ye found?" Chip asked, turning his attention to the little rodent spinning in circles before him.

"Fresh digging! The earth be soft enough to dig!"

Chip furrowed his brow. "Be ye saying that ye might dig down to the grave below?"

"Aye!" Humphrey replied excitedly.

He followed the small rodent over to a mound near the end of the last row. Like the others, all that marked the mound was a rock, no markings to signify who or what was buried there. Without waiting for instruction, Humphrey immediately began to dig, burrowing into the ground. Chip watched, thoroughly amazed at how fast the young rat could tunnel its way into the earth. After only a minute or so, he watched the rat's tail disappear from view.

Several minutes passed as he waited for Humphrey to return. Just when he began to worry if something had happened to his little friend, a twitching nose appeared at the edge of the hole. Humphrey reemerged, shaking the dirt from his coat and stretching.

"What did ye find?"

"Master, there be nothing but wood beneath the earth."

"Wood?"

"Aye. It be the same as what ye mongrels use to carry things."

"Did ye look inside the wooden box?" Chip asked, trying not sound impatient.

"I chewed me way inside. There be nothing inside the ... what ye call wooden box."

He had secretly hoped that the grave would contain a body and that Isabella's story was nothing more than an orphan dealing with death. Now that he knew her story was true, he faced his next obstacle. Empty graves were only one part of the puzzle set before him. Now, he needed proof that the orphans of St. Thaddeus were being sold to the Americas as slaves. He was tempted to chuck the rock that marked the empty grave over the nearest tree line.

"I doth well, Master?"

"Aye," Chip replied, keeping the growl from his voice "ye did well. Come," he extended his arm to the small rat, "let us rejoin yer pack and the young girl. I hath much thinking to do."

Humphrey scurried back up his arm and sat upon his shoulder. Chip then rose and slowly made his way back through the cemetery, towards the cobbled streets beyond. As he walked, a mixture of resolve and anger swept through him. Isabella and the children of St. Thaddeus needed someone to help them. As of that moment, he knew he might be their only hope.

———◆———

Chip turned onto the street in the south of Leith and stopped dead in his tracks, staring at the shop door swinging slightly on its broken hinges. He eased closer, looking for any signs of stirrings within. Slowly, he made his way around the corner and over the back wall into the courtyard behind the shop. He could barely feel his heart beat within his chest as he stared at the open cellar door. Mustering all his resolve, he clinched his fists and dashed into the cellar, ready for a fight. Unfortunately, all he found waiting for him was some of Humphrey's pack.

"Where be the girl?" Chip demanded, staring at the rats before him.

"The mongrel pup ran," a fat gray rat replied.

"Where did she go?"

"We heard a scream and then the mongrel pup be gone," the Master rat replied, sitting on the table. "We know not where the pup be."

"What happened before the girl fled?"

"We smelt a mongrel," a thin brown rat replied, climbing up onto the back of a chair.

"We heard footsteps in the above mongrel dwelling," the Master rat interjected.

Chip did not need any further answers. He knew what had happened.

"Shouldn't hath left the lass so long!" he growled, storming out of the cellar. *The men from the orphanage couldn't hath found her here. Someone else must hath come and claimed her.*

He searched for several minutes, but the streets were as vacant of her presence as the graves he and Humphrey had found. The small rat sat perched on his shoulder, constantly sniffing the air. He knew that his tiny friend searched for her as well.

"The mongrel pup not be here, Master."

"Aye. The question be, where she be now?"

"Would she return to the mongrel dwelling that she came from, Master?"

"Nay. At least not of her own free will. Though I hath not a doubt that it be where they take her. It shan't be long before they discover she be an orphan."

Chip walked back into the cellar. He looked down to see Humphrey's pack gathered together in front of him. "Ye rats want me to provide more food?"

"Aye!" the rats chorused in unison.

"Then ye shall assist me in finding the young mongrel girl. Master rat, I be needing several of ye scouts to come with me and Humphrey. The rest of yer pack need to search for the young mongrel girl."

Chip watched as four rats hesitantly scurried around his boots.

"Mongrel Chip, these rats shall go with thee and the rat ye call Humphrey,. They shall fulfill yer biddings. The rest of the pack shall search for yer mongrel pup."

"Thank ye, Master rat. Should ye find her, hide her and send for me. She shall follow ye. She believes ye to be her friends."

It sounded like rushing water as Chip watched as the large black rat and the rest of the pack scurried up the cellar stairs, up the flue pipe and out whatever crack they could find. Soon, only Humphrey and the four rats that sat near his boots remained.

Chip turned his head to look at Humphrey. "We shall visit the orphan dwelling."

"Master, ye shall go inside?" the tiny rat asked, sounding concerned.

"Should it be necessary. First, ye scouts shall enter."

"I shall go too, Master. I be a scout for me pack as well."

Chip nodded to his little friend. He wasn't sure how rodents measured courage, but he counted Humphrey as brave.

———◆———

Chip left the south of Leith, making his way up the streets towards the orphanage. He hoped that Humphrey's pack would find the girl hiding in some abandoned building. Deep down though, he knew what had happened and wondered if he would find her before something dire transpired.

Humphrey decided to hide beneath his coat collar while the four scouting rats followed in the shadows, staying close to the trees, shrubs and buildings. The number of passersby grew the closer they drew to the docks. He would have to be subtler about how he communicated with the rodents, lest someone thought him mad.

"Master!" Humphrey shouted, sticking his head out from beneath his coat collar.

A woman jerked at the sudden emergence of the small rat. Chip smiled and nodded to the woman, who looked to be appalled by the sight.

"Stay hidden beneath me coat," Chip whispered.

"Master! Look ahead," Humphrey hissed, ducking back out of sight. "It be the mongrel that be looking for the pup."

Chip scanned the street ahead and sure enough, the thin weedy looking man from the night he found Isabella walked several paces ahead of them.

Chip slowed his pace and decided to follow him. "Excellent work me little friend."

The man walked at a casual gate. Several times he stopped to peer into a shop window, looking as though the weight of the world had been lifted from his shoulders.

"This not be a good sign," Chip breathed aloud.

A few minutes later, the weedy man checked his pocket watch and abruptly increased his pace, no longer stopping to look about. *He must hath forgotten something,* Chip thought, hurrying to catch up.

Chip kept his distance, focused upon his prey, hoping that he might lead him to Isabella. It wasn't until the smell of fresh fish caught his attention, did he realize where the man had led him. They were near the all too familiar fish market. He had passed it countless times while headed to the docks. *The orphanage be near, but why would he stray this close to the water –*, Chip pondered, puzzled by this. *Unless the orphanage not be his destination!*

His momentary distraction nearly cost him, looking around just in time to see the man slip around the corner of a warehouse. Chip hurried to catch up, turning the corner and almost losing his footing on the wet pier. Fortunately, his prey was far enough ahead not to hear him grunt.

He watched as the weedy man made his way up a gang plank, boarding a cargo ship. Chip eased along the edge of the granite wall, drawing as close as he could to the ship without being seen. The man stood just topside, speaking with one of the ship's crew members. The weedy man handed a roll of parchment to the crew member before making his way back off the ship. The man spread his arms like wings to balance himself while he crossed the gang plank, his carefree attitude returning.

Chip slumped low between two stacks of crates, allowing the man to pass, before easing out to follow him. This time he had no question where the man was headed, the steeple of St. Thaddeus rising into sight as they walked up a small hillside street.

When the man reached the orphanage, he knocked smartly upon the door and waited. Chip drew close to a large tree to watch, peering around its thick trunk. Moments later, a Nun answered, allowing the man to enter. Chip rubbed his forehead in frustration, looking down to see the scouts from Humphrey's pack huddled together between his boots and the trunk of the tree, awaiting instruction.

"I must know whether the mongrel pup that be with us this morning be in that mongrel dwelling," Chip whispered, kneeling to address the rats.

"Master, doth ye wish for us to enter the mongrel dwelling?" Humphrey asked, crawling out from underneath Chip's collar.

"Aye. Might ye this for me?"

"We know ways inside that mongrels not follow," one of the scouts said. "The mongrel pup shall not be able to return with us."

"I understand. All I ask of ye be to see whether she be there."

"We shall search the mongrel dwelling, Master. Should she be inside, we shall find her."

"I shall wait here for thee, little friend."

Chip watched as Humphrey and the scouts scurried away towards the orphanage. He silently dreaded what they might find inside.

The sound of a door opening caught his attention. He straightened back up so that the tree would hide him from view. He could hear voices and peered around to see the weedy man leaving the orphanage, being escorted out by the same Nun. Chip bit his lip, deciding to do something potentially risky. He straightened his coat and casually stepped out from behind the tree and on to the path that led to the orphanage. Neither the man nor the Nun saw where he came from, being too preoccupied by their own conversation.

"Good day to ye," Chip said, clearly startling the man.

"Good day young man," the Nun said, greeting him warmly. "I be Sister Carmylle. What might we for ye?"

"Young man," Chip scoffed, flashing the gentleman. "Ye flatter me, Sister. I be not a young man for many years. I be round concerning the young lass that was missing."

"Missing?" Sister Carmylle repeated in a shocked tone. "I know not what ye speak of, sir."

"Really," Chip said, tilting his head to one side. "It be this gentleman here that be looking for a young lass. It be several weeks ago, indeed, but it crossed me mind when I saw St. Thaddeus."

"Sir, I know not of what you speak," the weedy man snipped, drawing himself up to his full height. "We have never met before, sir. You have me confused with someone else."

"Nay sir," Chip retorted, setting his jaw. "I remember clearly. It be ye that be looking for a young lass. Ye looked quite worried indeed."

"Young man," the weedy man's face contorting into a sneer, "you and I have never met before. To even suggest that I would be searching the streets for a lost sandy child is absurd!"

"Sir," Sister Carmylle interjected calmly "there not be any children missing from the orphanage. Ye must be mistaken."

"Me apologies." Chip nodded to Sister Carmylle and the infuriated man. "It must hath been another gentleman," His eyes locked with the man's cold soulless brown eyes, "for I not imagine the flash of a gentleman before me caring for a child."

Sister Carmylle's eyes went wide at his statement, glancing nervously from Chip to the man.

"Sir," the weedy man breathed, "I have much compassion for the children of St. Thaddeus. They did not choose to be abandoned by their fathers over a lost cause."

"Indeed," Chip said, his contempt for the man showing on his face. "When we remember why, we must remember all that hath happened to lead to this unfortunate circumstance."

"Indeed," the weedy man replied, straightening the ruffles of his shirt. "Shall I see you to the gate?"

"Thank ye, but I believe that I shall find me way. Good day to ye both." Chip nodded once more, then curtly turned on one heel and made his way back down the path, not daring to look back.

———•———

Humphrey hurried through the tall blades of grass, keeping his senses keen for the first sign of danger. As he approached the orphanage, the other scouts broke off, each going in a different direction.

He paused at the edge of the tall grass line before quickly

making his way over to an iron grate, slipping between the bars. The dark narrow shaft beyond stretched onward and upward. Humphrey moved quickly, following the path that he had traveled before. He had passed through this place many times, watching the mongrels clean their coverings. As the shaft began to shift downward, he slowed his pace so that he would not slip and fall into one of the hot tubs of water which sat below.

He reached the end of the shaft, slipping through another iron grate and easing out onto a small ledge that ran the length of the room. He could see several mongrel pups below, tending to the wash. None were the mongrel pup he sought. He continued around the edge of the room until he came to a doorway at the top of a flight of steps. He slipped under the door and into a long empty hallway. He quickly sniffed for any signs of danger, but there were no immediate threats about.

Suddenly, he heard footsteps coming his way and smelt the distinct odor of mongrels. He ducked under a nearby table and watched, shaking slightly, as two mongrels entered the hallway. They were laughing and sounded happy. As they drew closer, Humphrey could begin to make out what they were saying.

"How many more of the sandy filth is left?" the first mongrel man asked.

"There are enough," the second mongrel man replied. "At a hundred pounds a head, we shall find more when needed."

The first mongrel grasped the second by the shoulder, halting their progression several feet from where Humphrey laid silently.

"I understand many things, and am not naive to what we do. However, how might you guarantee that there shall be more to sell?"

"Do not ask questions that you do not want answers to, Blake. Besides, plague and fighting shall provide more than enough. Dogs shall tear one another apart over scraps of meat if there is no one to pull them apart."

The two mongrels laughed as they continued down the hallway, away from Humphrey. He didn't know why, but he knew that the way to find the mongrel pup was to go the way the mongrels had come. He scurried down the hallway, an aroma reaching his nose that made his fur stand up. Blood. Not alluring, like the smell of old blood was. No promise of a meal lingered with it. Whatever animal was bleeding still be alive. Hunting for the source of the smell, he found that it became stronger the closer he got to the end of the hallway. He reached the end, finding it blocked by another door. Beyond that door, the aroma of mongrels and blood overwhelmed his senses.

Easing under the door, Humphrey quickly hid under the first thing he could find. A mongrel man sat in the chair he chose and it sounded as though he was eating. Looking about the room, Humphrey could see several mongrels standing in a circle, conversing quietly. A small gasp caught his attention. He looked over to the far corner of the room to see the mongrel pup bound to a chair, her arm bleeding. She looked directly at him. Humphrey shrank close to the wall, lest the bad mongrels noticed him as well.

"Listen filth," one of the mongrels growled, turning from the circle to face the pup. "You were gone for weeks. Found looking quite healthy for a sandy gutter. You were with someone. Tell us who!"

The mongrel pup shook with fear as she stammered, "N-Nay, sir. I n-n-not be—"

"How many more times have us to ask her the same questions?" another mongrel man asked. "The little filth hath answered the same every time. I grow tired of this."

"You shall remember your place, Berkley! There is too much at stake, lest she ruin it!"

"I admire your attention to details, James," came a voice that made Humphrey shiver as the door to the room opened. "However, I do not believe that the young lass has anything more to tell you—do you child."

Humphrey looked up, not sure what to expect. Another mongrel man had entered the room, though he did not smell the same. The aroma of death which followed him, combined with his emotionless tone, made Humphrey want to flee.

"N-Nay sir," the mongrel pup replied.

"See," the mongrel quipped, stepping further into the room. His walking stick clicked against the floor, sending shivers up Humphrey's spine. "The lass shakes from pain and has a fresh wound. She shall not fetch much a price in her condition."

"We should send her as well?" another mongrel asked.

"What would you do with her?" the mongrel asked, tapping his walking stick on the floor impatiently.

"N-Nothing, my Lord," the mongrel man replied, looking at the floor.

"It's settled then. We all have things to tend to" the mongrel with the walking stick turned, and in a frightening move, looked directly at Humphrey, "and tasks to perform."

"Tasks?" one of the mongrels repeated, sounding confused.

The mongrel with the walking stick turned back to address the question and Humphrey wasted no time exiting the room. He hurried as fast as he could away from the room and that mongrel. Following the path that he knew well, he reached the outdoors once more, hoping to never have to enter that mongrel dwelling ever again.

He reached the tall grass to find the other scouts waiting for him. "Found the pup. Hurry! We must tell me Master!"

———◦———

Chip walked away from the orphanage, knowing the weedy man and Sister Carmylle were watching him. He walked until the orphanage was out of sight, before rounding back to the tree. He was certain that Isabella had been caught and returned here. Now, he just had to wait for Humphrey and the scouts to return and inform him as to whether she still be alive.

Nearly a half hour later, the scurrying of small animals

through the tall blades of grass caught his attention. Chip knelt as Humphrey and the four pack scouts approached his boots.

"Did ye find her?"

"Aye, Master. The mongrel pup be there, and she be alive."

"Well done, me tiny friend. Be she in danger?"

"The bad mongrels hath her bound. They be asking her questions. She not be telling them of ye. Another … mongrel with a walking stick entered and told the other mongrels to mend to her wounds. They be sending her away."

Chip sat back on his haunches as he pondered what to do next. *They must be sending her to the Americas aboard that ship*, he thought. *That roll of parchment must hath been shipping orders. If I could get me hands upon it, the authorities would be forced to believe me.*

"What doth ye wish for us to do, Master?"

"Ye hath done well little friend. It be me task to perform now. I must stow aboard the vessel that the mongrel we followed here boarded at the wharf. I must retrieve what he delivered to the mongrels."

Chip still felt odd referring to people as mongrels. However, when speaking of the weedy man and anyone who would knowingly sell children as slaves, the name fit.

"I shall go with thee, Master."

"Very well," Chip said, extending his arm so that Humphrey could climb up. "Ye must remain hidden under me coat collar or in a pocket."

"We shall travel with thee as well," one of the scouts said, looking up at him.

"Whether ye wish," Chip said, nodding solemnly to the rats.

A feeling of dread passed over him at the thought of what he was about to do. He shrugged away the feeling and resolved himself to do what he must in order to rescue Isabella from her prison.

FIFTEEN

———·◆·———

SHADOWS OF INVERNESS

Chip set off for the shoreline, retracing his steps back to the vessel. He hated leaving Isabella in the bowels of that place, but he knew that the best way to help her was to end this slave trade. Once he retrieved the parchment, he would seek out Captain Sinclair. Though he was no longer a member of the Royal Navy, Captain Sinclair was an Englishman and would have influence amongst the English soldiers.

His newfound confidence wavered as he approached the ship. Boarding without being caught wasn't going to be easy. He waited until dusk fell in earnest, the distant sunset casting a red glow across the bay. The reduced visibility allowed for Chip to edge closer to the vessel. He watched the dockers work, loading the ship with bags of grain and other supplies.

"When might I be going ashore?"

Chip looked up to see one of the crew members leaning against the ship's railing.

"Ye be ashore only this morning," another man answered,

just out of Chip's view, "and yer chores still not be done."

"Ye not be the Captain or the first mate," the crew member spat. "Ye not be telling me what to do!"

The two men begin to scuffle. Amazed by his good fortune, he took hold of a bag of grain and tossed it over his free shoulder. He followed a docker up the gang plank and onto the ship, keeping the grain bag high on his shoulder to hide his face.

The crew members and dockers were too busy watching the fight to even notice him sit the grain bag down and slip into the captain's quarters. Looking about carefully for any signs of life, Chip eased in, quickly making his way to the captain's desk. He knew that the parchment would be there somewhere. He shuffled through the parchments while keeping an eye out. If necessary, he would fling himself out the cabin window and into the waters below.

"What's going on here!"

Chip jumped as the shout echoed against the cabin door. He knew he was in trouble. He was about to forget what he came for and take his chances with the waters below when he found it. He unrolled a parchment and immediately his heart sank.

MANIFEST of cargo taken aboard the Nomas of Leith, Scotland whereof Captain Clark is Master, burthen 119 Tons, to be transported to the Port of Boston for the purpose of being sold or disposed of.

42 Barrels, Contents Thereof is Tea

12 Barrels, Contents Thereof is Whiskey

14 Barrels, Contents Thereof is Tobacco

16 Barrels, Contents Thereof is Sugar

25 Crates, Contents Thereof is Infantry Riffles

We, do solemnly, sincerely, and truly swear, to the best of our knowledge and belief, that the goods above specified, were not imported to the Colonies illegally and do not stand in contrast with the Navigation Act—So help us God.

Sworn to this Before

Sir James Blake

District and Port of Leith Scotland

Master of the Nomas,

Having sworn as the Laws directs, to the above Manifest, consisting of only legally traded goods, Permission is hereby granted to proceed to the Port of Boston.

Given under our hands to the Port of Boston,

The manifest spoke nothing of slaves. Chip inwardly cursed himself for thinking that the manifest would contain any information regarding illegal trade. *It would be foolish to keep such records, even if the recipient in Boston be in on the deal.*

"I still need to sign that."

Chip dared not look up to see whom had entered the cabin. He immediately rolled up the parchment and placed it back on the desk.

"Me apologies, Captain Clark," Chip said, straightening the desk. "Ye weren't aboard and the wharf master asked me to verify that the contents of the manifest matched the goods that we be loading in the hull. All be as it should."

Chip kept his head low and nodded to the Captain. He made to pass the man, but a hand caught his chest. Chip looked down and saw a glimpse of what looked like a star on the man's wrist, peeking out just beyond a ruffled sleeve. He remembered seeing the exact same mark only weeks ago on the wrist of the weedy Englishman. As though a dam had broken, the memory of the same mark on Mr. Tomlin's wrist from all those years ago flooded his mind.

"You are not a good liar," the Captain said, a hint of mirth in his voice.

Chip refused to make eye contact with the man. "Liar?"

"Yes, Mr. MacDougall."

The man shoved him backwards. Chip regained his footing, only to find himself staring down the barrel of a pistol. He looked up at the man for the first time, only to fall to one knee as he stared into the face of a dead man.

"Surprised to see me, Mr. MacDougall?"

"Ye be dead!" Chip exclaimed, staring into the eyes of Captain O'Toole's former first mate, Mr. Kellogg.

"You thought me dead, Mr. MacDougall?" Mr. Kellogg scoffed. "Tell me, did you mourn my passing?"

"How did ye survive? Did the crew throw ye overboard?"

"Throw me overboard?" Mr. Kellogg repeated, tilting his head to one side. "Are you inferring that the mutinous crew threw me overboard before we fired upon the *Ottoman*?"

"Ye betrayed Captain O'Toole!"

"Now you are catching up, Mr. MacDougall," Mr. Kellogg laughed. "For an uneducated man, you're a fast study. I heard that Captain O'Toole made you his first mate while up in Inverness. Should have stayed on after you returned to Leith."

"Lay down yer popper and I shall mourn yer death again, blaggard!" Chip growled, clinching his hands into fists, the blood thundering in his ears.

"Very poor form indeed, Mr. MacDougall," Mr. Kellogg sighed as three crew members hurried into the cabin. "Take hold of him! He has threatened your captain."

The three burly men moved past Mr. Kellogg to apprehend Chip. Two of the men, one bald with a long beard and the other sporting a long ponytail, grasped him by the arms and forced him back to his feet. The third man stood behind him, just beyond his view.

"How could ye betray Captain O'Toole?" Chip asked, struggling against his captors. "Ye were his first mate!"

"Touching," Mr. Kellogg simpered, placing his pistol back in the waist line of his breeches. "We may speak freely, Mr. MacDougall. You shall not bring any revelations to my crew. They know who I am. As for the dear Captain O'Toole. He's a good man, indeed. Loyal to his people and to his homeland. I do miss his witty remarks and bold speeches."

"Ye be an Englishman. Why join the Jacobites?"

"Come now, Mr. MacDougall. The crew aboard the *Persica* believed such, but you should know better."

"Why then?"

"Gold, Mr. MacDougall." Captain Kellogg and his crew chuckled darkly. "I was offered a captain's seat as a privateer. All I had to do was assist the Jacobites in overthrowing the *Persica*. A fair trade should you consider it. The pay of a first mate in the Royal Navy is fair, but the pay of a privateer captain, transporting trade goods to the Americas is where the money lies. Living as Captain Clark is but a small inconvenience by comparison."

"I respected ye! I thought about ye when the Captain made me his first mate! It felt wrong as ye should hath still been there!"

"Again … touching. Now, I would offer you a place aboard the *Nomas*. Unfortunately, I see that you wouldn't find the post accommodating."

Captain Kellogg walked past him. The two men holding him forced Chip to turn and face the desk.

"Scottish children be valuable trade goods to ye?" Chip growled.

"Slaves are always valuable trade, Mr. MacDougall. You shall bring a decent price yourself. Gentlemen, escort Mr. MacDougall to his new quarters. You shall love America, Mr. MacDougall. Supposing you're civil, we might even let you out so that you might enjoy your last voyage."

He continued to glare at the man he had once considered a friend. He wanted to break free and strangle him until the smirk was gone from his face. He struggled against the men holding him, but their grip was too strong.

The men forcefully removed Chip from the cabin, dragging him across the deck and down below into the hull. They stopped to gather up some rope and Humphrey appeared from under his collar. Faster than he could blink, Humphrey struck out and bit the hand of the bald man that was holding onto his arm. The other man shrieked in pain as the scouts from Humphrey's pack attacked the legs of his captors, just above their boots.

Chip hesitated before grabbing a loose plank and striking both men in the face, knocking them out cold. He waited for a moment at the ready, but none came to their aide.

"Thank ye me little friends."

"Hurry Master! Let us leave."

Chip nodded as Humphrey quickly scurried up to his shoulder. He hurried up to the deck, preparing to fight his way out. To his fortune, the path was clear to the gang plank. Several crew members gaped openly as he dashed past, headed for the side of the ship. A boar-faced sea-crab with massive arms lunged for him, barely missing.

Shoving an unfortunate docker off the gang plank, he crossed it in a single stride, sprinting as fast as he could through the wharf. Shouts and the sound of boots echoed behind him, but faded after several minutes. He dared not look back until he reached the safety of O'Bryan's tavern.

Reaching his room, he quickly gathered up some belongings, tucking them into his haversack. Barely an hour ago he had considered seeking out Captain Sinclair for assistance. Now, there was only one man he could trust that could help him—and silently, he prayed he would be able to find him in time.

———•———

"Captain Clark, Sir!" the *Nomas'* first mate exclaimed, bursting into the captain' quarters.

"What's the trouble, Mr. Bead?"

"The Scot has escaped."

Mr. Kellogg threw a glass of whiskey across the room, shattering against the wall.

"What should we do?" Mr. Bead asked, unfazed by his captain's reaction.

Captain Kellogg regained his composure. "Nothing."

"Nothing?" Mr. Bead repeated, his brow furrowed. "Sir, I do not understand. Suppose he should tell the authorities of what we are doing?"

Captain Kellogg sighed as he sat back into his chair. "What shall Mr. MacDougall tell them? That the captain of the *Nomas* is really the former deceased first mate of the *Ottoman*? That I was going to abduct him? Sell him into slavery in the Americas? None shall believe such a story, especially without proof."

"Very well, sir. What shall I do with the two that let him escape?"

"Send them to me," Captain Kellogg replied, a scowl covering his face. "I shall then decide what is to be done with them."

"Very good, sir." Mr. Bead left in haste to fetch the two seamen that had allowed Chip to go free. Captain Kellogg contemplated the sudden appearance of Mr. MacDougall and whether to report his presence aboard the ship. Shuddering at the thought of how 'they' might react, he fetched himself another glass of whiskey. The door to his cabin flung open and Mr. Bead forcefully shoved the two men inside, wearing a nasty grin.

"Here are the two, Captain."

"Thank you, Mr. Bead. You may go."

Mr. Bead nodded before turning to leave the cabin, slamming the door behind him. Mr. Kellogg rose from his chair and slowly made his way around his desk so that he could look the two failures in the eyes.

"Explain," he demanded, his voice quiet yet fierce.

"Sir, he caught us unaware," the bald man said, stoking his beard nervously.

"Unaware? You were supposed to be escorting him to the brig!"

"We were, sir," the long-haired man said, looking fearful.

"He be quicker and stronger than he appears."

"Stronger and quicker than he appears. This is the excuse that you bring to me?"

"It—it be the truth, sir," the bald man replied hesitantly.

"Mr. MacDougall's a topping man. Are you sure that he didn't pay you two to let him go?"

"Sir! We would never—" the long haired man began, but fell silent when the Captain held up his hand.

"Too bad," Captain Kellogg sighed, looking disappointed. "It would have been a better excuse that what you have brought to me. At least it would have made up for the wages that you shall not see for this voyage."

"Please sir," the long-haired man pleaded, "give us one more chance to prove our worth."

Captain Kellogg resisted the urge to smirk, standing there for several minutes in silence while scowling at the two men. He wanted them to sweat a little.

"I shall give you two one more chance," Captain Kellogg growled. "Fail me again and it shall not be your wages that you need concern yourself with."

"Aye, sir!" the men said in unison.

"Then get back to your chores! We have a voyage to prepare for!"

The two men fled for the door, shoving each other as they tried to exit the cabin at the same time. Captain Kellogg shook his head at the total lack of character and intelligence that the men displayed. He knew that Captain O'Toole would have run most of this crew through with the blade before even considering bringing them aboard one of his ships. They were a mix of thieves and lotmen of every sort. The qualifications necessary to be aboard the *Nomas*.

———◆———

Chip stared up at his destination. Whether it was a blessed sight or another curse upon his soul, he wasn't sure. All he knew was that the man that he sought was somewhere within. Nothing stood between him and his destination now, but his own apprehensions. He felt Humphrey stir beneath his collar and he knew that the tiny rat could sense his dread. Making up his mind, Chip approached the *Ottoman* and slowly walked up the sloping gang plank.

"Might I help you?" a man hailed, approaching Chip as he stepped onto the deck of the *Ottoman*. "Mr. MacDougall? Is that you?"

"Aye, Mr. Barrett. It be me."

"Good to see you again!" Mr. Barrett shook Chip's hand and smiled broadly. "What brings you aboard the *Ottoman*?"

"I hath come to see the Captain. Be he aboard?"

"Aye! He shall be delighted to see you! I shall let him know that you be aboard!"

Mr. Barrett hurried away towards the captain's quarters.

Shall he be happy to see me once he hath heard what I hath to say, Chip wondered.

"Mr. MacDougall!" Captain O'Toole hailed, clapping his hands as he emerged from his quarters. "To what doth I owe the honor of ye presence so soon since yer departure?"

Stepping forward, he shook Captain O'Toole's hand before being pulled into a half embrace. He forced a smile, though he didn't feel that he deserved such a welcome.

"Might we speak in private?"

"Of course, lad. As long as we doth share a round of whiskey."

Chip nodded in agreement, thinking that more rounds might be necessary after he heard what he had to say. The Captain wasted no time pouring them both a glass of whiskey from his private stock. Chip laid his haversack down then took a seat in front of the Captain's desk. He was surprised when Captain O'Toole pulled over another chair and sat down across from him.

"Me desk be for meetings and a bloody good way to intimidate me crew," Captain O'Toole said, as he took a sip from his glass. "This be how I speak to me friends. Tell me, what brings ye to see me at this late hour of the day?"

Chip took a deep breath and told his former captain all that had happened since he had left the *Ottoman*—omitting Humphrey and the rats. Captain O'Toole didn't interrupt, even when he spoke of Mr. Kellogg. He listened with his hands folded around his glass of whiskey, the look upon his face impossible to understand.

Once Chip finished his tale, Captain O'Toole continued to sit silently. Without uttering a word, he finished his glass in one, rose to his feet, poured himself another glass, then returned, bringing the bottle with him. While waiting for the Captain to speak, he could feel the tension mounting in his chest.

"Hath ye come to me for advice or for me help?" Captain O'Toole asked, breaking the strained silence and weighing his words carefully.

"Forgive me, Captain—"

"Call me Joseph, lad," Captain O'Toole interrupted. "It be what me friends call me."

"Forgive me … Joseph, but did ye not hear what I saith? Mr. Kellogg, ye former first mate, still be alive."

"I heard ye," Captain O'Toole replied, taking another sip from his glass. "Mr. Kellogg's continued existence be news to me, but not shocking. Nor be it that he be living under a new name. He would be considered a traitor to the Royal Navy should he be found. What be shocking be that he be living a lotman's life in the north of Leith."

"What doth ye think of orphans being sold into slavery?"

Captain O'Toole sighed, "This not be uncommon these days. It be illegal. There be not any question of that. The trouble be, what be ye resolve? Ye be a topping man, memory serves me. Hath ye not tried the power of persuasion?"

"I doth not believe that me wealth would help. The blaggards that be the heads of this I hear be powerful and of the topping."

Captain O'Toole sighed again, sinking back into his chair. Chip could tell that he wasn't taking this lightly.

"Could ye not report Mr. Kellogg being alive to the Navy?"

"Nay, lad. Should Mr. Kellogg be serving as the captain of a vessel here in Leith, the local authorities be on the cuff. Besides, me being a vocal Scot not hold well to get the attentions of Parliament."

"A vocal Scot?"

"Aye. I voiced me opinion a little too loudly over we Scots being banned from wearing our kilts. I received a scolding from me commanding officer for speaking me peace. I be surprised I still be the captain of the *Ottoman*."

Chip took off his cap, brushing his hand through his hair and blowing out a puff of air in frustration.

"Ye doth not drink enough whiskey," Captain O'Toole chuckled.

"Forgive me, sir, but how doth me drinking habits affluence me problem?"

"Should ye drink more, lad, ye would not be so stressed when problems arise. Not saying that ye need to cut the leg. Just enough to remove the edge." He drained another glass, admiring something in the bottom before continuing, "As for yer problem … how be it yers to begin with?"

"I told ye, sir."

"Aye, ye told me how ye found the lass and of her tale,"

Captain O'Toole said calmly. "Me concern be ye hath come to me, but not once hath ye mentioned yer wife. Nay, not once since ye begun hath ye mentioned yer family."

"Me whither and I be estranged. She knows not any of this."

"I see. That be why ye hath returned here tonight. Ye hath sought help from ye second family."

Chip couldn't deny it. He simply lowered his eyes to the wooden floor and waited.

"This be nothing new," Captain O'Toole continued. "Life abroad changes ye. Ye not be the first sailor to return home and all not be well. I know that ye were estranged before ye sailed with me, but I also know that ye found yer self while aboard this ship. Be it the same troubles or hath something changed while ye were away?"

"Me wife thought I perished aboard the *Persica*. None that knew me believed I had survived."

"Ye wrote yer family many times while we be in Inverness," Captain O'Toole said, causing Chip to look up in shock. "A good captain knows all that happens aboard his ship."

"Somehow, me letters never made it home."

They sat once again in silence. Chip knew that the Captain could never begin to guess all that was going on with the man that sat before him.

"Well, as for yer young orphan lass," the Captain said, breaking the silence "the law not be yer friend or yer answer. I doth not give advice lightly, but it be time that ye think like a scoundrel. I not be suggesting offing a gent, but supposing ye wait for the knobs to be of service then ye be waiting for not."

"What doth ye suggest?"

"In yer youth, did ye ever hear tales of the Shadows of Inverness?" Captain O'Toole asked, propping his arms on the rests of the chair, the whiskey beginning to serve its purpose.

"I shan't say that I did."

"Well, they be tales of Inverness's shadowy past," the Captain explained. "Me father would tell me and me brothers stories of how Clan MacKay ruled Inverness in secret. It not be until the Restoration and the rise of Charles the Second to the throne that the secret dealings of Clan MacKay with the Spanish and the French be revealed. The destruction of Cromwell's Citadel be what finally brought their secrets to light."

"Ye wish for me to destroy the orphanage?" Chip asked, smirking at his own wit.

"Not quite. Evil in any form flees the light of day. It seeks the shadows. People ignore what they shall, pretending all be well. When they not be able to deny it any longer, they shall revolt against it. Ye must find a way to bring this to the light of day. Ye know these docks. How might ye shed the light upon that which they do?"

"I know not."

Captain O'Toole pounded his fist against the chair. "Think, Chip! Think! Find the lotman inside ye. One must think like those ye fight against."

Chip sat and thought, wondering what he could possibly do to prevent Isabella and the other children from being shipped across the ocean.

"Ye grew up in a small township," Captain O'Toole quipped.

"How doth ye know that and what doth it matter?"

"Ye bear the markings, lad. Fortunately for ye, I wasn't. Inverness reared me as much as me mother and me father."

Chip watched as the Captain stood up, stretched and walked over to the wooden cabinet that enclosed the picture of St. Michael. He placed a hand on the cabinet door then turned to look at him.

"Ye spent over a year aboard this ship and under me command," Captain O'Toole continued, rubbing his face. "A portion of that time ye spent as me first mate. There be things that be needed aboard any vessel. What be they?"

"A captain, a crew and provisions," Chip recited without hesitation.

"Aye. Now, which be the easiest to off with?"

"I doth not wish to harm anyone."

"Ye doth not hath to harm anyone, lad. I said scoundrel, not murderer. Though ye be about the right path."

"Then what be ye suggesting, sir?"

"Ye need to delay the crew a bit. Wait until their special cargo be safely aboard."

"Delay them? What good be it to delay their voyage?"

"Think lad!" the Captain exclaimed, sounded slightly frustrated that Chip couldn't grasp what he was inferring. "Vessels not leave or approach port until the break of dawn. Any illegal cargo must be loaded aboard by the cover of night. Ye shall know when they be ready to sail when they board the children. Now, I assume that all the provisions be aboard the vessel, being ye sneaked on as a docker."

"Aye. There be enough provisions in the hull for a long voyage."

The Captain sighed. "That be too bad. Ye could hath burnt them or tossed them into the bay. Mr. Kellogg be not a morpus. He shall be watching carefully, lest ye return." He squinted his eyes as he thought, leaving Chip to wonder how many glasses the Captain had downed before he arrived. "That leaves the crew. Find a way to keep them from their vessel."

"They shall wish to go ashore before they sail."

"Now ye be thinking," the Captain said, walking back over to the chair he had vacated. "Delay the crew and ye shall delay the voyage."

"Ye still hath not told me what good there be in delaying their voyage."

"I might just be a worthless old Scot and seafarer to some, but I know many. Many that might take a slight to the enslavement of poor unfortunate Scottish children. Send word to me when the special cargo be aboard, and be clever about it. Delay the ship and leave the rest to me."

"Sir, should ye be discovered—"

"I be also a survivor," Captain O'Toole interrupted. "These same I know shall not turn. None shall know of me involvement. Should I be discovered, me merits shall keep me from the repository. Me life hath been filled with risks. I be too old to change now."

Chip realized that it would foolish to argue. Captain O'Toole wasn't a man that said or did anything in haste. If he was willing to help, then he had considered all the consequences.

"Thank ye, Cap—, um, Joseph," he said, standing up and tossing his haversack onto his back.

Captain O'Toole rose with him and they grasped arms—as was the custom when parting ways. He wasn't sure yet how he would delay the *Nomas'* crew from returning to the ship, but that was his task.

"Doth not think me the saint, lad. I be the vengeful sort. Mr. Kellogg be owing for the loss of the *Persica* and her crew."

"Aye," Chip agreed, nodding solemnly. "I not thank ye enough for all that ye hath done."

"It be the task of a captain. Yer crew be family. Not all be good, but that be family. I bid ye safe journey, for Mr. Kellogg shall not spare yer life twice."

Chip nodded again then turned to leave. Just as he reached the cabin door, Captain O'Toole hailed him.

"One last thing, Chip. Why the rat?"

Chip stiffened, for he had not once mentioned a rat. "Rat,

sir?"

"The one beneath yer collar," Captain O'Toole said. "Ye think that I would not notice? I know that some keep rodents as pets, but hath ye not seen enough of the little beasts?"

"I know not what to say, except I be accustomed to them."

A simple nod from Captain O'Toole told Chip that he had accepted his explanation. "There be some that be offended by yer pet. One might suggest a cage."

"This not be one for the cage," he replied, glancing down at the lump under his collar "but I shall consider what ye say."

Chip tipped his cap to the Captain and departed his quarters. Even though difficult and potentially dangerous hurdles laid ahead of him, they felt achievable knowing the Captain was on his side.

The moment his boots found the pier, Humphrey dashed down his front and onto the planks below. Before Chip could utter a word, he saw two other rats appear from behind some nearby crates.

"Master, the young mongrel hath returned!"

Chip squatted down and extended his arm, allowing Humphrey to return to his shoulder. "How?" he whispered, looking about in the darkness for signs of anyone that might be lurking. "What doth ye mean by returned? Where be she?"

"Master, I know not how. She hath returned to the pack. She be badly injured."

"Returned to the pack," Chip repeated, his mind racing and

293

his breathing shallow.

He realized that Isabella must have returned to the cellar, looking for him. He also knew that it would be the first place that the orphanage workers would look for her.

"Be she in the dwelling beneath the ground?"

"Aye, Master. She be in the mongrel dwelling that she be in before."

"Into me pocket little friend."

Humphrey obeyed immediately, scurrying into his open pocket. The moment the tiny rat was inside, Chip sprinted down the dark streets of Leith. Silently, he prayed that he reached the abandoned spirits shop before the men from the orphanage did.

SIXTEEN

———◆———

THE PLAN

Chip approached the abandoned shop carefully, constantly on the lookout for the slightest movement or sound that might indicate the presence of someone lurking in the darkness. The moon laid hidden behind a thick blanket of clouds and light from the street lamps danced like demons against the buildings.

"Humphrey," Chip whispered.

The tiny rat scurried out of his coat and climbed onto his shoulder.

"Aye, Master." Humphrey's whiskers tickled the side of his face.

"Doth ye smell, hear or sense any mongrels about besides me self?"

"Nay, Master. Ye be the only mongrel about."

With that knowledge, Chip eased his way through the street towards the shop. He worried whether the little girl would still be there or if she would have become fearful and left.

He approached the door to the abandoned shop and carefully pushed it open. He moved silently until he reached the cellar doors. As he crept down the steps, a small shriek greeted him before a pair of arms wrapped about his waist. Chip patted the unseen form as he pulled the door closed behind him.

"It be okay lass," Chip whispered, peering through the darkness for the table and the candle that sat upon it. "Ye feel as though ye be soaked to the bone."

He could feel her head nod against his chest. His eyes finally focused enough to spy the small table. He pressed forward, Isabella still holding onto his coat, until he reached his destination, fumbling for a moment with his flint before finally lighting what was left of the candle.

Chip was so shocked by what he saw that he dropped to one knee, gripping the candle. Isabella stood before him, drenched to the bone and her hands covered in blood. He sat the candle back down upon the table so that he could examine her hands and wrists.

"What happened child?"

"Not be mad with them," Isabella said, looking worried. "They did not mean to bite me."

"The rats bit ye?"

"They were trying to remove the ropes. Should ye not hath sent them, I would not be free."

Chip looked about the room at the multitude of rats that lined the floor.

"We returned the mongrel pup to ye," the Master rat said, climbing to the top of the table.

Chip stared at the large rat in awe. He hadn't even considered sending Humphrey's pack into the orphanage to rescue the girl.

"How did ye—I mean—when did ye …"

"A scout returned to the pack while ye searched out the ship. Doth this make ye happy, mongrel?" the Master rat asked.

"Aye. Ye hath done well, Master rat."

"Shall ye continue to feed me pack?"

"Aye," Chip nodded before returning his attention to the girl. "Tell me child, why be ye soaked to the bone?"

"When yer rats freed me, I made to run, but there be too many about," Isabella explained. "Had to hide amongst the wash. I waited till the men left to search for me before squeezing through the kitchen window."

"Be yer wrists yer only injuries?"

"Nay. I fell from the window and hurt me leg. Me other injuries be tended to and wrapped before me escape."

"Other injuries?"

"The men hurt me back and arm. I not tell them about ye or yer rats."

Chip growled as he chewed the inside of his lip, anger pulsing through him as he envisioned the blaggards torturing her.

"Ye able to walk?"

Isabella nodded. Chip thought long and hard about where would be the best place to take her. As much as he dreaded the thought, he knew that the abandoned groundkeeper's shack in St.

Anthony's graveyard might be their only choice.

"I believe that it be time to return to the graveyard. This place not be safe any longer."

Isabella nodded, looking fearful. Chip tore off the cuffs of his shirt and tied them around the girl's bleeding wrists. She winced slightly, but didn't cry. He gave her a small smile to reassure her, though he was far from confident himself.

He bundled the girl in one of his thicker shirts from his haversack. She was soaked, but there was no time to allow her to change. He stuffed some of her clothes he had purchased into his haversack then tossed it onto his back once more.

"Mongrel Chip, hath me pack proved its worth to ye?" the Master rat asked, gaining his attention.

"Aye. That ye hath. Shall ye and yer pack come also?"

"Long as ye feed me pack, we shall go where ye go."

"Be they coming with us?" Isabella asked, her voice shaking slightly.

"Aye, lass, they be a coming."

The Master rat sent scouts ahead to make sure their path was clear. They took the longest way possible back to the graveyard, lest they risked encountering someone from the orphanage or the *Nomas.*

The moon was still hidden behind the thick blanket of clouds when they reached the graveyard, making it incredibly difficult to see. As they entered through the iron gates, Chip took much caution not to trip on any of the smaller gravestones that were as plentiful as the stars. After Isabella stubbed her foot for the third time, he decided to carry her the rest of the way.

Chip waited for the scouts to check the groundkeeper's shack before entering. Once it was deemed safe, Humphrey's pack quickly made themselves at home again while he tended to the girl. He stepped outside briefly to collect some sticks and give her some privacy while she changed clothes. He then lit a small fire in the stove to warm up the drafty shelter. The scouts kept watch, lest someone attempt to sneak up on them.

Chip waited until the girl felt safe then left to spy out the area. He took several rats with him, including Humphrey, to help scout St. Thaddeus and the *Nomas* for activity. After a moment of consideration, he decided to scout the orphanage first. There was a stone wall that ran along the road in front of the property on the opposite side. He crouched down behind the wall, peering over the top at the orphanage, looking for signs of life. By all accounts from Isabella, they moved the children at night.

"Humphrey, might ye and yer fellow scouts search this mongrel dwelling once more? I need to know when they shall take the mongrel pups to the vessel on the water."

"Aye, Master. We shall scout the mongrel dwelling."

"Thank ye little friend. Hurry now. We must be cautious lest we be found."

Humphrey and his fellow scouts darted off towards the orphanage, squeezing between the cracks in the stone wall. Chip sighed as he sat there, squatted down behind the wall. He felt as though his entire life was out of his control. He cursed himself for being so gullible. Seeing the star on Mr. Kellogg's wrist had awaken him to the reality that he was deep in the middle of something much larger than he could wrap his mind around. What it could have to do with Mr. Tomlin was just beyond his grasp, but he couldn't dwell on that now. Luckily for him, he had Captain O'Toole on his side.

After sitting there for what felt like an eternity, Chip began to become concerned. He thought that surely the rats would be back by then. He was about to try and find a way to creep closer to the orphanage without being seen when he heard a scratching noise. Moments later several rats, including Humphrey, came scurrying over the wall. One of the rats looked to have changed colors. At first, he feared that it might be blood, but as the rodent drew closer the smell of molasses reached his nostrils.

"What took ye so long?" Chip whispered, staring at Humphrey.

"Sorry Master. There was much to see and hear."

"And taste?"

"Taste? Nay, Master. A female mongrel attempted to off us. Threw all manner of things at us."

Chip smirked at the thought of one of the nuns pelting objects at the rodents, though his mirth faded quickly as his mind registered Humphrey's words.

"Ye said that there was much to see and hear. What be happening this late at night?"

300

"Bad mongrels were talking amongst one another, Master. Saith they shall move all strong mongrel pups on something called a Thursday."

"Excellent. Ye hath done well."

"Master, what be a Thursday?" Humphrey asked as he climbed back onto Chip's shoulder.

"I shall explain later. Now, we must be getting back to the graveyard."

"What about the vessel?"

"We need not go there now," Chip replied, slowly easing away from the wall, the other rats following him like a herd of cats. "Ye hath heard what we need."

Chip returned to the graveyard to find Isabella asleep on the cot. She reminded him so much of his Anna that he almost shed a tear. Knowing that the children wouldn't be moved for a couple of days, he decided to camp out in the chair and get a little sleep. He would have slept on the floor, but knew that he would probably awake to find rodents covering him the same way they did the girl. Regardless of how he felt about Humphrey, he wasn't ready yet to bond with the pack.

The next morning Chip visited the nearby market for food, careful to keep himself bundled up so that none would recognize him. The wind was harsh and cold, so none would note his actions as odd.

That night, he visited Captain O'Toole to let him know of when the orphanage planned to move the children. The Captain informed him that he had volunteered for port patrol. This meant that the *Ottoman* could legally detain the *Nomas* for inspection. Now, it was up to Chip to find a way to peacefully delay the ship from departing at first light.

———•———

Mr. Wallace strolled up to the MacDougall home, feeling quite confident. He had not come around for several days, but had received a note from Mary requesting his presence at his earliest convenience. He knocked swiftly on the front door and waited, humming merrily to himself. It was a cold but sunny morning. He knew Mary's children would be off to school and he would be able to speak with her without interruption.

"Morning Mr. Wallace. Would ye like to come in?"

"Thank ye Ms. Douglas," Mr. Wallace replied, tipping his hat and stepping inside.

"Ye may wait in the sitting room. I shall let the Misses know that ye be here."

Mr. Wallace bowed then made his way to the sitting room. He smirked as he admired the woodcarvings around the edges of the mantel. It had been one of the things that he had first noticed when he was helping Mary find a more suitable place to live. He was overjoyed when she had commented how elegant the carvings were.

By now he had expected to be living there as her husband,

302

or at least preparing to as her intended. His house would never be welcoming to a boy in a wheelchair, with all the stairs and sloping floors.

"Sorry to hath kept ye waiting, Mr. Wallace," Mary said as she entered the room.

Mr. Wallace sighed at the sound of her greeting him so formally. He turned to see the vision of beauty that he so longed to embrace, smiling to hide his disappointment.

"Ye have not kept me, Mrs. MacDougall. How might I serve thee?"

"Hath me husband been by yer office on business?" Mary asked hesitantly.

"Not for several weeks. Why doth ye ask?"

He watched as Mary sat down on the sofa, apparently gathering her thoughts and choosing her words carefully.

"Ye doth not have to tell me, Mrs. MacDougall," he added, "but know that whatever ye say shall not leave this room."

"Thank ye, Jefferson," Mary said, smiling and looking up at him. "It just be that me husband hath not been around for several days. The last time he visited, Ms. Douglas said that she heard him accidentally call me daughter by another name."

"Another name?" he repeated absentmindedly. Hearing Mary call him by his first name and seeing her smile had robbed him of his senses.

"Aye. She saith that he called her Isabella, though I know not any by that name."

Mr. Wallace stumbled as his hand slipped off the mantel. He quickly caught himself, straightening his waistcoat as an attempt to cover his stumbling, his throat suddenly dry. He knew that Mr. MacDougall had sneaked aboard the *Nomas* and had attacked some of Captain Kellogg's crew, but if he somehow had the missing orphan and knew what the vessel was transporting …

"Jefferson, be ye alright?" she asked, not missing his near tumble.

"Aye," he lied. "I just lost me footing. Listen … Mary, doth not worry about yer husband. I be sure that he be alright."

"Who be this Isabella then, Jefferson?"

"Mary, I not imagine that any man could find someone to replace ye," Jefferson said, causing her face to turn pink. "Yer husband be going through challenging times with being away from ye. Give him time."

Jefferson didn't want Mary to give Mr. MacDougall another minute, let alone more time to work things out. However, he knew that he was saying what she wanted him to say. He was trying to play the role of the concerned friend until Mr. MacDougall was out of the way forever. Problem was, it sounded like her estranged wasn't being idle either.

"Forgive me, Mary, but I just remembered an important bank meeting that I must attend. To miss it would be negative to me post."

"Hurry then," she said, calling to Ms. Douglas to fetch his things. "I hope that ye not be in trouble because of me."

"Supposing I be, it be worth it."

He was satisfied to see Mary's face grow pink again at his comment, but felt nauseous at the thought of what Mr. Prose might do should he not deal with this issue swiftly.

———————

The following night, Chip stood across the bay and surveyed the orphanage from afar, looking for any signs of movement. The Shadow Clan, or whomever they were, had increased the number of workers at the orphanage. They had also restricted the poor children's outdoor activities to less than fifteen minutes per day.

Despite knowing when they planned to move the children, Chip had decided to keep a watchful eye upon the orphanage and the *Nomas*. He was certain that Isabella's second escape had delayed the movement of the children from the orphanage to the vessel. Humphrey's pack had also kept a watchful eye upon the *Nomas*, waiting for the first sign that the vessel was preparing to sail. He had no doubt that Mr. Kellogg would set sail the moment he was able to.

"Master?"

"Aye?"

"I be wondering, how long shall ye stare at this dwelling? Doth ye doubt what we heard?"

"Nay, me little friend ... I doth not doubt ye. I feel thought that I might be missing something. Should they board early, we might lose our chance to deal with the crew."

"These mongrels hurt their pups daily, Master. What harm would ye to the pups to not allowing them to enter that vessel?"

"That not be a choice. The children must board the ship, lest there not be any way to prove they be stowing them away."

Chip knew that while many of the children would surely die on the voyage to America, he also knew that many might die while fleeing this place as well if things did not go to plan.

"How be Isabella?" he asked, changing the subject.

"The young mongrel rests, Master. She does not understand us as ye. She tells me pack stories."

Chip chuckled for the first time in several days. The image of little Isabella telling nursery rhythms to rodents was quite amusing. He bent down and extended his arm, allowing the tiny rat to scurry up onto his shoulder. He then turned his gaze back to the orphanage, staring at it as though trying to pierce its outer wall and see within. He knew that if he was successful, it would change the lives of Isabella and all the children of St. Thaddaeus for the better. Doing nothing would result in he and the girl most likely having to leave Scotland and head for Europe. Even then he wondered if that would be far enough away to escape the wrath of this 'Shadow Clan'.

"Mongrel Chip!"

Chip spun round to see a large rat racing towards him. He squatted down as the rat reached him.

"What be wrong?" he whispered.

"The vessel be doing as ye described!" the rat exclaimed.

"Explain. What doth ye mean?"

"The mongrels be moving about swiftly, tightening large ropes and rolling what ye called barrels into what ye called the hull."

"It only be Tuesday," Chip muttered, thinking hard.

Humphrey hadn't known the days of the week until after he had given an exhausting explanation of how mongrel calendars work, to the delight of Isabella. Therefore, he wouldn't have been able to mistakenly hear Thursday. Something had changed. Regardless of why, what the rat had described was a crew preparing for a hasty departure.

"Rat, go back to yer pack and tell yer Master that I need half yer pack at the dock near the mongrel vessel in case I need them." Chip realized then and there that things were not going to go as he had planned.

He had come up with a fairly simple plan. Get the crew of the *Nomas* too drunk to sail. He had remembered how the crew of the *Ottoman* had returned many times too drunk to set sail, their excuse always that someone had challenged them to a drinking game. That was where good old Jonah, who was more than happy to play along, came into the plan. Chip had convinced him that he was delaying the *Nomas's* crew so that Captain O'Toole could catch them smuggling. He didn't want to tell Jonah any more than necessary lest Chip endanger he and his family.

Now, that plan was in great jeopardy. If the *Nomas'* crew

was preparing for a hasty departure, it meant that the crew would not depart the ship again before it sailed. He had to get down to the docks and investigate, knowing full well the risk that he was taking. If he was caught, he wasn't likely to get away again.

With Humphrey tucked away under his collar, Chip made his way around the mouth of the bay to where the *Nomas* sat tied to the pier. Just as the large rat had said, the ship's topside was alive with activity. Hunched down behind some nearby crates of tea, the aroma of Assam overwhelming, he pondered whether he had somehow missed the children being boarded. He and the rats had been watching the vessel day and night, so the only possibility was that the children were going to be brought aboard that night.

———•———

Jonah McCullah was about to head home after a long day at the wharf when he saw someone sneak past some crates to his left. He decided to follow, wondering if it might be one of the smugglers that Chip and Captain O'Toole were after. He followed the figure at a distance, hiding in the shadows, all the way to the last pier where the *Nomas* was docked. The light from an oil lamp caught the figure's face for only a moment and he was shocked to discover that it was Chip.

He watched as his friend crouched down behind some crates of tea and realized that he must be trying to get a closer look at the ship for some reason.

"Chip," Jonah whispered, easing up behind him.

Chip clutched his boots with his hands to keep from jumping, turned and stared directly into his face in disbelief.

"Jonah!" he hissed in a hushed voice. "What be ye doing here? Ye nearly sent me to me eternity box!"

"I saw ye creeping along the edge of the wharf and followed ye. Thought ye might need some help." He knew that Chip was concerned that someone had spotted him by the look upon his face. "I be watching for things since ye told me about the smugglers. It be not for that, I would not hath noticed ye."

"Aye, but someone else might hath noticed. Ye need to leave, Jonah. I thank ye, but yer family needs ye."

"Nothin' doin'. Ye were there for me when I needed ye. Now, I be there for ye."

Chip growled in frustration, "That not be the same. I covered for thee with the wharf master. These men be dangerous."

"I be good in a scrap. I not be goin'—"

Jonah was cut off by the scurrying of rats, flowing like a river about the boots of him and Chip.

"Saints preserve us," he whispered in awe.

His eyes tracked the movement of a large gray rat. The rat climbed atop the crate of tea and stared at him before turning its attention to Chip. The rat squeaked and barked as though trying to communicate. When Chip nodded to the rat, Jonah had to shake his head to push away the maddening thoughts flooding his mind.

"Jonah," Chip whispered, sounding unsure and a bit

hesitant.

"Sorry mate," he hissed, thumping the side of his head. "For a moment, it looked as though that rat was speaking to ye. Madness, I know."

———◆———

Chip pulled Jonah behind the crates of tea, as the sound of approaching footsteps interrupted what might have been an interesting moment. They peered up over the crates cautiously to see several men escorting what looked to be nearly a hundred children down the pier and onto the ship. There was no way this many children had come from St. Thaddeus. The sudden drop in number would be far too noticeable. His mind felt numb, as he considered how many orphanages could possibly be involved.

"What be this?" Jonah hissed, a touch of anger in his voice.

"This be what they be smuggling," Chip whispered, knowing he had no other choice but to involve his friend.

"Children? But why would … those bloody blaggards."

"Now not be the time to explain," Chip whispered urgently. "These people be powerful and dangerous. Somehow, they must know what Captain O'Toole be planning. Ye must go find Captain O'Toole aboard the *Ottoman* and tell him they be setting sail at dawn."

"What be ye going to do?"

"I shall what I must. Ye need to find Captain O'Toole. Doth not argue. Go. Now."

"I shall go and inform the Captain, then I shall return," Jonah said, placing a hand on his shoulder.

"Nay. Stay with Captain O'Toole. He shall need ye."

Chip could tell that Jonah wanted to argue, but relented, nodding in agreement. He watched, as his friend disappeared into the shadows, silently wishing him a safe journey.

"Humphrey."

"Aye, Master."

"I need ye and yer fellow rats to scout the vessel. I need to know exactly where the mongrel pups be."

Chip watched as Humphrey scurried down his sleeve and into the midst of the rats that had gathered along the pier. Moments later, he saw his little friend and ten other rats head for the ship. They climbed the ropes that tied the vessel to the dock before disappearing over the side.

"Be there any way we might help, mongrel Chip?" the large gray rat asked.

Chip stared at the rat sitting atop the crate before him, thinking of what could be done to delay the ship's departure.

"Aye, rat. See those ropes high atop the wooden posts that we mongrels call masts?" Chip pointed to the top of the three masts of the *Nomas*.

"Aye, mongrel. I see."

"Send a few of yer pack to the top and hath them chew

311

through the ropes, leaving only a small piece on each rope whole," Chip instructed. "Doth this for each mast."

"We shall."

Chip watched as several rats headed for the ship and up the ropes that bound it to the pier. He knew if the ship was to set sail with weakened ropes, the moment a strong wind caught the sails, it would rip them away from the mast. Replacing the ropes wasn't an easy task and would take the crew hours.

"Master!" Humphrey shouted, sprinting for his hiding place.

"What did ye find?"

"The mongrels hath the pups bound with ropes inside the vessel."

"Did ye hear the mongrels say anything?"

"Aye. They said many things," Humphrey replied.

Chip sighed aloud in frustration. "I meant, did ye hear them speak of when the vessel might leave?"

"One mongrel said they be waiting for the clouds to part."

"Clouds to part," he repeated aloud, looking up.

The night sky was cloudy, and there was a slight breeze from the east. Waiting for the clouds to part was something seamen did when sailing by night. *Would Mr. Kellogg risk be being caught by the Royal Navy or was this another extension of the power of this mysterious 'Shadow Clan'?* Chip pondered this question, as he decided what to do next.

"This way, you," a voice growled to his right.

312

Chip crouched, as low as he could, peering between the crates to see what was happening. By the light of a distant oil lantern that hung beneath the main mast, he watched with horror, as Jonah was roughly escorted by two gents in red to the gang plank. The two men hailed the ship, requesting to see Captain Clark. Chip eased out from behind the crates, daring to get as close as he could without being seen. He knew that if Jonah was here then he never reached Captain O'Toole.

"What have we here?" Chip heard Mr. Kellogg, aka Captain Clark, groan with interest.

"Sir, this dog was looking for Captain O'Toole. Said he had to warn him about smugglers setting sail."

"And you thought of me," Mr. Kellogg retorted, a smirk curling his face. "I be truly touched with pride."

"What should we do with him?"

"He looks like a strong back," Mr. Kellogg said, examining Jonah. "Would be a waste to drown the rat. Mr. Bead!"

"Aye, Captain," a crew member said, hurrying over.

"Escort this fine man down below and secure him well in the brig. He should fetch an attractive price, supposing he survives the voyage."

"I not be a dog, and I not be a slave for sale," Jonah coughed, sounding as though he was struggling for breath.

"Aboard my ship, mate, you be what I say that you be." Mr. Kellogg grasped Jonah by the face with one hand. "I do not need to know your name, nor do I need to ask why you were off to see

Captain O'Toole. I have only one question for you. Where might I find Christopher MacDougall? Tell me, and I might let you go."

Chip desperately wanted to rush aboard the ship and attack Mr. Kellogg. Instead, he held his ground, knowing it wouldn't do any good getting them both captured. Jonah stared at Mr. Kellogg, uttering not a word.

"Have it your way, mate," Mr. Kellogg hissed. "Take him below, and this time, Mr. Bead, personally escort the sandy down to the brig. It would not be well for two to escape our grasp."

"Aye, Captain."

Chip eased back behind the crates, his breathing sharp, as he fought to control his rage. He could hear Mr. Kellogg tell the two knobs to keep an eye out for him.

"Humphrey, be any mongrels with the child—mongrel pups?"

"Three bad mongrels watch the pups, Master."

"Stay with yer pack. I must sneak aboard. Should the ship not sail tonight, they shall surely murder me friend. I doth not wish for ye to be harmed lest something happens to me."

"Nay, Master. I go where ye go."

"Ye hath done yer work this night, me little friend. This not be yer fight."

"Yer fight be me fight, Master. I stay with ye."

Chip sighed. "Very well, little friend. Ye be a brave and loyal rat."

He stroked the tiny rat's fur with a finger, staring at the side of the crates of tea. Captain O'Toole's plan had failed the moment Jonah was captured, but now his task was clear. Free his friend and the orphans from this vessel of doom—no matter the cost.

————— ✦ —————

SEVENTEEN

FIRE AND WATER

Chip looked up at the masts of the *Nomas*. It was so dark that he could barely make out their outline against the night sky. The wind was picking up, and he wondered if a storm was brewing at sea.

He eased out once more from behind the crates, scanning the pier for any signs of movement. Mr. Kellogg and his crew had gone back to preparing their vessel for the voyage ahead, leaving the gang plank vacated for the moment. Chip knew that the moment he appeared on the deck of the *Nomas*, he would be apprehended by its crew or shot.

"Humphrey," he whispered.

"Aye, Master."

"Ye think ye might be able to climb up and chew through the rope that holds up those lights?" he asked, pointing to the string of oil lamps that lit the *Nomas's* deck.

"Aye, Master."

"When the lights fall, I shall board the vessel and go below. Join me there, lest I might need ye."

"Aye, Master," the tiny rat said, climbing down his sleeve and heading for the *Nomas*.

Chip watched and waited, mentally preparing himself to board the vessel. He wouldn't have but a minute to span the distance from where he was to the entrance of the hull. As the lights fell from the mast, it was as if time itself had slowed to a crawl. The lamps crashed to the deck of the ship, sending everyone aboard into darkness.

Chip bolted from his hidden spot, up the gang plank, through the sudden darkness, past stunned crew members and into the hull. He was certain none of the crew topside had even noticed him. Too bad that couldn't be said for the crew below deck.

The three crew members that Humphrey had warned him about, stared at him in shock, as he quickly appeared out of the darkness. The lanterns below shone bright, and there was no missing his entrance. The men were burly and boar-faced, but none looked to be bigger than he.

"The deck lanterns hath fallen and the Captain be needing more from below," he said, thinking quickly.

"Who are you?" one of the men demanded. "You not be one of the crew!"

"Ye be right," Chip replied, shrugging before punching the man square in the face.

The other two men lunged at him as their mate fell to the floor. Chip instinctively stepped to one side to avoid being tackled, grabbing one man by the scruff of the neck and tossing him into

317

the side of a barrel, knocking him out cold. The third man regained his footing and was about to reach his target when Chip's knee found his gut and his elbow found the back of the man's head. Mr. Barrett's training had not been forgotten.

He knew he only had a few minutes before he was discovered, and that only the commotion above had covered the sounds he made below. Chip turned to go the same way he had been taken the last time he was aboard the ship, only to see about a hundred children sitting on the floor of the hull, their arms and legs bound tightly by ropes. He hesitated before hurrying past them to find Jonah. He couldn't get them all off the ship, and he knew the *Nomas* wasn't going to make it far that night anyway.

He found Jonah locked in a room being used as the ship's brig.

"Chip!" Jonah hissed, running to the window in the door. "Leave now lest ye be caught!"

"Not without ye, me friend," Chip responded, looking for a key hanging somewhere.

"Looking for this?"

Chip closed his eyes at the sound of the familiar voice of Mr. Kellogg. The roar of thunder boomed, warning every one of the approaching storm, as Chip turned and stared defiantly into the eyes of his former crew member. He wasn't surprised to see Mr. Kellogg being flanked by at least half a dozen men.

"Let him go free, Kellogg!" Chip spat. "Ye hath me now. I be happy to trade for his freedom."

"Show our captain respect aboard his ship!" a burly crew member growled, attempting to reach him.

"Leave him be," Mr. Kellogg demanded, causing the man to take a step back. "Mr. MacDougall here knew me before I became a captain. We have history together."

Chip glared into Mr. Kellogg's eyes. He wouldn't show that he was intimidated. He wouldn't give him that satisfaction. Mr. Kellogg only smiled darkly, as he stared back into his eyes.

"Did you really think that you could best me?"

"Ye be risking the lives of children, yet ye treat it as but a game!"

Mr. Kellogg laughed. "Oh, Mr. MacDougall, they just be misplaced itchland leftovers, like you. Should we lose a few along the way, it not be any loss."

Chip spit in his face, earning a fierce slap from the bear of a seaman who stood behind the traitor. Mr. Kellogg wiped the sputum from his face with a handkerchief then sunk his fist into Chip's mid-section. Chip doubled over as he heard the door behind him open before being tossed inside head first.

"Welcome aboard the *Nomas*, Mr. MacDougall. I wouldn't make myself comfortable, though. Once we're out to sea, you shall be leaving us."

Chip pushed himself up to his feet, shaking off his pain. He immediately began searching the room with his eyes for any conceivable way out.

"Sorry Chip, but I failed ye," Jonah coughed, leaning against

319

the wall.

"What hath they done to ye?"

"They rib-roast me good."

"Think ye be able to swim?"

"Aye, but we be in a locked room."

Chip ignored his friend as he paced the floor, concentrating on how to escape from the makeshift brig. A roll of thunder sounded from overhead, reverberating in his ears and throughout the hull of the ship like the inside of a drum. No matter how hard he thought it through, he could not come up with a single idea. Hours passed as he paced, sat down, beat the floor, stood back up then paced some more. Silence filled the room, as the hopelessness of their situation grew like an unwanted weed, threatening to choke the life from them.

The thunder continued to grow louder, making it harder to think. Chip closed his eyes in concentration. He opened them and was shocked to see Humphrey sitting up on his hind legs in the middle of the room, staring at a kneeling Jonah, his head bowed, and hands folded in front of him.

"What be the mongrel doing, Master?"

"He be praying," Chip replied, thinking of how it would be the first thing Mary would do if she was in his position.

"Wouldn't hurt ye to pray, Chip," Jonah said solemnly, glancing up at him. "We be in dire straits."

"What be praying?" Humphrey asked, looking up at Chip as well.

320

Chip grasped the back of his head with his hands and closed his eyes once more. There was a part of him that wanted to join Jonah, and another that wanted to kick him. Then, as though he could hear Bro. Hesperus speaking in the back of his mind, he heard the words, "It be what ye make of it."

Without caring what Jonah might say, Chip dropped to one knee. Instead of praying, he looked down at his little friend, knowing his answer sat before him.

"Humphrey, I need ye to gather the scouts from yer pack and bring them down here. Hurry now. There not be much time."

"Aye, Master." Humphrey glanced at Jonah before racing off and around Chip, sliding under the door.

Chip looked at Jonah, who stared at him as if he had gone mad. "Jonah, now not be the time to explain."

"Were ye just speaking to that rat?" Jonah grunted, as though the question wouldn't stay in.

"Aye," Chip replied, rising to his feet.

"And ye believe it understood thee?"

Chip stared at the wall so as not to see Jonah's face. "Aye, Jonah. Rats be the voices that I told ye about."

He felt Jonah's hand on his shoulder, but he didn't dare look at him. He didn't care to see the look of concern that was surely there. For this same reason, he hadn't told Mary or Captain O'Toole. He still could not explain to himself why he had felt so comfortable telling Bro. Hesperus or where the man had disappeared to afterwards. He knew though what Jonah and Mary would tell him.

He felt Jonah's hand leave his shoulder. Chip turned to see Jonah staring at seven or eight rats squeezing under the door and joining them inside the makeshift brig.

"Excellent work, Humphrey," Chip said, spying his little friend amongst the newcomers.

"How might we serve thee, mongrel Chip?" a brown medium-sized rat asked.

"Think ye might chew through the wood about this?" he asked, pointing at the metal lock on the door.

"We shall try."

Chip watched as several rats attempted to climb up the wooden door to the lock. The smaller of the rats, including Humphrey, were the successful ones. As they began to gnaw at the wooden door, Chip glanced at Jonah, who had become a statue, staring at only the door. He wondered what his friend's reaction would be once reality began to sit in.

A cracking sound grabbed his attention. He blinked in amazement as he watched one of the rats chewing into the lock itself. At first, he thought the cracking sound must have been the rat's teeth, but as he watched, he realized that it had been the sound of the metal wearing down. It was an unsettling sight for someone who had slept in the company of these four-legged masticating machines for the last several weeks.

Near through with their task, the door started to move. He worried the movement of the door as it weakened might draw attention from crew standing guard.

"That be good enough, me little friends."

With that, the rats halted their chomping and slid down the door.

"We be almost done, Master."

Chip allowed Humphrey to climb up his coat sleeve and onto his shoulder before burying under his collar. He then turned to see Jonah staring at him in awe, no fear present in his countenance.

"Be ready," Chip whispered. "Should there be any crew down below, they shall try to stop us when I kick through the door."

"I be ready."

Chip took a deep breath then, as the thunder rolled once more, he booted the door as hard as he could and stepped into the corridor beyond. For one brief moment, he found himself staring into the widened eyes of one of the men he had punched only a few hours before. He could see fear as he lunged at the man, shoving him against the far inner wall of the ship, slamming the man's head against it. The man slumped to the ground. Chip grabbed some rope laying atop a nearby barrel of gunpowder and bound the man's legs and arms, stuffing a handkerchief in the man's mouth.

"What now, Chip?" Jonah whispered, looking anxious and ready to fight. "There not be any time to summon Captain O'Toole, should they sail tonight."

"The rats hath already chewed through the ropes that tie

the sails to the masts. This ship not be leaving tonight. The only reason I be aboard be to rescue thee, lest they change their minds and murder ye."

"Supposing we escape now. What shall happen to the children?"

Chip sighed. "This night hath not gone as planned. We must get to the *Ottoman*. We shall surely be captured once more should we attempt to rescue the children now."

A loud commotion from above deck caught their attention. They eased closer to the stairs to hear what was happening. The scouts from Humphrey's pack were nowhere to be seen. Chip placed a finger to his lips to signal for the children to remain quiet as they eased past them.

"Hoist the main sails and lift anchor!" Chip heard Mr. Kellogg's first mate shout. "Make haste!"

"They be leaving amid a storm?" Jonah quipped.

"Something must hath happened."

Chip felt a gentle, familiar nudge under his feet. It was a sign the main sails had been raised, and the ship was beginning to leave port. He looked down at the scared faces of the children, reality of what was happening beginning to sink in.

"I thought ye said—"Jonah began, but was drowned out by shouts from the deck above.

Chip could not help but smile, for he knew what had happened. His humor faded, as he realized that if the ship's sails had ripped free—

"What be wrong?" Jonah asked, spying Chip's look.

"Quick, help me grab the Englishman," he said, hastily making his way back towards the makeshift brig.

He knew that the spare sails would be kept with the supplies inside the hull and that several crew members would be making haste to retrieve them. Jonah grunted, as they dragged the unconscious Englishman into the room and closed the broken door behind them. Chip hoped the men would be in such haste they would not notice the damaged door.

"Master, why hath ye returned to this place?"

"Hiding."

Jonah glanced at the rat, then at Chip, but did not say a word. They waited. Chip kept a palm extended to Jonah to remain silent. The sound of several men running down the stairs into the hull to retrieve the spare sails thundered like the storm that raged above, the familiar shouts of "Danger!" ringing inside the hull. To Chip's shock, the scouts from Humphrey's pack were still aboard the ship. He crouched near the door and waited as the men carried sails and ropes past the room and up the stairs to the deck above, several cursing loudly as they went.

"They hath more sails," Jonah whispered, sounding concerned.

"Aye, but they shall take time to replace. They hath dropped anchor, but they not be docked any longer. This means that they hath not any way to unload the children. While they be busy tending to the ship, we must find a way off so that we may warn Captain O'Toole. This night may still be ours after all."

They peered around for signs of movement. If they could time it correctly, they could make it from the hull entrance to the side of the ship without getting shot. The trouble was they couldn't see what was happening above without being caught.

"Humphrey, summon the scouts from yer pack."

Humphrey raced down his arm without reply and moments later returned with the other rats.

"What shall ye hath us do, Master?" Humphrey asked, his nose twitching.

"Send two of yer scouts to the top of the stairs and call out when there not be any mongrels about."

"Aye, Master."

"Mongrels?" Jonah repeated, his brow furrowed.

Chip just shook his head. Now was not the time to explain. He watched as two rats scurried up the hand ropes. He hoped silently the crew would be too busy trying to replace the sails amid a storm to think to check on their cargo and prisoners.

He looked over and saw that Jonah had his head bowed. He was praying again. The sudden sound like a canon blast jerked both men from their thoughts.

"Danger! Fire!" the rats shouted from the top of the stairs.

They had just enough time to hide behind barrels, as the sound of men rushing towards the hull entrance thundered overhead. Several men raced down the stairs, grabbing blankets and whatever else they could before rushing back to the deck.

"What be happening?" Jonah asked in a hushed tone.

"Humphrey," Chip hissed. "What be going on above?"

Humphrey rushed up the nearest hand rope. A minute later, he descended, climbing onto Chip's shoulder. "The storm hath struck a wooden tree that stands atop the vessel, Master. One mongrel be dead, and fire be burning. The other mongrels be trying to end the fire."

"Lightning hath struck one of the masts," Chip said, relaying the message to Jonah.

"Should the ship go down, they shall surely leave the children to drown."

Chip nodded in agreement, staring into the faces of the young boys and girls who sat scared and bound. All of the sudden, as he stared into the eyes of the children, his anxieties melted away, replaced by determination and rage.

"Rats, chew through the ropes that bind the mongrel pups!"

Immediately, the rats raced to do his bidding. Several of the children watched in awe as rats began to chew their bindings. Humphrey made to go as well, but Chip held up a hand, blocking the tiny rat from leaving his shoulder.

"Stay with me, little friend."

"Little friend," the voice of Mr. Kellogg repeated, descending the steps, his pistol drawn and aimed at Chip. "Even for a Scot, that must be demoralizing to be called his little friend," He scoffed, glancing at Jonah then returning his attentions to Chip. "I had come down to gather up more supplies, only to find my guests have decided their accommodations are not to their liking. I must admit I find myself impressed you were able to escape."

"First yer ship loses its sails, and now it be stricken by nature itself," Chip recounted, glancing at the barrel of the pistol. "Perhaps ye should reconsider starting yer voyage another day."

"Now Mr. MacDougall, you know I do not have that luxury. Now, be so kind and pick up that rope." He pointed to a piece of rope atop a nearby crate.

Chip reached over and picked it up. Before Mr. Kellogg could instruct him on what to do, Chip lashed out as if it were a whip. Mr. Kellogg fell backwards, his arms flying over his head. As he hit the floor, his pistol fired. The slug found one of the barrels of gunpowder that lined the outer wall of the hull. The explosion violently rocked the *Nomas*, throwing Jonah and Chip from their feet as it breached the hull of the ship. Water poured through the hole and into the vessel as shouts of "Danger!" filled the air—the *Nomas* was going to sink.

"We must get the children to safety!" Jonah shouted over the roar of the water rushing in, struggling to get to his feet.

Chip rolled over to see the rats had nearly finished their task. Many of the children were free and struggling to stand up.

"Get them up the stairs and over the side!" Chip shouted, pulling himself up by the hand ropes.

"Aye!" Jonah shouted, helping several children to their feet.

"Think you have the advantage?" Mr. Kellogg scoffed. "I think not."

His pistol lost, Mr. Kellogg now brandished a short knife as he lunged for Chip. Chip grabbed Mr. Kellogg by the wrists, to prevent him from running him through the chest. Jonah made to intervene, but Chip shouted, "Go! Take the children and go!"

Jonah didn't argue, ushering the children up the stairs, as Chip and Mr. Kellogg struggled for supremacy. None of the *Nomas's* crew came to their captain's aide, nor did they attempt to hinder Jonah and the orphans. Their lack of loyalty amongst lotmen becoming apparent. Chip heard Jonah in the distance shouting instructions to the children to help one another, as they jumped ship.

"Yer ship be going down!" Chip grunted as he struggled to keep a footing. "Shall ye go down with it, Captain Kellogg?"

"You think this is the end, Mr. MacDougall?" Mr. Kellogg edged the blade closer to his chest. "The *Nomas* is nothing more than a ship. Those filth you and your dog have saved this morn shall be boarded onto another ship and be traded in the Americas as intended. Nothing you have done shall change this. All that has changed, is that you shall die aboard this vessel, and your body shall rest at the bottom of this bay. I shall commandeer another ship and continue on. I might even send your dog down to join you as well before I be done."

Chip was locked in a fight that he was slowly losing. Mr. Kellogg was the stronger of the two and if Chip didn't do something quickly, Mr. Kellogg's words would come true. He felt and heard it before he saw it, as Humphrey flew like lightning down his arm, sinking his teeth into Mr. Kellogg's hand. Mr. Kellogg screamed in pain, stumbling backwards into the rising water, Humphrey being flung into the air and landing in the churning swell.

"Humphrey!" Chip shouted, wiping the spray from his face, as he prepared to dive after his little friend.

Suddenly, the ship shifted violently to one side, the weight of the incoming water pulling the vessel over. Chip reached out in time to grasp one of the hand ropes to keep from sliding beneath the rising water. To his relief, he spotted Humphrey, climbing the opposing hand rope, headed for the deck and safety.

"Help!"

Chip saw Mr. Kellogg struggling to stay above the water. "Grasp the wall and pull yer self up!"

"I cannot!" Mr. Kellogg exclaimed. "Something is wrapped about my leg!"

Chip let go of the rope and plunged feet first into the abyss below. He plummeted beneath the water's surface. Through the dark murky waters, he could see a rope wrapped and knotted around Mr. Kellogg's leg. Just as he began to attempt to loosen it, he heard an odd thumping. He spun around to see the Englishman he and Jonah had bound earlier struggling to get free. Chip abandoned his attempt to free Mr. Kellogg's leg and pushed himself towards the man. He grasped the struggling man and pushed off towards the surface of the water.

The moment the man was free, he climbed what once was

the ceiling and made for the hull exit.

"Help me save yer captain!" Chip shouted.

"Free him yourself!" the man retorted, disappearing through the opening.

As water continued to flood the *Nomas's* hull, Mr. Kellogg found himself barely able to keep his face above the surface.

"Leave me," Mr. Kellogg howled. "Everyone else has."

Chip took a deep breath and dove again into the murky waters. He struggled against the knot, unable to comprehend how it had become tangled about his leg. Regardless of how, the knot wasn't budging.

He decided to turn his attention to freeing the rope from the ship itself. He grasped the rope and began to pull as hard as he could. Chip could feel the rope give a little, but he had to return to the surface for air.

"The rope is tied to the side of the hull," Mr. Kellogg said, gasping for air as he broke the surface with Chip.

"Where be yer knife?"

"I lost it when that beast attacked me!" Mr. Kellogg shouted.

"Hath ye another?"

"It not be any use! Save yourself."

"I shall not leave ye."

"Then you shall die with me," Mr. Kellogg countered sternly. "Leave me to my fate or kill me now and save me the suffering of drowning."

"Nay! There must be another way!"

"This is the only way. Remember me when you pray," Mr. Kellogg breathed, causing Chip's heart to nearly fail.

Before he could utter a response, Mr. Kellogg dove beneath the water. Chip immediately followed, but was met with a hand to his chest. Their eyes locked, as unspoken regret poured from the man's soul. Tears would have flowed down Chip's face had he not been beneath the murky waters. The two men nodded to one another before Chip forced himself to the surface. He climbed the ceiling to the hull entrance and pulled himself through to find the waters much higher outside the ship. He looked back, but could not see Mr. Kellogg below.

Chip gripped the side of the ship, then covered his face with his free hand. The pure frustration of not being able to save Mr. Kellogg was overwhelming. He knew he had done all he could to save the man, even if the man had been a traitor and a self-serving murderer. All the same, Chip felt remorse for his demise.

"Mr. MacDougall!" a familiar voice shouted over the swelling sound of water and thunder overhead.

Chip looked up to see Captain O'Toole standing at the bow of the *Ottoman*, amazingly less than a hundred yards away.

"Swim for the *Ottoman*!" the Captain demanded.

Obediently, Chip climbed to the edge of the hatch he had been clinging to and leaped into the swell. He knew he had to swim as hard as he could to keep from being sucked below. It felt like an eternity before he reached the mighty ship. The end of a rope fell into the water before him and he grasped a hold as the ship's crew pulled him up. He was greeted immediately by the firm handshake and the embrace of Mr. Barrett before being quickly escorted into the Captain's chambers, a blanket being tossed about his shoulders. He was shocked to see Jonah sitting in a chair, staring at the floor, a blanket wrapped about him.

"Jonah," he breathed, causing his friend to leap from the chair and nearly tackle him.

"The saints be merciful!" Jonah exclaimed, smiling as he grasped Chip by the shoulders. "I thought ye be a gone for sure."

"But ... how be the *Ottoman* here?" Chip asked, trying not to shiver.

Captain O'Toole entered the cabin behind him and shut the door. "The *Ottoman* and I be here because I be a thirsty man."

Captain O'Toole's grin broadened, as he walked past the furrowed brows of the men who stood in his midst. They watched as he took a seat in front of his desk and motioned for them to join him.

"Would either of ye care for a glass of whiskey?"

"Aye," Jonah replied, while Chip shook his head no.

The Captain casually fetched all three of them a glass, sitting one for Chip on the side of his desk in case he needed it.

"I decided to wander down to the local pub last night for a shot of the kill-devil and maybe find me a new maltoot," Captain O'Toole explained. "There I met a gent that had tongue enough for two sets of teeth. He piped on until I was about to declare me self rammaged and retire for the night when a distressed woman approached me. She be with child and looking for her fellow. She saith his name be Jonah and I spied it might be ye.

"I assured her that I would find her lost mate before making haste back to the *Ottoman*, casting off for the northern harbor."

"What would ye hath done supposing it not hath been of me?"

"I would hath logged the voyage as precautionary," the Captain said dismissively. "That not matter, as I arrived to find the Nomas a flame and floundering. It twas Mr. Barrett that spotted ye in the waters."

"What of the orphans?"

"Drink ye whiskey like a good Scot and I shall tell ye." Chip downed the glass in one and waited. "The children be below, along with several members of the *Nomas's* crew. I be holding the crew members for illegal slave trade smuggling."

"What happens now?" Jonah asked.

"There shall be an investigation. The orphans shall be moved to another orphanage, and the ship's crew charged. Ye two shall remain aboard the *Ottoman* under me care until things be sorted out."

"Why must we remain aboard the *Ottoman*?" Jonah asked.

"The *Nomas's* first mate be in the custody of the new port authority. He be claiming that Mr. MacDougall be the one behind the illegal smuggling, and that he be paying Captain Clark to deliver

334

the children to one of the Colonies."

Jonah leaped to his feet. "That blaggard!"

"Sit down, lad!" the Captain ordered. Jonah immediately obeyed. "Now," continued the Captain, giving Chip an eye, "where be Mr. Kellogg?"

"Drowned," he replied, looking down.

"Tell me what happened."

Chip recounted exactly what happened and how he had no choice but to leave Mr. Kellogg behind. Jonah confirmed the struggle between Mr. Kellogg and Chip, though that was all he had seen.

"Was wrong about the rat needing a cage," Captain O'Toole smirked. "Unfortunately, this poses an even larger problem. Mr. Kellogg's death shall be framed as a murder. Mr. McCullah shan't able to testify for ye, for he would be dismissed as a fellow Scot. Any testimony from him would only lead to his imprisonment for assisting ye."

There was a knock at the cabin door and it might as well have been a cannon blast. Jonah and Chip jumped in start, their nerves on edge.

Captain O'Toole sighed as he responded, "Enter."

"Captain," Mr. Barrett said, entering the cabin. "Two knobs request your presence on deck."

The Captain nodded, then smiled at Chip and Jonah as he rose to go and greet the soldiers. Chip felt his stomach tighten, as he sat preparing to be led away at any moment. Several minutes

later, Captain O'Toole re-entered the cabin with Mr. Barrett, sitting
back down with Jonah and Chip.

"No worries," Captain O'Toole said in a reassuring tone. "I
explained to the gents in red that ye were aboard me ship in me
custody for assaulting me first mate. They be taking the *Nomas's*
crew into custody."

Chip glanced up at Mr. Barrett, then looked back at the
Captain.

"As for Mr. McCullah," the Captain continued, "they not be
aware of his presence, and I would recommend that ye be getting
home so yer whither might tend to the injuries of a Scot that hath
had too much whiskey."

"Sir, I not be leaving Chip," Jonah said firmly, realizing
what the Captain meant.

"Ye doth not Mr. MacDougall any good remaining here,
Mr. McCullah. I commend yer loyalty, but trust me when I saith
that Chip be in good hands."

"Jonah, I trust the Captain. Go home to yer family."

"I shall see ye soon," Jonah said, standing up, grasping Chip
by the arm.

"Until then." Chip rose to embrace Jonah, who winced
slightly.

He watched as Mr. Barrett escorted his friend from the
cabin. Chip bit the inside of his lip, wondering if he would ever see
Jonah again. Suddenly, Jonah burst back into the cabin, an odd look
on his face.

Jonah reached into his pocket. "Almost forgot. Found this little one on the pier, standing beside me boot."

Jonah extracted the familiar form of Humphrey, looking as though he had just awakened.

"Master!"

Chip took the tiny rat from his friend and smiled his thanks to Jonah. Jonah returned his smile then proceeded out of the cabin.

"Doth not understand yer fondness for such creatures," Captain O'Toole sighed, "but I doth understand loyalty—human or not."

"What now?" Chip asked, sitting back down. "I know ye be holding back in front of Jonah."

Captain O'Toole chuckled. "Ye know yer old captain too well. Now, doth ye still trust me?"

"With me life."

"Then ye need to listen," the Captain said, leaning closer. "Ye shall not receive a fair trial. Ye be a Scot who murdered a noble Englishman. Ye not hath a credible witness and yer service in the Royal Navy doth not matter. At this moment, I would wager me boots they be sharpening the blade of the maiden and preparing the cite stage."

"What shall I do?" Chip asked softly, feeling lightheaded, as the weight of what was being told to him sank in.

"Supposing ye want me to be honest … leave Britain."

"What about me family?" Chip asked, breathing hard, as he contemplated never seeing them again.

"Chip, I know it be hard for ye to hear, but should ye stay ye shall surely die." Captain O'Toole stood and fetched the whiskey bottle.

"I should not hath sent Jonah to tell thee," he sighed, looking at the floor. "Should hath come me self."

Captain O'Toole poured himself another glass of whiskey. "All plans fail the moment conflict begins. Any captain worth his salt knows this to be true."

Chip stared at the cupboard that hid the painting of St. Michael. Light shone through the windows on either side. The morning light peeked through the clouds, as the storm began to pass. The *Ottoman*, once his refuge, now felt like his prison. He thought of his family and how he might never see them again. He thought about Isabella, how he had vowed to keep her safe. Though now it felt like utter madness, only but a few short days before, he had envisioned himself making a mends with Mary and they inviting Isabella to join their family.

Chip found it hard to speak. "Captain, I know I not hath any right to ask any more of ye, but I need yer help with a matter … now that I not be able …"

Chip felt as though he was making his final requests and that his time upon the face of the Earth was coming to an end.

"I shall what I might," Captain O'Toole said, his eyebrows raised.

"The orphan girl, Isabella. She still be in hiding. She needs a good home. I know all children be needing a home, but I swore to keep her safe."

"Aye. This I for thee." The Captain scratched the whiskers on his chin. "Bring the lass to me ship. I shall make sure she be well taken care of and personally see to it she be placed with a proper family. When ye go to fetch her, doth not be tempted to see yer family. Soldiers shall be watching yer family's home for yer return. Fetch the lass and bring her straight back to the *Ottoman*. Wait until we hath returned to port, and not approach until it be dark."

"How shall I bring her to ye?" Chip asked, feeling confused. "Ye be releasing me?"

"Of course not! I could not possibly detain a lotman such as thee for long—let alone for a day's time. I not be certain what I be thinking!" The Captain chuckled, as he drained another glass of whiskey. "Ye, Mr. MacDougall, be going to escape."

———◆———

EIGHTEEN

THE CHOICE

Mary hurried out of the kitchen to see who was knocking on her door so early in the morning. Ms. Douglas had headed off to the market to fetch some produce for supper, so it was only her and the children at home. Secretly hoping it was Christopher, she straightened the front of her dress then opened the door.

"Mr. Wallace," Mary said, shocked by his presence. "What be ye doing here so early in the morn?"

"Forgive me, Mrs MacDougall." Mr. Wallace bowed his head, tipping his cap. "Might I come in?"

"Of course. Please," she replied, stepping aside to make way.

"Me apologies for interrupting yer morning. I have received disturbing news, and I wanted ye to hear it from someone ye know first."

Mary felt her chest tighten. "What be wrong, Jefferson?"

Mr. Wallace sighed, "I know not how to say this, so I shall state it the way it be told to me. Though first ye might want to sit down."

"I hath suffered ill news, Jefferson. Lest ye be telling me, me husband be deceased once more, I shall be steady."

"Very well," he said, biting his lower lip. "Mary, ye husband be sought for the murder of a privateer named Captain John Clark. He—"

"Tell me, why me husband would murder this Captain Clark?" she interrupted, her face hardening, as she felt anger begin to pulse through her.

"I know this be hard to hear." Mr. Wallace recognized the change in her tone. "I doth not believe it me self. An English soldier came to me office this morning, demanding to see Mr. MacDougall's ledger. I, in turn, demanded to know why. He stated his superior officer believed Mr. MacDougall hath been paying a privateer to smuggle orphans to the Americas. I scoffed at such a claim. He saith last night the agreement ended, and that Mr. MacDougall murdered the captain and sank the ship to make it be believed an accident."

"Leave me home this instant, Jefferson Wallace!" Mary demanded, pointing towards the door. "I shall not stand here and listen to another word!"

"Mary—"

"Address me as Mrs. MacDougall when ye speak to me, sir." Her tone turned as cold as winter wind.

A knock at the door interrupted any response. She walked over and jerked the door open far too hard, causing the English soldier on the other side to take a step back.

"Pardon me, miss," the soldier said, removing his hat "but might Mrs. MacDougall be home?"

"I be Mrs. MacDougall and me husband not be here," she replied, her fury and pain threatening to overtake her. "He hath never lived here."

"I presume then you have heard why I be searching for your husband."

"Aye, I hath." Mary batted her eyes to hold back her tears. "Mr. Wallace hath brought the news this morn."

"I must insist I be allowed to search your home." The soldier glanced at the door facing then back at Mary.

"I hath not a thing to hide."

The soldier entered the house and commenced to search the entirety of the residence, room by room.

"I shall stay while he searches ye place."

"Very well," Mary snapped, wiping a tear from her face. "When he leaves, so shall ye."

"M—Mrs MacDougall, I only—"

"Not another word. I hath things to tend to in the kitchen. See yer self out when the soldier be done with his searching."

Without giving Mr. Wallace a chance to respond, Mary returned to the kitchen so that she could be alone when her emotions finally got the best of her.

————◆————

Chip stood on the edge of the wharf, staring through the morning fog at the place where the *Nomas* had sank. It had been nearly a week since Captain O'Toole had helped stage his escape. He felt bad about having to punch Mr. Barrett in the face, but the Captain had said it was necessary.

All the orphans had been transferred from the *Ottoman* to a new orphanage on the south side of Edinburgh in New Town. Chip and Humphrey, with the help of his pack, had continued to watch over Isabella and the other orphans from afar, making sure that the new orphanage was what it seemed. As promised by Captain O'Toole, Isabella and several other orphans were adopted quickly by a Scottish family leaving for the British Settlements in America. He had snuck in to tell her goodbye and to give her the wooden cross he had received from the *Ottoman*. It had helped him find the faith to believe things could get better, even when all looked its darkest. Though his future looked bleak, he no longer needed a tiny wooden cross to keep the faith.

He knew it was for the best, though he couldn't help but feel a pang in his chest. Being a wanted man, he'd lost Marcus and Anna. Seeing Isabella go felt like losing another child. He glanced at Humphrey sitting on his shoulder and smiled. He knew the tiny rat shared his sadness at seeing the lass go too.

Chip's eyes returned to the bay and focused on the waters. He could see the shadow of the *Nomas* below. The hull of the vessel laid on the bottom of the bay, and he felt as though his former life had sunk with it, lost in the abyss. It was as if his soul laid beneath the waters alongside the body of Mr. Kellogg. The plan had failed miserably. He had wanted to save those poor children from a life of slavery, but it was as if, in return, he had sentenced himself to something far worse.

Captain O'Toole had offered him a place aboard the *Ottoman* under a fictitious name in order to flee Scotland. The vessel was set to sail for the Colonies in a week's time. Chip knew most of the crew, and their loyalties to Captain O'Toole and their former first mate, would keep their silence should he join.

He felt as though he was trapped between two locked doors. One led back to his life with his family, but as long as he remained sought for murder, that door was firmly locked. The other door offered a new life, but even though he held the key he did not wish to use it.

"Someone approaches," Humphrey squeaked, perched on Chip's shoulder, a hint of fear in his tiny voice.

Chip spun around and searched the foggy wharf for signs of life. The fog was so thick amongst the buildings and streets of Leith that the morning sun was unable to penetrate its dense covering. He squinted hard as he searched for any movement. Suddenly, he heard clapping—a slow methodical clapping.

"Show yer self," Chip said coldly, prepared to fight for his freedom.

"Greetings, Mr. MacDougall," came a voice from his

nightmares, a shadow slowly emerging from the fog.

"Mr. Prose?" Chip was taken aback. He pinched himself to be sure he was indeed awake.

"I must say, you are full of surprises," Mr. Prose said, drawing close enough that Chip could finally make out his face. He was dressed just as Chip had last seen him, carrying his walking cane under one arm, like a sword still in its sheath.

"The bakery was a delight, but expected." Mr. Prose removed his walking cane from under his arm, the metal tip ringing out like some distorted church bell, as it made contact with the cobbled street. "This, however, be the true masterpiece. Though one does wonder ... how."

Mr. Prose was pointing to Humphrey. Chip felt the tiny rat draw closer to his neck, as though the old man intimidated him as well.

"This not be yer rat, Mr. Prose," Chip said, stroking Humphrey's head with one finger. "How did ye find me?"

"Of course not. My rat was old. This rat be younger and smaller." Mr. Prose drew closer, ignoring Chip's question.

"How did ye find me?" Chip asked once again.

"Terrible thing that hath befallen thee," Mr. Prose sighed, continuing to ignore his question. "I mean, it not be bad enough your wife and children have become estranged to thee, but you be a wanted man for the death of the departed Captain Clark and the sinking of his vessel."

"How doth ye know all this?"

"The truly amazing thing is how you have accomplished the feats that you are *really* responsible for. Not every day that you meet one with such … talent."

"Talent?" Chip repeated, feeling his apprehension being replaced by a growing anger. "I not be in the mood for riddles, Mr. Prose."

"Riddles?" Mr. Prose lifted his eyebrows in amusement. "I be referring to your amazing gift of speaking to rodents."

Chip growled, "This not be talent. I know not how ye know of me ability to speak with rodents, but I trust ye did not hear such from the only three that know me secret."

"Are you referring to the orphan, the carpenter, and the man of the cloth? No, Mr. MacDougall, they did not betray your trust."

"Then how doth ye know?" Chip demanded, taking a step closer to the old man who had haunted his dreams. "How doth ye know whom I hath told?"

"I have my ways. You have a valuable talent, and I be always looking for potential treasures."

"How doth ye call this talent? It hath taken all I hold dear away from me!"

Mr. Prose chuckled, "Now be truthful, Mr. MacDougall. It was you who drove your wife away. It was you who parted from your life to find anew. In the end though, it was probably best to keep it from her. How could you possibly expect her to appreciate your gift?"

"I shall ask once more, Mr. Prose," Chip breathed. "How doth ye know all of this?"

"Again, I have my ways, Mr. MacDougall. I have eyes and ears everywhere."

"How doth ye find me now?"

"I never lost you, Mr. MacDougall. I have known the comings and goings of thee since the day you completed my task."

The air was suddenly frigid. Chip felt the as though the fog was collapsing all around him. Squeezing him. Swallowing him whole. The man from his nightmares stood before him. Any moment, he expected to be in a fight for his life.

"Why?" Chip asked, his voice starting to crack. "Supposing ye hath known, then why hath ye waited until now?"

"One does not interrupt a brilliant artist while he paints his masterpiece, Mr. MacDougall." Mr. Prose brushed some dust from his coat. "You wait until he lays his brush down and steps away from the canvas before you congratulate him."

"Ye call this a masterpiece?" Chip exclaimed, his rage rising. "Ye think me life be a painting?"

"Mr. MacDougall, every life be a painting. Some be more colorful than others. Some be merely filled with a single color while others capture the rainbow. What you have created be something truly special—not what I was expecting."

Chip resisted the urge to step away from the specter before him. "What was ye expecting?"

"That be of no importance now. What be important now

347

be what I offer thee for it."

"I took yer money," Chip spat. "I even buried yer rat, as ye requested. Ye hath nothing more to offer. I not know how ye hath done this, but this—talent—as ye calls it be yer own doings. I was never cursed until I met ye."

"I did not curse thee, Mr. MacDougall," Mr. Prose said calmly. "Supposing this be a curse, it be of your own doing."

"What hath I done to be cursed in this manner?" Chip shouted, startling Humphrey and causing him to squeak.

"Were you honest in upholding the task I set before you?" Mr. Prose asked, his eyes narrowing mischievously as he stared at Chip.

Chip started to shout again, but instead held his tongue.

"Let me help you remember, Mr. MacDougall," Mr. Prose continued cheerily. "You were supposed to repay me the twelve schillings I gave thee in good faith. Then you swindled Mr. Tomlin four hundred pounds at the closing of the transaction. Did you think by doing business with Mr. Tomlin you were repaying him? You had every opportunity to make things right, yet you allowed greed to decide your fate."

"Poor decisions, I shall admit, but I did nothing with ill deeds in mind. I shall repay ye. I shall repay Mr. Tomlin as well."

"What about the captain of the *Nomas*? How might you fix that? Have you enough money, should all that is yours be available to you right now?"

Chip's heart sank as he remembered how he tried frantically

to free Mr. Kellogg, to no avail. Mr. Prose's eyes danced again with mischief as he watched him.

"You reap what you sew, Mr. MacDougall. I not be responsible for your actions, nor did I ever ask you to be dishonest."

Mr. Prose slowly began to circle Chip, who twisted his body to keep his eyes upon the old man. Molten lava boiled in his chest as he caught a glimpse of a smile on Mr. Prose's face.

"I did everything I could to save the captain of the *Nomas*!" Chip growled. "Everything! Even though the man be a fraud and a blaggard! Ye probably already know, but I shall confirm nevertheless. The man betrayed the King's Navy!"

"I know who Mr. Kellogg was, Mr. MacDougall. That does not change the fact that supposing you had not attempted to escape, he would surely be alive."

Chip's muscles tightened as Mr. Prose's words pierced his skin. "He be the reason his body lies beneath the waves! Not me!"

"Do you remember his final words to thee?"

Chip's eyes widened as Mr. Prose continued to circle him, looking more like a predator than a man. He felt his heart racing. He knew the animal before him was ready to strike.

"Who be ye?" Chip breathed, his eyes narrowing.

"This morning, I have come to make you an offer, Mr. MacDougall," Mr. Prose said, ignoring his question. "A way for you to pay me back. In return, I shall clear your name and reunite thee with your family. Your life shall be restored, and you shall be hailed a hero. Mr. Wallace shall be gone, and you shall be able to return home. You shall be happy again."

"What ye say be impossible … unless ye—"

"Do we have a deal, Mr. MacDougall?" Mr. Prose pressed, the clicking of his cane against the cobbled street echoing eerily around the vacant wharf.

"What doth ye want?"

"I want you to come work for me. I could use a lad like thee in my organization. One with your talents."

"Doing what?" Chip asked, more curious than caring.

"Whatever I ask—and without question."

"What be yer organization?" Chip knew the answer already, but he wanted to hear him say it.

Mr. Prose shrugged. "Purely investments. I invest money and time. In return, people pay me back for my assistance."

"So, be this it? Be this what ye be after all along?"

"Oh no, Mr. MacDougall," Mr. Prose replied, halting. "You have thoroughly surprised me. For most, there be only one outcome. However, let us not dwell on such things. Let us look to the future and how happy your children shall be to have their father once more."

"Leave me children out of this!"

"Why must you be so difficult, Mr. MacDougall?"

Chip could see the first sign of frustration on Mr. Prose's face. The conversation wasn't going the way the old man wanted.

"I've learned from yer last task to be more careful," he

replied coldly. "Ye never know what be going to happen."

"Thus, is life, Mr. MacDougall. Whether you are serving a post with me or running a bakery, or even sailing the high seas."

"Aye, that be life. But life must hath honor. I hath sailed the high seas with honor. I started a bakery with honor. What honor be there in serving ye?"

"Mr. MacDougall, I'm offering you the chance to not be a wanted man. To be a hero. To be reunited with your family. Yet you stand here before me—questioning me about honor." Mr. Prose slammed the tip of his cane against the cobbled street. A sound that could only be described as breaking glass filled the air. "What honor be there in being removed from thee family—they believing you a murderer? What honor be there in knowing that another man stands in your place with your family and your money?"

"What would happen to Mr. Wallace? What would ye with him?"

"Mr. Wallace?" Mr. Prose repeated, sounding shocked. "You speak of a man, who desires to take your place and be with your wife."

"I be measuring the man before me. Should Mary choose to be with him, that be her decision. I shall not hold Mr. Wallace entirely responsible. What happens to men who not be valuable to thee any longer?"

"Oh my, so ignorant of thee it's almost endearing," Mr. Prose chuckled, wiping a tear from his eye. "You actually believe she has a choice. Should your beloved Mary be with Mr. Wallace, it shall be because I wish it. Mr. Wallace shall remain valuable to me, regardless, as long as he continues to breathe."

Chip closed his eyes and grasped the bridge of his nose with his hand, as anger flooded his being. Humphrey twitched next to his neck, before scampering down into his jacket pocket for safety.

"Go ahead, Mr. MacDougall," Mr. Prose whispered. "I sense it. You wish nothing more than to order your little rodent friends to attack me. I know they follow you about, watching, and waiting in the shadows. Go ahead—do it."

"Nay," Chip refused to open his eyes. "I shall not give in to thee. I doth not know how ye know the things ye do, but I shall find another way to return to Mary."

"There be no other way, Mr. MacDougall. Unless you come work for me, she shall never be thine again. What shall it be, Mr. MacDougall? Shall history remember thee the hero … or shall it shut the door upon thee?"

Chip contemplated his life. He could hear Mary encouraging him to keep the faith. To stand strong and resist the temptation to give in to the anger. He opened his eyes and glared at the man before him. "I hath already failed Mary once. I shall not fail her twice."

"Then we have a deal, Mr. MacDougall?" Mr. Prose asked, extending his hand in acceptance.

"Ye misunderstand me. I would be failing Mary again, should I accept yer offer. She would not wish me to, thus I shall not work for thee."

Mr. Prose sighed. "You sound so much like your dear departed father, Mr. MacDougall. He was worried about failing his family as well."

Chip felt as though the freezing waters of the harbor swelled around him as he contemplated the demon that stood before him. "Ye knew me father?"

"Of course, I did. You think it be fate that we met?"

"Doth ye know how me father died?" Chip asked, barely able to speak.

A sick smile curving his face. "That I do. I shall tell thee all that you wish to know. I shall give you back all that you have lost. All you have to do is to come work for me."

Chip clenched his fists tightly. "I shall be a dustman before I work for ye again!"

"Before you die, you shall work for me again—just like your father," Mr. Prose sighed, as he smoothed the hair above his ears with his hands. "It's your destiny."

"Never again!"

"Never say never, Mr. MacDougall," countered Mr. Prose calmly. "Never be a long time."

"I could live for all eternity, and I would never work for thee again!"

Chip defiantly stood his ground as Mr. Prose slowly began to approach. "No man lives forever, Mr. MacDougall. Though you shall feel as though you have lived far too long before you pass.

This I promise."

"I know what you be, Mr. Prose."

"Really, Mr. MacDougall?" The sick smile returning to his face. "In my life I have been called many things. Tell me, what would you call me? I doubt you could come up with something new."

Chip stood defiant. He tried to speak, but could not utter the only word in his mind, *Demon*. He felt the old man's cold eyes boring into his soul.

"How ... disappointing. Before you die, Mr. MacDougall, you shall watch all that you care for perish. You shall watch everything you hold dear crumble before your eyes." Mr. Prose was nearly nose-to-nose with him now. "It shall happen over and over again until you beg for death. Before you die, you shall regret this moment ... this choice."

"Crawl back into the hole ye came from and leave me be," Chip growled, his voice returning. "I doth not fear ye."

Mr. Prose backed away, straightening the cuffs of his shirt and chuckling darkly. "Oh, I shall not be crawling back into any hole, Mr. MacDougall. No, I shall be enjoying what looks to be the beginning of a marvelous day. The bustling of a growing city. There's always so much to be done and deals to be made."

The further he was from Mr. Prose, the warmer the air became. He continued to stare at the old man defiantly as the sun started to burn away the morning fog, removing its hold from his heart.

"There not be any deals to be made here," Chip said, folding his arms as his confidence grew.

"A lemon has pips, a boatyard has ships, and I always get what I want, Mr. MacDougall."

"Not today!" Chip roared.

Mr. Prose sighed, "Agreed. Though tomorrow is another day. As for today, it be best you be getting back to the shadows, lest an English soldier sees you flashing the gent. As for me, I have important things to tend to." He started to turn away, but stopped midway. "One last word of advice. I would turn down any offers to leave Scotland. Remember what happened the last time you decided to flee your troubles. Good day, Mr. MacDougall."

Mr. Prose turned completely on his heel before walking away, whistling to himself, the clicking of his walking stick fading eerily. Chip watched him disappear into what was left of the morning fog. At that moment, he knew not how, but he vowed that one day he would find a way to clear his name and stop Mr. Prose from hurting anyone else.

Humphrey crawled back up onto his shoulder as he headed for the shadows. For the sake of his family he had to run, to hide, to survive. The only options he had was to flee into the Highlands … or to sail.

A Lemon Has Pips …

A Boatyard Has Ships …

And Here Begins the Legend of Chip.

ABOUT THE AUTHOR

By day, Stanley Campbell is the owner of a small business in his hometown of Louisville, Kentucky. By night, he is a member of the local Scottish Society and a writer. Above all of this, he is a husband, father of two young boys and a Christian. Stanley has studies eighteenth century Scotland in his spare time. This is his first novel. He is currently writing the second book of the series, along with other works.

CPSIA information can be obtained
at www.ICGtesting.com
Printed in the USA
LVOW03s1918211217
560427LV00002B/645/P